THE
KEEP

BY THE SAME AUTHOR

FICTION

The Union

The Virgins

L: A Novel History

The Stench

Secret Love and other Stories

MORDEC THE VIKING SERIES FOR TEENAGERS

Mordec Raids England

Mordec's Quest

Mordec and the Hidden Hand

Mordec and the Lost Boys

Mordec the Conqueror

NON-FICTION

Hitler's Children:
The Story of the Baader-Meinhof Terrorist Gang

The PLO: The Rise and Fall
of the Palestine Liberation Organization

MEMOIR

The Last Days of Sylvia Plath

'In her power to present a large panorama, and fill it with lively, telling detail, Jillian Becker is a writer born' – *Cecil Day-Lewis, Poet Laureate*

'I don't know which I admire most: Mrs Becker's gift for detailed characterization or her powerful sense of dramatic form. Like a great wave, the novel crashes to its conclusion.' – *The Sunday Telegraph* (London), 16 July 1967

'The horror in Becker's first novel is infinitely subtle and impressive.' – *The Daily Telegraph* (London), 17 August 1967

'Jillian Becker's first novel is quite different in character from anything that has so far appeared in the category of South African fiction in English. In terms of a vivid splendour of characterisation, of drama, humour, irony and tragedy, in terms of profundity and living relevance in philosophy, *The Keep* is a rewarding and important novel.' – *English Studies in Africa* (1968)

'Her extremely impressive first novel is a vivid evocation of what it meant to live in South Africa in the late 1930s and early 1940s. *The Keep* finely bears out the truth of George Eliot's old axiom that there is no private life that has not been determined by a wider public life. But though the people are certainly products of their time and place and illuminate our understanding of both, their individuality is intense enough to convey a vision of life which is more than a question of a local habitation and a name. The violent disasters are enforced by prose that carries an unnerving authority. The tension between imaginative urgency and literary poise can only be the work of a striking talent.' – *The Observer* (London), 16 July, 1967

THE
KEEP

JILLIAN BECKER

To my daughters

Claire, Lucy, and Madeleine

1

THE DEAD

Josephine, a dark unchildlike child, too solemn, too clear and correct in her speech, so that adults felt criticised and attacked her cheeks in self-defence, stood on a lawn and watched her older brother Simon, who was to have an effect on history, come rolling down the steep bank from the terrace below their house. Her head slightly to one side, her hands in fists, she gave herself up to the force that tumbled him over and down, felt her face press, again, again, into the warm and prickly grass, her arms flail, her legs spread. When he lay on his back, an arm across his eyes, she walked slowly over the sunbright green and stood at his feet, her shadow upon his face so that he could look up at her.

'You must go upstairs and change your clothes,' her voice told him. 'It is Wednesday and we may go to tea at the Dead House.'

Simon sat up. Grass clung to him. His hair reflected the sun and crackled as he rubbed his fingers through it. It was gold thread, a spindleful of metallic flax. Observant people commonly remarked that the big fair boy and the scrawny girl did not seem at all like brother and sister. It seemed a something suspicious, even a little offensive.

'There will be two kinds of cake, chocolate and yeast. And there will also be meringues, ginger-snaps with whipped cream in them, hundreds-and-thousands on bread and butter, and pickled cucumbers.'

'How d'you know?'

'It is the third Wednesday of the month, and on the third Wednesday of the month those are the things we have for tea at the Dead House.'

As Josephine knew that Simon would come with her to the Dead House, the menu was not to entice him. But there would be no harm in coddling his willingness, which was only a few weeks old. It was bearing up; but it puzzled her quite as much as it pleased her; and, as it lived without a discoverable cause or origin, it retained a chimerical quality, and wasn't to be counted on.

A year ago Great-Aunt Jenny Kronowsky, who lived, so to speak, in the Dead House (which had, at that time, no name at all), told Mother and Nanny Binny that the children should pay their Wednesday visits only if they chose to. No one sought a special reason for her charge. She was always kind. Simon stopped going, not because the Kronowsky garden was worse than their own; on the contrary, in several respects it was better; but because a visit was not worth the grooming. So Josephine was walked there and back alone. There was no question of her remaining with Simon in the usual daily hope of keeping close to him. She saw as plainly as her Mother and Nanny Binny, without their pointing it out, that Great-Aunt Jenny's feelings were not to be so entirely disappointed. Neither Mrs Leyton nor Nanny Binny had attempted to cajole Simon. 'Great-Aunt Jenny,' they had trusted, 'will understand. She knows what Simon's like.' ('In other words, impossible,' his mother might have added.) ('A bit wild, a real boy,' Nanny hoped to imply.) Josephine did try all she could to get him along with her, but without success, until just a few Wednesdays ago when, to her greatest surprise, something she said made him change his mind.

It was a stormy afternoon and Mother fetched her home in the car. The hail started as she reached the top of the stairs, assailed the windows and the roof, and filled the house with noise and a strange grey light. But beyond Nanny's room the Nursery (as the room which she and he still shared was still called) was amazingly bright. Simon was there, scuffing up and down between the old toy-chest and the window, destroying, rather than dismantling, a locomotive which Uncle Fred Kronowsky had made up for him out of a construction set, which Uncle Fred himself had given him on a birthday in earlier days when people had still had hopes of Simon. Nanny Binny was darning, her lips drawn in tightly, since if Simon was quiet and happy there was no sense in saying anything, although they must have been dear, things like that, and there was many another little boy who'd be glad. Josephine, picking her way among the scattered bolts, cogs, and shards of tin, called: 'Great-Aunt Jenny showed me photographs today. She has a lot of books full of photographs of our ancestors. They are all dead.'

Simon paused in the rending of a steamship, and looked at her.

'Oh dearie me,' said Nanny. 'And just 'ark 'ow it's coming down. The poor flowers will be dashed to gymrags.'

'What, what, what, what do they look like?' Simon shouted. The house was resonant.

'Oh. Sad. Sad and funny.' She put her head on one side and considered. 'Finished.'

He examined the thing in his hand and twisted a piece of it more carefully.

'She has shown me some before,' Josephine called to him, since he'd asked. 'She often shows them to me on rainy days. That is usually what we do on rainy days at the Dead House.'

'At the what did you say?'

'At the Dead House,' she cried.

The storm hushed. A few last taps and it rolled away. The house felt peaceful, and everything lit up as the sun came out.

'Well!' said Nanny, 'that's not a nice thing to call your own Uncle and Aunty's lovely 'ome.' She bit off her thread. 'Your own flesh and blood.'

'Wh-wh-wh-why d'you call it that?'

'It's my name for it.'

'But why, hey?'

'Because of the ancestors. And because there are so many dead things there. Aren't there? The animals, and those things that once belonged to someone and now stand on shelves all over the place.'

She stopped at that, but there was something else that was harder to tell of and impossible to show Simon: how she felt deadness in her Uncle's house as unmistakably as she felt safety in their own.

He went on looking at her as long as it seemed she might be going to say something else, but when she shut her mouth and started on her buttons he dropped the wrecked ship and ran outside to the heaps of glittering hail.

And the next Wednesday he had come into the Nursery just as she was getting on her mackintosh – though the sky had cleared after lunch – and announced: 'I-I-I-I-I, all right, I'll go and see them. I'll go with.'

'With me to the Dead House?'

'Yes. The Dead House. Hey, will she show me those pictures? Hey? Jo?'

'If we ask,' said Josephine, holding button and hole apart as she watched him reach, voluntarily, for his hair brush, 'I am sure she will.'

The button went in the wrong hole and she had to do the lot again. She could not see, she simply could not see. She felt puzzled and happy both as they walked together, behind Nanny Binny, all the way to the Dead House. That day of storm and sun. (He even let her hold his hand for part of the way.)

Simon, at least, had never puzzled her before. He was a big, bright fact, like the sun. Not that he was ever familiar, ever close enough. But she had been certain of the sort of thing he would do, of how he would always do: – with a run, with a shout, with his hands; not with his thoughts; not by wondering. For the first time, on that Wednesday, she would have liked to ask him why, but the one thing he could not do was tell.

And it wasn't until the feast at the Dead House was over, that afternoon, the empty plates with the stained doilies cleared away, the crumbs swept from table and floor, and she kneeling beside him to study the pictures of the Dead in the leather-covered album which Great-Aunt Jenny placed before them, that she at last began to see.

No sooner was the book down, hardly had his great-aunt's hands left it than he whipped it open and stared down at the faint picture of a man, definitely a man, though in billows of shadow. He narrowed his eyes to peer at him as others do to see through glare. He had to see things to believe in them.

'Dead,' he tried.

'Yes, I'm afraid so,' said Great-Aunt Jenny.

'Hey. Hey, he's not dead. Not here he's not dead. Is he? Hey? Look his eyes are open.'

'Oh they've all been dead a good many years now, I'm afraid.'

'Aaaaaaa. I can see. He's not dead. Here he's not dead.'

'What do you mean, dear?' Jenny's voice was especially gentle that afternoon. She was truly glad that Simon had come. But she'd never denied he was hard to understand.

Josephine, however, was beginning to understand what he was after, if not yet why.

'The photograph,' she explained, 'was taken while he was still alive.'

'Who was it then?' he challenged. 'Him.'

Josephine leant against his flannel shoulder.

'Which?' Great-Aunt Jenny bent over them, grasping the thin gilt shaft of her spectacles the better to see. 'Take your finger off. It makes smudges. Oh that's your Great-Uncle Jacob who died in the Civil War.'

Who'd been all but blotted out, it seemed. So that was it. A face in smoke. If Simon had added a mark of his own it was not to be distinguished here.

'A-a-a-a cannon-ball gottim. I suppose. Hey?'

'No, no, no, poor man. He fell out of a top window when a parade was going by. A parade of the – Red Army. If I remember rightly. Or was it the White? Do you remember Freddy whether it was the Red or the White? It was the Red.'

Uncle Frederick tipped down the corner of his journal and looked at his wife from under bristly brows.

'Are you asking or are you telling?'

'It's all right, dear, I'm sure it was the Red.'

'So,' said Uncle Frederick, 'what difference does it make?'

To Josephine it would have made a difference. 'A parade of the Red Army' – those words had proved the transparent kind, six panes in a window, which, furthermore, opened outwards, and this was one of those times when she could see through to the event. Her head straightened, her eyes widened, and she gasped softly. For when vision was sudden it seemed to knock her in the chest, so that she drew breath audibly, with a catch like a sob. Huhuh, at the very first sound of the drums, tramping feet, the flight of bugles, and there, rounding the corner, wavering between the trees of the avenue, flashing behind the thick clustering but distinct green leaves of summer, the flag, and Great-Uncle Jacob was drawn back from the front line on that gasp of air, and, whole again, was stationed here at his own window, and the coats of the men who passed below were scarlet. The band-brass swirled with reflected scarlet as the old bearded fellow tipped over the sill. Down he plummeted, head first, yet Josephine had time to notice the red-checked pattern of his carpet slippers before he crashed among the spectators.

'Who, who, who took the photos, hey? Did Uncle Fred take them?'

'Oh no. Uncle Fred left Russia long before the Civil War. Long before the Revolution. Uncle Fred wasn't in Russia very long at all. He went to school in Germany, you know, and he was the first to come to Africa. Ooh and I had left before Jacob died. Uncle Fred's pictures were all taken in Africa. I'll show you Uncle Fred's albums if you like. I'll show you your grandfather and grandmother when they were in Africa. Saul and Rachel dear – I was saying you took their photographs.'

'They must be here somewhere.'

'Oh, yes, dear they're not lost!' As if they could ever really lose anybody once they had him by a relic!

'Show me,' said Simon.

His attention remained unusually fixed throughout that afternoon. He even examined some of the faces through one of Uncle Fred's magnifying glasses (of which Uncle Fred had a variety kept in a big sweet-smelling chest, along with microscopes, telescopes, periscopes and one kaleidoscope for which Josephine had the warmest admiration. With microscopes however, she never had luck: she always saw her own eyelashes and, dimly, her own eye staring back at her though Simon managed to see the insects with obvious delight. And as for periscopes with which Uncle Fred claimed to look round corners and through crowds, she had no need of them). And although there was not a single study of a corpse in any of the albums, he went again the next Wednesday, and the next, and still his curiosity remained unsatisfied.

On this third Wednesday of the month, after he had eaten both kinds of cake, ginger-snaps, meringues, bread and butter and pickled cucumber, more or less simultaneously, he was ready again to examine the faces. For them too he had an appetite.

'What you want to sit in the house on a fine day?' Uncle Fred deplored. 'Let them play in the garden. Hey my boy?'

Simon did not look up.

'You want I should come with you? Hey? Simy? I'll take you round the collection hey? What you say to that my boy?'

'Oh,' piped Great-Aunt Jenny, 'There's poor old Uncle Alex who emigrated to Australia.'

'What's so poor about him?' Simon wanted to hear, and folded his arms the other way. 'Is it like dying? Is, is, is, is Australia like dying?'

'We begged him to come to Africa but he wouldn't listen. And no one ever saw or heard of him again,' Jenny mourned.

'Except Australians,' said Josephine.

'And look at him there, smiling!' mused Great-Aunt Jenny, and she clicked her tongue.

'Takke!' said Uncle Fred, giving up, and returning to his journal.

'Soldiers,' called Simon, pressing regardless.

'Ah yes! Fanny's boys!' And sighing and smiling at once Aunt Jenny showed how *particular* Fanny's boys, or Fanny herself perhaps, had been. Oh what had they done, Fanny's boys? Was it something great? Something tragic? Something wicked, something brave? What kind of deed was it could keep Jenny smiling while her cameo went up, and paused, and fell on a sounding breath? Even for Josephine these uniforms and moustaches told too little. One was stout, one was vague and one was sharp and fair. Was that a river in the distance, a town with battlements? A few more shapes, best of all a story or two, would have to be made out from the blotchy pages and great-aunt's random memories if she were to restore all their carpet slippers.

'Were they killed in the Civil War?' she prompted.

'No, no. The Great War,' sang Aunt Jenny.

They looked at Fanny's boys. Three at one blow.

Simon sighed, out of pure concentration, and Josephine could smell his boy's smell of hot flesh and flannel.

'There's your grandfather. When he was about fourteen, I'd say.'

'In Russia?'

Of course.

All the Dead had posed in Russia. In uniforms, or long coats and hats of fur, or waistcoats and moustaches, or dresses bellying here and here so that the wearers looked as though they had been cut in half and the top part of their bodies stuck back on the rim of the lower part.

And everyone who was old now had been a child in Russia. Once upon a time, in a land far away.

'Was it a sad place?' asked Josephine.

Jenny went round the table and sat down facing them. She leant forward on her arms.

Ah, Josephine felt.

'It was very, very cold. Ooh, I remember how the pond used to freeze. And do you know there was one little duck, I remember –' and the children froze, and watched their Great-Aunt's lips purse a little (for this had been a scandal), 'who used to send her mate down through a hole in the ice to look for food. And when he was down there in the icy water she used to –' Jenny pressed on the table, lifted her broad silk bottom, shifted it to one side and lowered it again suddenly, 'sitonthehole and there. The poor daddy-drake drowned of course. And it wasn't just the once. She did it every winter. And every spring she took a new husband.'

The children watched until the lips smiled, which meant that the little figure on the flute was over.

Then Simon opened his jaws and laughed his hideous laugh. Josephine knew it was 'put on' and that he found it no funnier than she did. She waited until he'd finished, and then asked, 'Was it horrid then? Russia?'

'Well. In St Petersburg –'

Josephine uncurled her legs and slipped her hands, palms down, under her thighs.

'– in the winter, there were bells on the horses of the troikas. The troikas. They made tracks in the snow which I always thought were just like scribbling on a sheet of paper –'

Josephine held her breath, but Jenny was finished.

'Were you poor?'

'In the country we were very poor.'

'Is that why you went to St Petersburg?'

'We went to St Petersburg because of the Cossacks.'

'What are they?' Simon asked, standing up on his chair.

'Sit down, Simon.'

'They were men who rode horses,' said Josephine. 'And wore boots.' Giants, she perceived, catching her breath: giants in priestly robes, with jewelled scimitars. Their horses were coal-black and foaming. They rode with their legs straight from saddle to stirrup. The tumultuous hooves came close, and before they passed, in dust and an effluvium of hot metal, leather and sweat, she noticed the face of one in particular. He had long pale yellow hair, a yellow beard, a pleasant face, while the others were indistinguishably ferocious and many bared their teeth. Whatever that one took was given to him freely, she felt sure.

'What else did they do? Hey?'

'What did they do?' Josephine asked.

'They used to – grab people and – steal – and – be very rough.'

'Why didn't you –'

'Rough and nasty.'

'Why didn't people hide when they saw them coming?'

'We did. Mother used to push us all into the cupboard.'

'And they didn't find you. They didn't think of looking in the cupboard.'

But Josephine felt the banging in her own chest and could change nothing.

'Oh yes they did.'

'And what did they do?' asked Simon, clenching his fists, not in fanciful defence of Great-Aunt Jenny but because he couldn't wait, and if he were to have the story at all he'd have to wrench it out whole from the moulded vault of her bosom.

'They – they were very rough. They hurt my poor sisters, your Great-Aunt Judith she would have been, and your Great-Aunt Lydia.'

'But what did they *do?* Did they, they push you and, and, and hit you and, and –' Simon spoke through closed teeth, jerked his arms.

But for Josephine the only thing to do now was to move on.

'So then you went to St Petersburg?'

'Oh no.'

'But you said –'

'We only moved when Father's brother, your Great-Uncle Sascha he would have been – no, let me see, your Great-Great-Uncle Sascha, found a place for Father in his business. Well, we couldn't rush. It had to be gone into. It all took time. The Cossacks came more than once before we could get away.'

'And did they *always* find you?'

'Every single time?'

'Yes.'

'In-in-innnnn the cupboard?'

Speech was always a stony slope for Simon, and eagerness greased the stones.

'Yes. Sit *down* Simon!'

'Why didn't you hide somewhere else?'

'The cupboard was the place to hide,' said Great-Aunt Jenny, quite rebukingly, as though it had been suggested she should cheat.

Simon's mouth began to stretch, so his great-aunt stabbed her finger at a young woman who seemed poised quite comfortably among endless mountain peaks.

'There's Esther,' she proclaimed, her haste to prevent the nasty laughter making her sound so urgent that she raised Esther very high indeed in the hopes of the children. Then, as they waited, she frowned to remember.

'Our cousin she was. Uncle Sascha's daughter you see. Oh it was sad about her. She was *so* beautiful. And well there you are. She would have been your Great-Aunt Esther.'

The children studied the red and white.

'And *so* clever she was. Would you believe it she was only twenty-two when she died.'

Both lifted their heads and looked at her. What else?

'She was the soul of kindness too, she really was. We used to call her "Angel".'

'Who?' Fred demanded.

'Esther, dear. Sascha's daughter. The one who died.'

'The one with the adenoids? Who wanted to come out here and be a florist? *That* one? Hm!'

'Perhaps if she'd come to Africa in time she might have lived.'

Simon tilted the album and an ancestor slid out on to the table.

'Who's the one not pasted in?'

'Not what? Oh dear. That's my cousin Peter.'

'What happened to him?'

'Well now as a mattrafact. He ran away with an equestri-enne from a French circus. His father, my father's brother in Petersburg, that was, Sascha as I said, he was Esther's brother you see, so Sascha was his father too. Well he cut him off. Cut him off. With the proverbial shilling I'm afraid. There now.'

The doorbell drew Great-Aunt Jenny off with the rest of the tale untold. Spangles had flashed in the corner of Josephine's eye, and the lady was plump. But that would be Nanny Binny come to fetch them home.

'What's an eck?' asked Simon.

'An equestrienne is a lady who stands on her hands on the back of a horse while the horse trots round and round the circus ring.'

'And what's the?'

'The Proverbial Shilling? That was the name of the lady's horse.'

Nanny Binny stood waiting in her hat and gloves while Great-Aunt Jenny kissed Josephine goodbye.

Josephine did not go in for kissing, but looked at Great-Aunt Jenny's cheeks and saw they were gently resilient like padded purses.

Simon was patted on the hair first by Great-Aunt Jenny's ringed hand and then by Uncle Frederick, who rose, laugh-ing, from his deep chair and let his journal slide to the floor. At home it was the paper, but here it was a journal. He stood in his tobacco suit under the animal heads on the wall and laughed, the dead faces of the buck looking on with their eyes of amber glass. In the hall there was a hippo, with jaws stretched wide, killed in mid-laugh, or mid-bellow, or mid-yawn. Uncle Frederick had shot him long ago, and now Uncle Frederick stood there with his mouth wide, the keeper and survivor of the Dead.

'Goodbye, Great-Aunt Jenny, and thank you for the tea and the things to eat. Goodbye, Uncle Frederick.' And Josephine turned, but Nanny Binny blocked the way and already the laughing man was advancing with finger and thumb outstretched. Having no choice she stood and endured.

At the top of the veranda steps the children turned to wave to Great-Aunt Jenny, who always called 'Goodbye, goodbye,' until they were out of sight. Then they descended into the shade of the drive; but once out of the gate, which shut behind them with a clang, they were back in the real sunbright world. They had grown-up shadows before them on the street. Behind hedges smelling of dust the houses kept their windows inscrutable, reflecting the huger inscrutability of the sky. The facades could possibly be melted. A face at a window, looming behind the blue and the passing cloud, unless its consternation should fly away on an aeroplane, could help the dissolution from the other side. But necessary as it was to see through to what lay beyond, lives should not be naked to the street. And the street itself, all the big outdoors, was busy and bright and noisy with birds among leaves, with their own footsteps. And yet, and yet, just such a world must have sounded *their* footsteps, those beige relations who'd stiffened for the camera.

An automobile clanked past.

Strapped to the luggage-rack behind was the white stone body of a woman, one arm upraised and protruding, a strip of crimson cloth tied about the wrist. The children turned and watched it out of sight.

'Wha-wha-wha-wha-what made her die then, hey? If she was only twenty-two or whatever she was?' Simon asked as they walked on.

'Well it couldn't have been adenoids,' said Josephine thoughtfully, 'so I think it was probably consumption. That's a sickness people used to get as a result of being very artistic or beautiful or especially good.'

'What happens?'

'You cough, and your cheeks sink in, and your eyes burn like living coals in your head, and you can become religious.'

'And then?'

'You die.'

'But, but, but, but not in Africa. She said.'

Josephine pondered.

Africa had not been a place of survival for all of them. After all, out of the quite considerable number which had arrived from Russia, only the Kronowskys and Great-Aunt Lydia were extant. The rest, even here, had come to dust. Their grandfather and grandmother, and the rest. Dead and gone, long ago. And this was odd to think of, because, to Josephine, Africa if it was anything was here and now. Europe was a tale of war and death, but Africa was pervading certainty, like the sunlight, not particularly to be noticed, but the general condition of being. Africa was not a word that had to be seen through. Africa, though almost totally inapprehensible, suffused and supported, overlay and underlay. Only at some few points it stuck out at you, with something, and you could feel its special feel, see it, smell it. There was the sprawling thorny shrub that grew against the wall of the kitchen garden at home, flaunting on its dry sticks, very occasionally, such blooms, so perfumed, that the English wallflowers secluded between the pea-rows and even the twelve tulips which Mrs Leyton had the gardener coax into rigid existence every spring in the wall's shadow, were humbled into a modesty that golden-brown and purple could never ordinarily express. At such times it incited admiration. But at others it merely looked savage. Twice Mrs Leyton, visiting her tulips in the seedling stage, before its evil glamour had begun to cast its own unconquerable spell, had ordered its destruction. But either its roots went too deep, or the gardener was in league with it, for twice it rose again, stretched out, clawing at the pea-vines, and again, in due season, shamed the tulips. Except that there was a unanimous certainty of its being Indigenous, nothing was known about it and nobody could put a name to it: not even Uncle Fred, who had made a study of local flora and fauna, and had his own 'indigenous collection'.

*

Uncle Fred's African studies had begun when he'd 'smoused' through the Free State and the Transvaal with the customary donkey-cart (that motif of the pioneering days so common that along the frieze of the century it fits between the ox-waggons as a Greek triglyph between the metopes). They had continued when he had turned prospector, exercising his hopes with a sluicepan. And they were given their widest scope when, after making his fortune in partnership with the owner of a mining store who'd had a side interest in brandy and a side door which the mine boys preferred to the other, he had gone with a party of intrepid men into the bushveld and shot his subjects dead. More recently they had been pursued chiefly through books, museums and camera lenses. But throughout, their chief purpose had been to assist Fred Kronowsky in fixing his claim to be a True Man of Africa.

'Jews,' he instructed the children, 'have always had to be adaptable. You can't say a Jew's like this or a Jew's like that. The most typical example, of any nation, on this earth, that you may care to name, is its Jew. The most Russian Russian. The most German German. And so on. Maybe not the Esquimaux. All right, about Esquimaux I'm not arguing. But Indiannnns, Chineeeeese, I'm telling you. And in the Middle East, like it or not, there are Jews as black as kaffirs.

16

Blacker, if you'll excuse me. I'm telling you if we had to live among leopards, we'd come out in spots. All you've got to do, you've got to put a Jew in a New Country, and you've got a New Man.'

It was something to do with his being a New Man that kept the 'Great' from growing on the 'Uncle' like an old man's beard. He *was* their great-uncle from being married to their great-aunt, who was older than he, but he would not be venerable. And it was because of his newness and trueness that his library consisted of so many books about Southern Africa, and his walls were hung with the heads of beasts; with maps, tusks and, faded to reddish lines on yellowish grounds, framed round photographs like sick eyes. If one looked very closely at these one could make out hatted, moustachioed cronies. Among this lot, his fellow Uitlanders, he had stood and booed President Kruger at the Wanderers Ground when that rheumy old tyrant had dared to come to Johannesburg. (As he'd passed in his open carriage, Fred Kronowsky had been able to see little more than his top hat, for being a short man and his confederates tall, he had done what he could with his teak periscope to witness the historic event.) Before the eyes of this lot he had brought his hippo down. With these he had celebrated the Jubilee. In himself, to himself, he seemed a piece of history, and as triumphantly resultant as any other current event.

The koppie behind his house was stocked with dwarfish trees, succulent and flowering plants which he had gathered together from as far afield as Namaqualand, Mozambique, the banks of the Limpopo. He would point out how natural the arrangement looked, while in truth, he'd confide, nothing except the hill itself and some of the larger rocks had been found 'in situ'. No, no. At great expense and over several years he had constructed that wild and natural seeming hillside, spiky and blooming with native vegetation. Its making had cost more both in time and money than all the rest of the garden at the sides and front of the house, with its terraces, its lawns and rose-gardens, all of which had had to be dug out of the hill-slope, and which had been planted, at his wife's desire, with 'European and Australian imports'.

When he had bought his house, an imposing Victorian pile with a corner turret, its green roof tiles shaped and laid like a fish's scales, its verandas trimmed with wooden lace, it had had no garden. But it had been one of the biggest houses in the most fashionable suburb. Since then fashion had loped off northward, and the city itself came barking at its heels. But with or without the accolade of fashion, Fred Kronowsky's house had éclat. He had bought it at a bargain price, in the year of the Jameson Raid, from an English Knight who had suddenly needed to return home. He must have been something of a plotter, for in the thick door of the hexagonal turret room there was a revolving shelf with so many miniature doors of its own radiating from its axis, that while documents, glasses, plates or other small articles could be turned upon it into the room, at no point could anyone on the outside, whether messenger, waiter or spy, catch any least glimpse of the inside of the room. Furthermore, it was rumoured, on certain moonless nights the gentleman had had all the lights of the house extinguished except those in the turret and all but one of the servants sent to bed; and closed carriages were hauled up the steep drive, and nameless visitors admitted by an old blind Hottentot who would conduct them with a single candle straight up the narrowing stairs to the tower.

This room had been the chosen retreat of the Kronowskys' niece Freda for some years before she married Rayfel Leyton. Freda had gone to stay with her aunt and uncle while her parents went on a pilgrimage to Palestine at the end of the Great War. On the way they had despatched, from an Egyptian port, an enormous fancy pouffe made of liver-coloured leather, and had died of influenza a few days later on board ship, the very day they were due to set foot in the Holy Land. The news of their demise reached the Kronowsky household in the same hour as the pouffe, and Jenny had wanted to withhold the thing from her niece for a day or two for fear that delivering it to her at the same time as her loss would make it look like a kind of consolation prize. However, Fred Kronowsky, who believed that everything in the world could best be sorted out in terms of nationality, dismissed her scruples by saying, 'Prize shmize. The cushion's Egyptian, so where's the confusion?'

Freda received the news in silence, but pronounced the pouffe 'the most superbly ugly thing I have ever seen in my life'.

Jenny wavered between considering this a disrespect to the dead or an oblique expression of grief.

Fred seemed to approve his niece's judgement when he declared (prodding the thing gently with a cake fork) that you couldn't expect much from Egyptians.

In her high room the orphan, a tall, handsome girl who alternated spells of excited loquacity with brooding silences, read poetry. (And possibly, her uncle suspected, perpetrated it.) After leaving school she was uncertain what kind of future to commit herself to, and her guardians advised her to take time to consider. She seemed to like her own company best, and from her point of vantage she watched two filtered summers bloom. For the glass in her windows was red, blue, yellow, green, in wide strips and large fixed squares, set about small centre panes of white that could be opened but were not. She would gaze at garden, or street, or valley, or walls and city roofs through the colours, her hands coifing her face. Through the red the koppie could be seen, and Uncle Fred, for the most part oddly bleached behind a transparent wash of diluted syrup, but the twisty dark-barked native trees were gnarled and clotted flames. The window edged with green faced a gap between trees in the drive, and, distantly, a gap between the hills, so it was mostly sky that was green, a rank and vegetable sky through which coniferous flocks of birds grew sideways out of sight. The city was blue, a cold ash that a poker's tap would settle into a soft and shapeless clinker. And through the yellow, a golden mine dump golder yet, but nearer, between walls of butter, walking corpses dead of jaundice strode in saffron clothes along a primrose way. Only the white was unacceptable. Except at sunset. Sunset through all the colours was moving. It would make Freda feel there was no time to waste, and she'd leave her room and go downstairs where nothing was happening except a clock, and after wandering about a while, she'd creep up to the particularly big, particularly black piano in the dim drawing room (while beyond the French windows the garden expired in its last and deepest glow) and play sweet melancholy Chopins, or the big black-bassed works of lesser Germans. Aunt Jenny Kronowsky, rolling a sensible piecrust beyond green-baize, would be stirred in her depths, not knowing that it was a fortissimo in the lowest register coming up soundlessly through the floorboards, and would wonder whether there were something odd about her niece, or whether her choosing solitude could be on account of cleverness. Though her niece had not done well at school. Oddness must have its bright side. So perhaps Freda was clever in a surreptitious way. The thought was disturbing. It made her tingle in her toes.

When Freda was nineteen they took her to Europe. She wanted to hear music and watch plays, she said. But once there what seemed to please her most were ruins. Castles, churches, temples, cities, the more broken and fallen, the wider the devastation, the better. (Fred, who had been reluctant anyway, complained when he got back that the trip had been 'nothing but a goggle at tumbled stones'.) Freda read aloud from the guidebooks, apparently delighted to know how big, how important, how beautiful a building had been, though she ignored details of what kind of architecture it might example, or even to what use it had been put where such things had to be pointed out. All that mattered to her, she once made it clear to Aunt Jenny who was asking the wrong questions, was that it was *down*.

Not long after her return Freda, persuaded into some sociability by her worried aunt, met Rayfel Leyton. He asked if he might call on her. He was eloquent, smaller than she, and looked delicate, so she allowed it. Still, she might not have considered him as a career had he not ambushed her in her own territory; by accident, she had to assume.

They shared a stiffish afternoon (it was a Wednesday, a public holiday) in the drawing room, the black-and-white man (such dark hair, such pale skin, such a gleaming collar, such a deep-dyed suit) seated on one of those humorous chairs with a back raised on two sides so that one feels one must straddle the point where the other two meet; and she, desultory on the liver-coloured pouffe. He seemed embarrassed by the brittle quality of the meringue he had chosen. But rose above the litter of white crumbs to dilate on his plans and prospects. He was very political, very ambitious, and very detailed. However, the roll, the rise, the carol, the cantation charmed her, with the result that despite pins and needles she saw him to the gate. He turned to look up at the house and asked, 'Which is your room?'

'The tower,' she admitted.

'Up there?' he said, and, suddenly sending his voice into a register it had not risen to all afternoon and using a forefinger as a metronome, he intoned, 'But who hath seen her wave her hand? Or at the casement seen her stand? Or is she known in all the land, The Lady of Shalott?'

Freda smiled. 'There I weave by night and day A magic web with colours gay. A curse is on me if I stay To look down to Camelot.'

And in a pleasant duet (though the sun was going down inside the tower) they murmured, 'And moving through a mirror clear That hangs before her all the year, Shadows of the world appear –'

And so it came about that Freda got, as she supposed at the time, her loyal knight and true. Soon, moved by his plea, she acceded to his application. It was only after she had let herself in for Rayfel Leyton, possibly even then because no real alternatives presented themselves, she discovered that this was the only poem he knew, having had to learn it by heart at school as a punishment (unjustly administered), and retaining it ever after in his safe of a memory (a white elephant he had supposed, had he not happened to remember overhearing that the Kronowskys' niece, who was Saul Levin's daughter who'd been in gold and died of the Spanish flu, practically a millionaire, and his wife at the same time, a dreadful thing to happen, was said to be artistic and very keen on poetry).

Perhaps what Freda would have liked most would have been to stay in her lofty room, only she would not presume. She had a fortune of her own, but her guardians expected her to take off along some customary course, for her own sake. Proceed she must, marry she may as well. On the day of the wedding, however, her reluctance asserted itself. Her two aunts, Jenny and Lydia, left her ready dressed and came down before her. They waited and waited, and Jenny went up again to fetch her when time ran short. The door was shut, and no amount of calling or hammering brought any response, the door in any case being virtually soundproof.

They sent Fred post-haste in the Ford to fetch Rayfel him-self from an anteroom in the synagogue, where the smell of polish, a dripping tap and his best man's smile were making him feel nervous.

'What if I don't break the glass when I stamp on it?' Rayfel asked his friend, one Naty Bloch.

'No one will know. It's wrapped up in a white cloth,' Naty reassured him.

Rayfel followed Fred in his Ford, preceded him through the front door, took the first ten stairs two at a time then walked up the rest of the way. He looked at the door. He asked for paper, unclipped his mottled-maroon fountain pen from a recess of his morning coat, and printed large words that were mostly incomprehensible to the hatted ladies who stopped rebuking, reassuring and restraining one another with their hands to lean over his shoulder and read, 'My brazen greaves! The bridal bells ring merrily! Tirra lirra?'

'Vos is dos?' Aunt Lydia growled.

Rayfel made no reply, but with a trembling hand laid the paper upon the little shelf in the door and sent it spinning in to where their imperialism could not reach.

A breathless minute. Their chins sunk, they watched the tiny roundabout. It creaked, and round came the pa-per. Underneath his message was printed, in lipstick, 'Wait downstairs.'

Rayfel's breath came out again, rough as a ratchet. He was devoted to persuasion, but this was to be the only time in all his life that he was to succeed with few words.

They stood at the bottom and watched her come down, down, down, in her dress of white lace, the heavy floor-length veil covering her completely like a tent, so that they could not read her face. She put out her hands for the bou-quet of arum lilies, but said not a word until they were about to part to their respective motor cars.

'Rayfel,' she called, standing in the shade of the veranda.

He stopped on the steps, and began to turn his topper round and round between his sliding fingers.

'Yes – my dear?'

'I want a tall house on a hill,' she said.

'You shall have a skyscraper on a mountain,' he promised with relief, and would have magnified the proposition further had urgent action not been required.

*

But in the end they had gone to live in the fashionable valley near the Zoo, in a merely two-storeyed house.

It had wallflowers and roses in the garden and oaks in the drive, which was something.

Fred and Jenny, staying on alone in their large house, did not miss their niece, though Jenny thought she did (her dutiful cameo going up and down) when she went into the tower room and indulged a long-frustrated desire to open the white windows, which she did every morning, letting in a rush of birdsong and the sibilance of the city. They took possession of a room which retained no speck or thread of the girl who had denied them admission. Somehow Freda had not impressed herself. Jenny gave herself to dusting and baking, as she had unstintingly done since the first days of her marriage, and Fred saw to his collection, read his journals, worked happily in the red light of his darkroom, as he had done since the early days of his retirement. In time, there were the children on Wednesdays, to whom he told the names of plants, showed his books and pictures, and boasted of his courage and his aim. He would have been incredulous had anyone ever told him that to his grand-niece not only did he and Jenny belong to a past era far more remote than the old ordinarily sprang from, but that their very tenure of the earth was of the most provisory character.

They were simply permitted by the Great Curator to retain their fleshly existences only in order that they might dust the relics, preserve the archives of an ancient culture, display, maintain and expound them. (There were even showcases in the house like the ones in museums. And when in the deep dark caverns underneath the city where men crushed and hacked gold from the walls the explosions occurred which made the earth rumble and all the hefty houses tremble, there was such a rattling of glass in the Dead House, in the tops of the showcases and the fronts of cabinets and in all the windows, that a shattering catastrophe seemed inevitable. But Great-Aunt Jenny and Uncle Fred never seemed to fear for their safety.) Insofar as they fulfilled this function – and others closely related, such as storing up specimens of the present for future memorialising and research, so that the whole of the 'indigenous collection' spelt doom to the native vegetation of the land – they were functioning necessaries, devoted to the past as a cause, a profession, an ideal and a raison d'être. In all other respects they were obsolete. And all that they had to do with, even the hard and pallid (but rooted, watery, flowering, leaving) plants, and especially those heads on the walls (ah, dying herds) had a quality of deadness in Josephine's view which was not to do with the natural end and alternative to life, nor even of rocks and sand, but of unnatural things, like celluloid. So it was no wonder to her that if Simon was looking in this place for death, he should find nothing to satisfy him. What was frightening here was different from the other sort of terror that lurked in shadows, pits, caves and darkness, though here too there were recesses. When Josephine rang the front doorbell she felt nervous as she waited, because when the door opened she knew she would look straight into the wide jaws of that immense hippo, stuck there immediate-ly opposite across the narrow hall, so that it seemed one step more would start you through the stockade of teeth, over the pink cement ramp, and on down a long corridor into oblivion. Uncle Fred himself usually opened the door, stepping aside with a gesture of invitation. ('Will you walk into my hippo?') Josephine always turned quickly towards the library door.

There, in addition to the albums which would furnish a roll-call for Judgement Day, were the framed etchings of men in pith helmets, leopards on rocks, Africans in skins and feathers, desert landscapes, waterfalls, hills crowned with circles of baboons. There were guns in glass cases that receded behind a mist as Simon breathed his hazy interest on the panes. But they were, Uncle Fred regretted, in honourable retirement, and were not to be disturbed. With that one, once, he had got the lion which lay beaten flat but snarling on his bedroom floor. (It was from that skin that Josephine had learned the smell of Africa.) And with that one –. His stories, like the stories in his books, like Jock of the Bushveld himself, seemed all to belong to an old forgotten place, quite different from the country she glimpsed through the windows of the car when Father took them for a drive of a Sunday afternoon, the real veld gold and green, the mauve hills, the orange rocks.

And then again, all the furniture in the Kronowsky house was inherited. This jardiniere had belonged to a cousin, that bookcase to an uncle. All their relations had looked upon their house as a final repository for their domestic possessions, a veritable grave of movables. And whatever came, stayed. Even personal things like clothes were taken in once bereaved of their owners, and put away in mothballs, as though, like Egyptian mummies, the cousins and uncles, nephews, aunts, nieces, parents and grandparents might one day have need of them again. Yet what a sorting there would have had to be, for possessions were so mixed with possessions, uncles' commingled with nephews', aunts' confounded with nieces', it would almost have been like restoring a stew. As neither Jenny nor Fred could in most cases remember what had come from whom, the house, to themselves, was less a pavilion of memories than a museum. But sometimes they did remember. Four times during that year, when Josephine went alone to tea, her great-aunt in gratitude perhaps, took her to this or that cache and allowed her to choose some small object to keep for herself (a coin, a small gold key, a bead necklace), in memory, Jenny was able to say a couple of times, of Uncle This or Cousin That, whom Josephine in fact had never known.

Josephine's conviction that her great-aunt was herself a relic made her no less fond of her. She would follow her happily down the long dark passages, black floorboards rocking underfoot, to one of the six spare bedrooms in which nobody had slept since the English Knight had slipped away and his family and friends dispersed (to turn up again, perhaps, somewhere quite different with surprising and well-known identities). The cupboards in these chambers had doors which seemed to climb, groaning, up and down invisible steps as they were opened and shut. Everything had a smell of age and camphor. Though there were no cobwebs to be seen, and no dust. Even the light, strained through acacia-shade and window-lace, seemed to have matured on the way here, and arrived softer, yellower. Once Josephine received a bunch of artificial poppies out of one of these cupboards, the red armistice sort that did not grow in Africa according to Uncle Fred, and a cedar-box which had once held the pieces of some game, the name of which, once gold, was rubbed away, leaving a semicircle of black on the lid. But on one side was written, quite clearly, in ornate gold script, 'Directions within'. Great-Aunt Jenny couldn't recall who had owned the box, but she told

Josephine that the poppies had come on a hat from Paris. 'It's Peter's wife sent me those. I could wear the hat but not the flowers,' she'd explained, though as this was some weeks before Josephine heard who Peter had been, and saw his plump and glittering wife upside-down on the saddle of her prancing horse, they were just poppies, but lovely. 'Lovely,' she'd said. 'But she does have rather exotic taste,' said Jenny, who often spoke of the Dead in the present tense.

Lately Simon too had been offered souvenirs. But although he had begun to look closely at anything which was part of a deceased estate, he wouldn't take anything. Things in his hands were either to be worked upon or with. But he looked and looked, without the curiosity abating. Simon curious! His sister, never having managed to rouse his interest in anything before this, had him now by that inexplicable curiosity, but not securely since she was still not sure enough of what it boded to attempt to pull the reins in tight. On this third Wednesday of the month here he was keeping beside her as they walked home behind Nanny Binny, though he did not hold her hand again. She looked ahead, and he, she was certain, at her face. He must believe she had an answer that he wanted.

'N-not, not, not in Africa? Hey? She wouldn't have died in Africa. Hey, Jo?'

'She might not have died of consumption. She might have got better here because of the good weather. But she would have died eventually.'

'And, and, and when you're dead?'

If he supposed that she had a knowledge of death, he was partly right. Josephine had gone into death; but it wasn't out of pondering that she had learned what she had. Luck, or some nameless process of nature had served her. For twice, without even trying, she had comprehended it. Simply, surprisingly, and briefly, once as she sat in a stationary tram and the bell clanged and it started to move, and once as she reached the top of the stairs at home and looked out through the landing window over roofs and trees to the far blue hills beyond which distance lay and so much unknown life, she knew (chilled, stilled) that one day she, Josephine Leyton, would stop being alive and would never be alive again. She saw to nothingness. The impossible had come to pass. But the circumstances, she knew, were irrelevant to the vision. She did not see through them; they and the vision just happened to coincide. Describing them would convey nothing. For all the strength of the experience, there was nothing to tell. Like toothache, it was unshareable. And like toothache the true knowledge faded with the fading of the sensation. Only a memory that it had been felt survived. But she did conclude a positive principle; that all most desirable knowledge would come in just such a way; not through the straining, pondering, gaping that she was inclined to go in for, head on one side, frowning; but easily, naturally, unexpectedly, as with the Chinese puzzles of intertwined metal loops that would not come apart with force but, when held and moved in the one right way, accidentally the first time, slipped out of one another.

Besides, how could she, she wondered, show Simon what was not already obvious? Even with a torch of curiosity he could no more follow her into the secret places of the mind than she could pursue him into the must and cobwebs under the privet hedge, or into any other holes where slime turned into reptiles.

'But they, they, they, they bury you, hey?' Simon persisted.

'Yes. And –'

'And?'

'And then,' what then? 'you slowly crumble up.'

He looked away. He would run on ahead soon if she could not postpone that unacceptable end.

'Except your hair,' she admitted. 'And your fingernails. They go on growing and growing like – like old roots under the ground, twisting over each other and other people's and weaving in and out and the hair becomes red and winds round and round the bones and the stones and everything that sticks down into the earth.'

'Then, then, then they're still alive.'

'No, they're absolutely dead.'

He stopped. She too; and turned towards him, showing that solemn truth was in her face.

'And the bones,' he asked, 'do they grow too?'

'No. Not bones.'

He looked hard, and then, 'Aaaaa who says so?'

'I just know.'

'But how d'you know?'

If authority were needed she'd choose the highest.

'Father,' she said, and instantly regretted it.

'Well, I don't care, it's not true. Hey, Nanny?'

'No, duckie. Step out now. Don't dawdle.'

He broke into a run. She started after him. The limp front of her coat opened into tawny wings and she was a bird, a bird.

'Mind how you go, you two.'

Josephine slowed. She had a stitch, and she had no hope of catching up with him anyway. He'd run ahead all the way home. Oh why had she, why had she –? She knew he didn't like Father, knew it so well that now she wondered whether *she* liked him. She brought him to mind, sitting in his chair with his legs crossed, and focused her attention on his socks, his smooth, neat, fine black socks, between the trouser cuffs and the polished shoes. For socks like that one could feel nothing but respect.

So far ahead that he could afford the delay, Simon stopped and stood on his hands in a patch of sidewalk grass; ran on and paused again to peer down a drain – what was it he hoped might be there? – and further to leap at a branch, and swing. Josephine dropped her gaze to the gravel passing beneath her feet. The world did not stretch the distance Simon could not run, the height he could not leap, the depth he was not willing to explore. Simon.

'There's no holding him,' said Nanny Binny proudly. She preferred boys.

Josephine reached for her hand.

When they had turned in between the stone gateposts and crunched up the drive, between the oaks, there he was already at the front door, reaching for the tight little nose of a bell. Through the hall, up the stairs, while the dog leapt for joy at their return, Josephine went after him, but he was not in sight, nor even to be heard. In the Nursery there was only the grey flannel jacket, peeled and shaken and pushed off and flung down on the bed, seam-side up, with two humps of striped sleeve-lining. The room was calm again, though it smelt of cloth and Simon.

Nanny Binny hung up Josephine's coat and Simon's ambassador, put on her own white overall in the pocket of which her bunch of keys chimed, and it was into the garden with Josephine until suppertime.

She looked for him in the orchard, in the sunken garden, down the rose-walk with its noise of bees and its green smell of parsley, beneath the oaks and across the fallen strips of bark and scattered pearly leaves of the furthest gums. There was no one in the branches of the jacaranda in the corner of the big lawn. The small lawns were empty. Then most likely he was lurking under the pergola beyond the tennis court, where spiders spun, and toads and worse hunched at the ready. She ventured as far as the first arch and called into the gloom of tangled creeper.

'Si-maaaaaaaaaan.'

Only silence, with birdsong.

Back she went, listening now for the burr of the mower or the snap of shears to guide her, for often she found him with Willy, the very thin very black gardener who had stiff spiky whiskers on his cheeks and who kept a handful of little white bones in the big pocket of his blue apron. He said they had once been part of a man and had magic. Simon liked to hold them and arrange them in the dust. Some were like arrows and some like reels.

The dog, whose name was Alan Jesus, came round the corner of the privet, but turned again to follow her. Perhaps he had come from Simon. He padded and panted after her and there, as she rounded the corner into the wild and sandy part of the garden, she saw Willy squatting among the yellow-flowering pumpkin plants and weeds, and Simon looking down into his hand. So they were playing with the bones again. She would watch. Alan Jesus went nosing off after something among the rusty coils and everlasting sun-bright empty tins. She stood beside her brother and looked down into Willy's pink palms, but little of them showed, for it wasn't the bones that he held but a handful of grey fur; a kitten, making a noise that wasn't so much a noise as a stroking upwards of the scales of air.

'Is no good,' said Willy.

'I-I-I-I'll bind it up honestly I'll get them to take it to the animal doctor because you see, you see, you see there's a special doctor for animals and, and, and we took, we took Alan Jesus there once. Honestly. It's all right. Honestly.'

Simon kept nodding and he held his own hands out. Willy must be made to understand and deliver the creature, which for some reason must not be grabbed, into Simon's hands.

'Give it to Simon, Willy,' Josephine ordered.

'Is no good, Mosser Simon. Is nothing, nothing no doctor can do with this little cat.' Willy's voice went suddenly soaring.

'It's alive, it will keep alive,' said Simon.

'Is two legs broken, Mosser Simon. An maybe he all broken inside. He cry, cry. He ver sick, Mosser Simon.'

'He's alive,' repeated Simon obstinately. 'If he's alive he, he, he, he'll stay alive you see. I-I-I-I-I'll keep him and, and, and look after him.' His cupped hands urged up against Willy's. But Willy would not let go.

'Let me hold him.'

Willy stood up.

'Let me just look then.'

'You take him he hurt more.'

But Willy put his hands low and held them out so the young master could see without having to touch. With a snuffle Alan Jesus poked his head, curious and with bent back ears, between the legs of the children. His nose trembled over the fur, and then, with a stifled bark, he had it in his teeth and was shaking it.

'Ow,' said Willy, and the children slapped at the dog. 'Let it *go*, put it *down*, it's *hurt*!' Josephine screamed. That words should now of all times have no force!

Simon gripped the collared nape and forced the brute head down until it let go. The kitten dropped, and as Willy pulled the dog away, Simon and Josephine bent over it.

'Is it still alive? It's still alive.'

The head was lifting and weaving, the tiny tiger mouth stretched wide, and that least of grainy sounds grated over the bulging tongue. The two good legs pushed stiffly into the sand.

'Ow,' said Willy again, in awe of the huge anger and pain of the baby creature. Alan Jesus, kept at bay, pricked his ears and cocked his head as he too kept his eyes fixed on it.

Simon's mouth stretched also, but no sound came out. He whirled about, looking for something, anything he could wield, and quickly. His hands held out, he raced up a mound where a spade was planted. At head height he seized the iron bale of the handle, but pulled the thing up and out and dragged it, bumped it down the slope. Beside the kitten he lifted the spade as high as he could, rising on his toes, and then brought it down swift and hard. The blade sank an inch or more into the dry sand and the kitten's head was severed from the body.

Simon, his hands still on the burning metal, stood a moment, seeing that the act was done. Then he lowered the spade carefully to the ground and set off towards the rose-walk. Josephine had reached the corner of the privet when she saw him break into a run and go pounding up towards the big lawn, stumbling against the walls of pink leaves and thorn which caught at his skin and sleeve but could not hold him. She hurried after, and Alan Jesus, glad of the fun, cantered past. Willy went loping round the other way, through the orchard. He was the first to come upon Simon, who was kicking up the turf, tearing handfuls of grass, rolling this way and that, bellowing. But Willy could not get hold of him. Alan Jesus ran round him barking. The noise sent a window flying up and Josephine saw her mother standing there in a white dress, sheltering her eyes from the sunset glare with a saluting hand. The kitchen door banged and Nanny came bustling down the stone steps and across the lawn with a tin of metal polish pressed to her chest. 'Run, run, run, run,' the keys clamoured.

But not even Nanny could make him get up. They could only wait until he was quiet, and Alan Jesus sitting back and panting. Then he was led, filthy and docile, to the bathroom. Alan Jesus padded after him. Mrs Leyton called to Nanny to let her know what on earth it had all been about, and pulled the window down. Willy went off fingering the needles that grew out of his cheeks, clicking his tongue and shaking his head.

Josephine stood there alone, fetching her breath, in the middle of the big lawn on which the last strip of sunshine was filling in with shadow. She watched its end.

'He was putting it on a bit,' she said aloud. 'He wasn't that pleased really.'

Still, she was sure that he would not come with her to the Wednesday teas any more.

How in the jacaranda brown birds squawked with causeless excitement! And an arrow of wild duck flew westward against the last current of the light.

*

On the following Saturday, in the afternoon, a table was set for tea (as usual) in the corner of the lawn under the jacaranda, which no longer afforded much shade. Out of the house came the great-aunts in hats (as usual) and Uncle Frederick, sporting (as usual) a white dustcoat, cap and pushed up goggles, though the age when motoring required an armour was long since past, and he drove a closed sedan. He was strapped to a camera and carried a tripod (which was not usual on his Saturday visits). And at the rear of the procession a stranger came on, smiling because he had dropped in uninvited. Saturday afternoons, as long as warm weather lasted, were relegated to the great-aunts and Uncle Frederick. Even Mr Leyton was never here, but gone afield to address gatherings. (And none of all these except him, not even the stranger who never expected increment from any source but his own mind, had woken that morning with any special expectations of this day.)

On they came between the two tall poplars, down the stone steps flanked by the grassy bank, and across the lawn.

'I'll be mother then,' said Great-Aunt Jenny.

Mrs Leyton, content with this at least, crossed her legs and the shadow of her long pointed shoe lay down on the grass. But she wasn't at ease. The stranger sat at the other end of the bench observing her private relations. Why of all days had he chosen this one? Not, she assured herself, and the shadow of her shoe swung a little on the grass, that it mattered vary greatly that this young man (who had an ostentatious mole on his forehead) might judge her erroneously from the evidence of her more distant connections. Still, at that party the other night she had been particularly lively, while her Saturday policy was somnolence, non-committedness. Torn between two roles then, she decided on a third. She would be charming.

Giving little time for anyone to prepare themselves properly for the new conditions of the occasion, Great-Aunt Lydia started in straight away.

'Nu, Freda, vere's the kinderlach?' she quizzed. She had a voice like a cheese-grater and had come to the country too late to get a wieldy grip on English. 'Vere's Josy and Simy?'

'Nanny will bring them down,' Freda Leyton assured her, and smiled. Great-Aunt Lydia, who expected skewers if anything from her niece, stared at her a moment suspiciously before going on.

'He's vell, bless him, Simy?'

'He's a strong and healthy little boy,' said Jenny firmly, anxious to deflect the point that Freda usually made in answer to this question.

'Gott tsu danken. But he's a big boy, he's not a baby, he must learn not to vorry his Mama.' Up and down the phrases went. Consonants fell in grains. Unaware that she was a desiccator, she persisted in trying to improve matters by working away with voice and words, yet nothing, neither in memory nor expectation, and especially not her niece, ever seemed to soften for her. 'Come here Josy.' (For Josephine had arrived in her stiff dress.) 'Come here my kind. You know your Aunt Lydia loves you. You must give your Aunty a kiss. Fffffpfa.

That's a good girl. That's a nize good girl. Now look what I have here for you. Shocalutt, ja? You like shocalutt?'

Great-Aunt Lydia always brought red cylinders of chocolates. They came to remind Josephine so strongly of Great-Aunt Lydia's cheddar-coloured, freckled skin (and that black felt hat with its tin and tortoiseshell buckle from which it could not be dissociated) that she lost all taste for it. It wasn't just that Great-Aunt Lydia was the giver of it; the chocolates themselves on being unwrapped appeared pale and speckled, through age or weakness, or a sudden despair when they were bought by Great-Aunt Lydia. Knowing that her distaste for this great-aunt was unfair since a relation was not something to eat, Josephine reminded herself of the Cossacks, making them very rude fellows indeed as Lydia kissed her cheek. (Simon, however, had shouted out in the bathroom that if he'd been a Cossack he would have socked her too. Which Nanny had seemed not to hear.)

'There he comes,' Great-Aunt Jenny announced, looking up from her cake-cutting which she executed with the well-raised elbow and vigorous jerks of one not afraid of hard work.

Mrs Leyton sighed, the branches stirred, the shadows fluttered over the tea table, and on the white cloth lozenges of light flicked and dissolved. But Simon, in all his solidity, came on.

Nanny in her Sunday silk was shepherding him. He was scoured and brushed and smoothed and buttoned and tied. His hair was flat and weirdly dark. And after a haircut that very morning, the back of his neck had turned out innocent. Mrs Leyton noticed this, glancing at him when his back was turned, and felt a teeny bit reassured.

'Now. Say good afternoon,' Nanny ordered, turning him this way and that. And when he had she took her hand off his shoulder, gave him one last look of approval, an artist's look, seized the silver teapot which needed recharging, and bore it off like a trophy. She was always telling Mrs Leyton there was nothing wrong with the boy. Now they could all see for themselves that he was a proper lad. That old fusspot Aunty Whatsitsname.

The proper lad went, with his vulnerable ears, to receive his cylinder. Lydia had long since ceased to demand a kiss from him, and now contented herself with a seizing and shaking of his chin, or rather of her own hand gripping his chin, for Simon's head moved not a centimetre, while the sun passed through a cloud.

Then the sun came out extra bright, Nanny came back briskly with the teapot, and Lydia and Uncle Frederick broke into Yiddish, Uncle Frederick bringing the backs of his hands gently but repeatedly down on the table to show how sure he was. Lydia always disagreed with Fred in Yiddish, though she was often his ally in English, particularly against Freda. She was the only dependable opposition ill-judging fate had supplied him with. The hostilities got under way. The children did not matter any more. They were free to eat. And, eating, they turned and looked at the stranger.

The two on the bench had also been set free by the outbreak, and were conversing in quiet intelligent English.

He had come because he was going away very soon. Going away? Yes, in a few days. But where –? Spain.

Spain?

Spain.

To –?

Yes, to fight in the war.

'To fight in the Spanish Civil War?' Uncle Fred's voice boomed.

The young man shifted and faced him.

'Yes.'

Light and shadow blotched their features, netted them all together.

'Heh, heh, heh, heh,' laughed Uncle Fred, for some bitter-comic angle which he himself had on the event. He pushed back his white coat, and his tweed jacket, slotted his thumbs in the two neat little pockets of his waistcoat, leant back, shrugged his elbows, nodded his head, and probed in disbelief, 'You're going to fight?'

'Yes, I am.' The young man lifted his chin and spoke crisply.

'And please. I would like you to tell me. On which side? Which side are you going to fight for tell me please?'

'For the Government, of course. For the Republic.'

'For the Government?' And this time the old gentleman's domed front sprang up and down on a laugh too deep for utterance. 'You mean the Communists? Hey? And the Anarchists? Hey?'

'Yes, well that's very nice too,' said Jenny the peacemaker. 'Is anybody ready for another cup? If Mr Er wants to fight for his principles I think that's very brave of him. What about you, Freddy?'

Her husband ignored her hand, held out for his cup, but re-envisaged the crumpling legs of beasts, though he did not take his amused look off the eyes of the young man. He was not going to be rushed into argument. Next to specimens he liked politics. And it wasn't often he could get at them. Rayfel Leyton was a political man but very seldom available.

'So you're a Communist, hey?'

'I didn't say –'

'Well, nu, for a young man I don't say it's not the right thing. You've got to live a little to know what is the meaning of that little four-letter word – freedom.'

'The alternative in Spain,' said the young man, flushing, 'is not freedom.' He hoped he would not become too explicit in case he proved himself guilty of the charge of youth.

But Frederick wasn't listening anyway. The advantage of seniority established, wisdom would climb upon it to overlook facts. He turned to Freda, who was neutral.

'I'll tell you Rayfel used to believe in it, you know that, Freda? Before he went to study in England he was forever saying about the bourgeoisie, smug, money-grubbing, all the nasty names he could think of. But when he came ba-ack –' the note was held and he lifted a forefinger, 'it was a very different stor-reee.' The finger pointed down, and the music, and the corners of his mouth. The arc of experience was both to be seen and heard. It wasn't expected that anyone should benefit. Esteem was all that was asked.

'Now Freddy, Rayfel's not here to defend himself,' Jenny interposed. She had once been awed by her husband; but by now she had not only forgiven, she had accepted the duty of protecting him. 'Won't anyone have a scone? Or this piece of cake? It's a pity to let it go waste. Simon? Josephine?'

Simon could not have heard. He was a thorough devourer, and the only reason, Nanny Binny said, why he did not grow fat was that he was 'always on the go'. Others, less partial, faced the fact that he was greedy, and if not actually fat pretty strapping for a mere boy. Clumsy too. And *restless*. Though something was holding him now. He was watching the young man.

'I take it,' the young man said, foolhardy, unable to stop now, 'that you are aware what the issues are that are being fought out on the battlefield of Spain?' He was himself aware that he was bordering on insolence, but what sort of crime was that when weighed against the perils he had chosen to face? He stretched his neck and sat stiffly.

'It von't vaste,' Lydia comforted, as Jenny still held out the cake on a pleading china trowel. 'The *sh-shwartze* will have it.'

She had nearly said the *shiksa* but was afraid to in-
criminate Nanny Binny whose thinness, Englishness and
brusqueness established her as a one-woman Outpost of
Empire in the eyes of the eternally refugee Russian Jewess
who had suffered at the hands of Cossacks.

'I am aware. Yes I am aware, and that is precisely the
reason why I say a pox on the lot of them.'

'But –'

'A pox on the lot of them. I agree with Shakespeare.'

'Excuse me, Sir, but I think you're talking nonsense.'

That struck below the belt of superior understanding.
Fred shot forward, the goggles fell smartly on his nose, and
he turned their gross glare on the volunteer.

'And you'll excuse me –' he began, but the voices of the
aunts rose against him.

'Vy get exshited over nutting?'

'If you take those off, Freddy, I'll put them in my bag. Let
me give you a hand with the buckle.'

The fall of the goggles released Simon from a spell. His
hair dry and rising, chocolate on his fingers, face and shirt,
he sprang from among the fallen silver papers to the side
of the bench where the young man sat bridling. His voice
rose above all others.

'Are, are, are, are, are you a soldier, hey?'

His cheeks still targets of indignation, the young man
relaxed, turned to the boy and said with that lightness of
voice and gravity of face that protects the man from the
child, 'Yes I am. Would you like to be a soldier?'

Simon put a foot on the bench, a knee on the arm, a hand
on the back, and chocolate on the shoulder of the young
man.

'And, and, and, and do you want to kill people? Hey?'

'Well, not really.'

'Are, are, are –'

He was being allowed to go on, scrabbling and gabbling, though even he did not know where to, because just then he was necessary to them, no matter what he might come out with. Even Mrs Leyton, whose stomach was tightened by the sound of Simon's voice, suffered him now. At least children could fill in gaps. Only, through her teeth, she murmured, 'Get *out* with it.'

'– are you going to kill people? Hey?'

'Well I suppose I shall have to.'

'If, if, if, if you don't want to why are you going to? Hey?'

Completing his hat-trick at last Simon tipped over into the man's lap.

'Well,' said the man, hoisting Simon back to his precarious perch, and holding on to him, feeling the dangers of losing balance, 'if I want the right side to win I must help it.'

'Right shmight – Communism?' Uncle Fred boggled.

'But,' Simon got right on to the arm and stood up, slowly leaving go of the back. The young man kept his arms outstretched on either side of the crumpled socks. 'But it must be nice to fight, hey?' His arms began to jerk and whirl.

'That's enough now, Simon. You're plaguing Mr Colley. Get down and go and play.' Mrs Leyton's voice had the plaint which always sounded specially for Simon. Now he was about to fall again, possibly among the tea things. Oh, in a world of china Simon was a flail! He teetered, but steadied; and climbed down.

Mr Colley took the offensive. Steadying himself at the height of his resolution, he bent down to offer a little leaden question.

'Would you like to be a soldier?'

'I-I-I-I like fighting. I'm going to have a big army all my own, you see.'

'A real Aryan type,' said Uncle Fred, examining Simon anew though he'd often come to this same conclusion before. 'Colouring, everything.'

Simon about-faced and marched stiffly off into the orchard, bellowing, as though he had made another conquest, and so that Mrs Leyton shut her eyes very tight.

'Onward *Christian* so-o-ilja-as
Marching as to-o *war,*
With the cross of *Jee-ziz*
Going on before.'

And only when, in the clash of cymbals, the roll of drums, the manifold triumphs of brass, he had been borne away into the distance, Mrs Leyton looked again.

'And I,' she apologised, 'wanted a son who would be a poet.'

'Oyoyoyoy,' said Uncle Frederick, hauling up his anchor of a watch and raising his eyebrows at it (it told the day, the month and the year). 'A ruffian isn't bad enough, now she wants a fairy. We must start thinking about going.'

Usually when Simon led the way out, Josephine followed. But this time she didn't go. She knew what the young man would be, but not what he was. She stayed to watch and learn.

'But tell me, vere is he learning to shing sutz shongs?' Lydia wondered, and then, after looking doubtfully from Mr Colley's curly hair to his Queen Victoria face, nodded to him briefly and added, 'Ekshkuse me.'

'Does it matter?' Freda asked wearily, feeling charm grow weak in such a climate.

'You sink you can do mitout religion? The kinderlach don't know nutting about their own religion or their own pipple. You don't shend Simy to shool –'

'Ach, don't start,' Fred pleaded, rapping the backs of his hands on the air. It wasn't that he wanted to save his niece from anything, but that Opposition, generally, kept him buoyant.

'I must stand by and votts my own nephew and niece bringing up to be heathens?'

'You have no choice,' Mrs Leyton reminded her, raising one shoulder and closing her eyes. Under no circumstances would she attempt to explain to Lydia. And in this instance, at least, she wasn't even willing to explain to herself. For in place of Nanny Binny's conviction that a nightly Our Father was as essential to the forming character as a daily bowel movement was to the growing body, she had nothing to substitute. And while she gathered from her husband that this nothing was the intelligent, up to date and challenging piece of cake, terrible hat, to believe in, two things prevented her from replacing whatever image of Heaven and Jesus the children might have with a radical blank. First, the policy she had established from the beginning of non-interference with Nanny's governorship. And secondly, if only her aunts were thin ladies with white hands who smelt of lavender and wore pearls! When she had been a boarder at St Catherine's School how she had wished on visiting days that her mother (bringing boxes of teiglach) would not talk so loudly, or that, if she must, she would sound like Josephine Mills's mother, whose dentures had so aristocratically clicked on the last syllable of her daughter's name.

'Well that was a lovely tea, Freda, most enjoyable. And the children are well, and now we must be on our way.' Everyone rose. 'If they would like to come to tea on Wednesday they're more than welcome but it's just as they like. Oh dear, yes, of course, Freddy wants to take his snap. Right-ho dear, just let me put your glasses down.'

She laid them on the bench. She could not really have forgotten what Freddy had so plainly planned. Taking up her place with a sentry's straightness she confirmed her hat, her cameo, her coat collar.

Josephine remembered, but too late, what curiosity can do. Now she'd have to stay, and her face would be put into the collection. Ready. Neither she nor Simon had ever been caught before; not by Fred's marksmanship.

Politely, Mr Colley left the family group and as though technical by inclination, strolled over to stand beside the photographer, who was mounting his machine. Mr Colley lifted his feet rather high, Josephine noticed, as though he were overcoming invisible obstacles at every step.

'Back, back,' Fred ordered, 'yes, you too please, Mr Er, a group's a group. Where's Simon? No, no, don't go, I'll get him another time. We must hurry now before the light goes. Yes please, Mr Er, over that way that's it next to the child, move close to the bench Josy, right now, Jenny over please, squash up a bit, Freda closer to Jenny, is something the matter? Okay Lydia, if you want to sit, sit. Hold it, smile, still a little more to the left please, Mr Er, that shouldn't be hard for you hey? No offence meant. One step forward please Freda I don't want a straight line like soldiers, that's it now, tha-ank-you! One more please, don't move, just the same.'

'Well,' said Jenny. 'Right. Now then. *Goodbye*, Mr Er, and I wish you the very best of good fortune, now let me see. Yes, thank you, Josephine, here you are, Freddy, I'll strap them on for you in the car.' Before tackling the buckle, she had to manage the disentanglement which leave-taking always was for her.

'Goodbye, young man,' said Uncle Frederick. 'No ill feelings. Good luck to you and a safe return.'

Then the three who remembered wars started on their way home, promising a return next week unless the weather should prove hostile. Mrs Leyton and Josephine saw the car out of the gate, Frederick in the front, alone, the hands of Jenny and Lydia in the back.

'Show Mr Colley up to the lounge, then run along and play.'

'Thank you,' said Mr Colley when the child delivered the message, and he wondered whether he should tousle her hair. Action came hard to Mr Colley. He kept his hands in his pockets, waded after her across the lawn, ascended the steps, said 'Thank you' again to the child's pointing finger, and shaped his course on to the veranda and beyond.

'A soldier,' said Josephine, watching him go, but seeing nothing in him to confirm his claim. She couldn't even imagine him angry, or making a din like Simon.

No drums for Mr Colley.

But she thought no more of him then, for she had to hurry. It must be nearly supper time. Where to start looking now? Had he conquered in the orchard, fallen beside the sundial, or was he in ambush under the pergola? No, there he was, quite easily found, perched on an isthmus of the rockery, cutting up the headless body of the exhumed cat with Nanny Binny's ruby-eyed stork-scissors.

'Oogh,' pronounced Josephine, not because she believed the piety that only outsides are in good taste, but because she was afraid of hot tacky insides, where she guessed that there were tongues that licked but did not speak, fingers which gestured in mud neither to grip nor to charm, and many mouths.

'Look,' Simon commanded, and she obeyed, but with her face half turned away. Deliciously, with his fingertip, he dented a resilient smooth pink bag marbled with veins of red and blue and some of their subtleties, and out of generosity, for he did not much care what anything was called, 'That,' he said, 'is the biladder I believe.'

And he pressed.

'I am quite certain,' said Freda Leyton, looking at Mr Colley in a way that assumed his sympathy, 'that I need a drink, and I have a feeling you might enjoy one too. I can't mix cocktails, so it will have to be sherry.' She rambled on, having risen again to be cool and witty. 'Do sit down and relax,' she encouraged, taking out a decanter and holding it up to the light.

He did as he was told in part, perching himself on the very edge of a deep wide chair made for lounging in. It was the golden age of the lounge, but Mr Colley's heart rebelled against his generation.

'I hope you don't mind me dropping in but. I don't know how to explain it.' He ground palm on palm. 'I suppose I need some reassurance really.' And though the strong can confess to a weakness, he pinched the top of his nose. 'I thought – I've only met you once but I thought –'

'I'm very glad you've come,' she said firmly, accepting the role of the equally strong, and a dash of the wise added too. 'And I'm most interested in your decision. I hope you like it dry?' And with great care, almost a nurse's gesture, she set the little glass down on the small table beside his chair, keeping her tone sympathetic so as hardly to seem to be moving from the central topic at all.

'Thank you, yes, marvellous,' he said, with so much enthusiasm and so little attention that he belittled the thing.

'It's imported of course,' Freda impressed, filling another glass. There was a third on the tray which remained empty. She had taken out three although she knew that her husband was to be late that evening.

'Fine, anything at all,' he said, impatient to get on.

Well, a decided preference for imported sherry wasn't, she supposed, all that important. She sat down, watching his face, as though ready now to listen, but thinking, now that she'd had time to climb back to objectivity, that it wasn't only the mole; the face was altogether rather too smooth and white, rather like a marshmallow, a wee bit puffy. Still, he was certainly unusual, definitely sensitive. She set her glass down carefully on the leather pouffe.

'Now tell me please. When are you going? When did you decide –'

'I leave in a few days. You see –' he eased back a little in that chair designed for more contented men, looked about the room, caught sight of the empty glass beside the decanter and sat forward again. What was her husband like, he tried to remember. And feeling an urgency to have his say before rival notions should arrive on heavy masculine tread, began, 'Mrs Leyton –'

'Aren't you going to invite me to call you by your first name?' she asked, not intending to invite him to use hers. That way she'd gain an advantage which she might need should he turn out to be too unusual, or positively original, or have no sense of humour, or holes in his boots.

'Oh yes, please do, yes, though I'm afraid' – a quick half-articulated laugh – 'it's rather a formal sounding name.'

She waited.

'Benedick. No T on the end. Like Beatrice and.'

So he did have a sense of humour. Thank God, he was no *real* political fanatic.

'Hah!' Cool at her height, she smiled, she sipped. 'Never Benny – or Dick?'

'Oh dear, rather not I think.'

He laughed nervously, and fixed his gaze on a porcelain dancer on the mantelshelf, stepped upon the toes of orange shoes, spreading her skirt forward and back into a pair of butterfly wings. Her cap of waved black china hair. Her white arms. But what if her tongue were sharpened not by understandable exasperation, as it had seemed to him on their first meeting, but by malice?

She spread her bangled arm along the back of the sofa and said, 'Good. Abbreviations are silly. Now tell me about the designs you have on the unsuspecting Falangists.'

Ah yes, he had remembered her rightly. A woman, he had recognised at that party, through whose eyes matters could look bigger, in their true and generous proportions: who would know how much it took of a man's resolution to reason his way right from pacifism to the International Brigade. Any kind of travelling makes one feel older, and he'd felt like an explorer come in among coenobites.

'I'm not very good at party conversation,' he'd said, with false humility.

She had half shut her eyes at him. (It was his sincerity, she had told herself, that got in his way, like an umbrella.)

'You couldn't really talk to anyone here,' she'd sympathised. 'We've all had our minds chromium-plated to match the furniture.'

'I didn't really mean to be rude,' he apologised, dropping his freshly lit cigarette down the long hollow pipe of a standard metal ashtray whose bowl was instantly flushed with his own discomposed face. 'I really did mean that I'm the awkward one. I'm an intruder from –' (how could he say, aloud, 'from the terminus of unreversible commitment'?) 'the Eastern Province,' he said.

'I thought you couldn't have been long in Canaan,' she consented.

'Canaan? But this is the great cultural hub of our land, isn't it?' (He had never been sarcastic before, but was happy to share what was offered.)

'Well, I can tell you this. If you mention a book everyone will ask you what odds you're offering.'

He looked down into the pale amber shallows of his glass, and smiled.

'You wouldn't,' he said.

'I escape now and then to Yoo-rip,' she explained, 'Athens, Rome –'

'And your friends —'

'Mm. There are always a few who have minds. But most of them have the sense to take them where they're wanted. I –'

Freda had been about to unfurl an umbrella of her own, when she heard Maisie Gould, her hostess, say, 'We always treat our servants like human beings,' which meant she was within earshot.

'And there are some who're just dears,' she murmured, bowing her head so that he looked at the straight, narrow and very white path through her dark hair as he asked, 'Could I come and call on you?'

'Please do,' she had said emphatically, flattered into forgetting Saturdays, 'just arrive, I love surprises.'

In fact it had been a surprise to Freda to hear herself say so. Her whole life was organised to prevent anything from happening. Yet sometimes, in the still afternoons of the weekdays, as she lay on her couch listening to Beethoven, she felt that she was being held in reserve, that the clear decks of her days, the oiled routine, her lack of commitment to anything more demanding than a dinner date or holiday trip were necessary to an obscure policy of fate which would sweep her into action of enormous, transfiguring significance. She would know when it came. There would be signs. What form it would take she didn't attempt to imagine. Yet could it be love? she wondered. It could be love. But looking up at young Mr Colley, who was having great difficulty finding the exact words to describe how he felt about life and its purposes, she rejected his pudgy face with its mole from her pillow. She would accept his respect, his admiration, his confidence. Love was another thing.

'It's true that I, well, that I haven't *tasted* much of life, I mean life *itself*—'

He stopped talking, lifted his head, listened. The door-knob turned slowly. He grinned at it. But as the door opened, it was respectfully knocked upon, and nobody came in to interrupt, only a black man in white clothes as stiff as paper. An African, as Mr Colley would have said.

'Yes, Sixpence?' said Mrs Leyton.

'Yes, please, Mam, the curtains, Mam.'

'Yes, right, go on then.'

Mr Colley went on.

'I'm only twenty-four.'

Zzzzzzip.

'But I mean I could live to be an old man and do all the accepted things and I mean just never really do anything worth doing.'

Zzzzzzip.

'I mean what is one's life *worth* if one doesn't use it for for –'

Freda Leyton hated inarticulateness, and watched the adjustment of the curtains. The only feature she had ever found attractive in her husband was his phraseology. But she would be sympathetic, she would keep criticism at bay.

'Of course,' she said. 'Good Lord.'

'Excuse me, Mam, the light?'

'No thank you, Sixpence.'

Sixpence went out with a crackle, and the knob turned slowly again this way and that.

'I mean most of the people I've known here,' the young man continued, 'have been well not even *alive* at all really if you know what I mean. I mean they have their virtues, naturally, I don't mean just to condemn them, but somehow, how shall I put it, they have the whole of their lives so neatly organised, and they're terribly comfortable. I mean my parents for instance, I don't believe they care about anything except comfort and security. But I mean when everything's

so sort of ready and set, I mean like a sort of background, well where do they go from there? I mean they're *ready,* but for what? You know. They make money to make money to make money. And hell but this is a terrific country I mean from the point of view of sheer *geography!* Why don't they –'
The effort at saying what they ought to be doing with that landscape which lay beyond the curtains made his voice grate in his glottis until it sounded like a spill of beads in a wooden box. 'They're not alive at all,' he insisted, that at least being clear. An Orpheus among the shades he rose and paced. And ragged as his tune was, still it covered him; neither tooth nor talon would have at him. He was capable of camouflages too.

'One has one's life, one *has* it. One can let it just drift by like a long dream, or one can *spend* it on something one considers worth while. But it's one's own choice – one *makes* one's role –' And he turned to her, pressing his upward curling fists (gripping his life) together, and gritting his teeth defiantly.

'Now he looks' – she let the thought raid her chaste intentions – 'like a squirrel with a nut.'

And at the time, failing to see that her waiting and his going were for the same thing, she felt nothing but relief when he left her quiet lounge and went to arm himself for war.

*

Josephine knelt on the broad sill of the stair window. She wore her pyjamas, dressing gown with the twisty cord, slippers with the felt faces of flat rabbits; the warm and easy but ceremonial dress for supper; bedtime story; prayer. Her face felt a little tight; the hair on her nape was damp. One arm round Alan Jesus, forehead against the pane, she saw the big stars and the small hung at their different heights. And down there she could see her mother shake hands with the stranger on the doorstep over which the yellow light was melting. He, on the lower step, was half dissolved. But her mother was a distinct and opaque figurine on the top of the stand, on the gold-bright threshold between the house and the night. Josephine longed to have a glimpse into her mother's rich and secret life. But it would seem to be the last and most impenetrable of mysteries. Within a circle that Mother drew about herself, only Mother could withdraw. Where otherwise did she go after she had walked down a passage and shut a door? The signs were hard to interpret: the sound of the gramophone, books left lying on tables. Sometimes when she was out Josephine went to her room and breathed its pastel air, or, in the wardrobe, air camphorous, furry, blunted by crepe. Looked into all the mirrors. Gathered on her fingertips the grains of pink powder from the glass top of the dressing-table, lifted the lid of the tortoiseshell goblet on its thin stem and marvelled at the lightness of the swansdown which it trapped. The room had a weather of its own, cool, glass-light. But in places between chests and chairs shadows gathered a thick pile and they could stifle and wrap you away forever. She had told Simon that there were little hidden doors in their mother's room, and he had gone in one day on his own and had done something wicked, she didn't know what.

Now, above her, shining tiles were streaming with the noises of his bath. She also listened to Mr Colley crunching up the drive. (What was his part in her mother's play?) Watched her mother go in and, even on Mr Colley, shut the door. Saw the darkness pale a little as that rival light was called in from it. Heard a car door slam, but no sound of engines starting. Out of sight, in his dark car, Mr Colley sat, one of the lesser mysteries.

But up above a door opened, and the flying cries and the echoes came down to land. The click of a light switch,

Nanny's 'Do be careful now that slipper's not on the 'eel and watch that cord', and an outflow of heat. Simon pushed his way on to the sill the other side of Alan Jesus, wrenched at the curled handle and shoved open the window. Steam rose from his parboiled flesh and clouded the stars.

'He's got into his car and he's just sitting there,' said Josephine.

'Why?'

'I think he's afraid to go to the war.'

'He, he, he's going to be killed,' Simon asserted, not even adding 'Hey?'

'No he's not,' Josephine hoped, remembering how he'd smiled for the camera in a careful secret sort of way that people practise in mirrors. She'd smiled for herself in mirrors, trying to look at her own face as if it were a stranger's, but had frowned into Freddy's lens this afternoon.

'Yes he is,' said Simon, as one who had dominion over death.

There was a grinding and a cough and the leaves of the plane tree on the pavement outside the gate became some a bright peppermint green and some the matt gold of biscuit. He was going.

Simon, done with him, thumped on down the stairs, in one slipper only and with the useless cord trailing and unravelling in his wake.

*

There's nothing so tiring as sitting down, Nanny Binny thought as she rose from the edge of Josephine's bed. She always read to Josephine at bedtime. The child seemed to enjoy it so, although good gracious the child could read better than she could, even those words which Nanny Binny just couldn't get her tongue round.

'Good night, duckie,' she said, bending for the kiss. 'Whoo!' she said, straightening.

But she couldn't go to sleep herself, not just yet. She must first see to all those odds and ends which tied up the day ready for its storing in the past. Frances the cook and Sixpence the houseboy must be done with the washing-up by now, and the kitchen ready for her inspection. People who needed seeing after! Nanny Binny thought with contempt.

'Once to-oo-oo ev'ry
Man a-a-and na-ation
Comes the-e-e mo-oment
To-oo decide,'

she quavered softly as she hung up a wet cloth, removed a spot of grease from the draining board, made sure the window was tightly fastened, and, because of the coal stove and the mischief children can get up to even in their sleep, locked the kitchen door. She went as briskly as ever up the stairs, though her legs did ache a little. Alan Jesus followed her and jumped on to her bed as she drew the folded cotton nightdress from under her pillow. She remembered that the button at its throat was loose. I'll do it before I get undressed, she said, a stitch in time, and tiptoed softly into the Nursery.

Josephine had not closed her eyes yet since Nanny Binny's lips had stopped rustling like tissue paper as they unfolded the story of Alice. She lay still and watched Nanny – glad that she'd come in, knowing it could only be to fetch something – cross to the table, take up what? her round basket it must be (in which were nested the many-coloured reels, the darning mushrooms and the scissor-stork), and carry it from the room. She would have liked to call out, bring Nanny close again with her nicest smell in all the world of ironed cotton and soap, of kindness and safety. Nanny was quite distinct in her white overall (which had beautiful buttons made of bone, each with a silver eye). Nanny? Nanny! But Nanny went out, leaving Josephine again to the mercy of the shadows which shifted on the walls, against which even Simon was no protection since he always fell asleep as soon as the light went out. And sometimes she would hear the footsteps of the old washerwoman coming up the stairs to carry her away, who came openly only on Mondays and stood among piles of clothes in the steamy wash house, the blackest woman imaginable, with her black dress and her black apron and the tight black doek which almost covered her eyes. And her eyes were red in her black head. Like the black stove in the kitchen – when Frances, who was yellow and cross and spent all day banging pans, opened its door, or lifted one of its little black lids, red fire licked out.

But for the moment there were no footsteps. Only comforting rustles from Nanny's room. The blinds were still though the windows were open. Even the shadows hardly moved. Millions of cold stars pulsed with the high-pitched song of crickets, a sound that composed silence.

It was at Nanny Binny sitting stiffly on the wooden seat of her bedside chair that the powers of darkness clawed. She looked down at the thing she held in her hands. She was still dressed when the front doorbell shrilled faintly in the fastened kitchen. Her back was very straight as she went downstairs and along the passage, Alan Jesus after her.

'Oo is there?' she called, for one opened one's door to nothing unless one was sure.

'Only I without my key.'

'Is that you, Mr Leyton?'

'Yes, it's all right, Nanny.'

'Ho ho, I forgot to transfer my keys to this suit this morning,' Mr Leyton explained very loudly as he came in. Picking up envelopes from the hall table he asked affably as Nanny relocked and chained the door, 'What news from the domestic quarter?' He looked into the mirror and felt his chin.

'Oh it was the Saturday tea though it seemed to me we'll be needing fires before long.' Her voice, too, was raised.

They always looked past one another and called.

'Usual crowd?' he hollered, striding on and rubbing the backs of his hands. He did not see her look of obstinacy, the outward sign of a firm resolve she had made on her bedside chair that she would protect her boy, give nothing away. He opened the lounge door.

'Hello, everyone gone to bed?'

'Mrs Leyton had a tray and went up early.'

'*I see.* Good. Well off you go to bed Nanny. I'll see to the lights. Children all right?'

'The children are fast asleep and as good as gold,' she replied with fervour. 'I give 'im a proper scrub and 'e looked like a angel. They didn't 'ave a word to say against 'im!' And this time she was ready to meet his eye.

'Tha-at's it! Fine!' He rubbed his hands again. Something was making him heartier than usual, making him confident enough to extend the time he usually allotted for the exercise of his Common Touch, but not enough to turn and see her face as she declared for Simon. She went on standing there, her feet planted positively, and he went on looking into the dark room, peering this way and that, not for anything he suspected was lurking there but in order not to have to see into a pair of seeing eyes. It wouldn't do. It had long ago been understood that each of them for all the heartiness of their meetings, had a reserve; he of pride, she of humility. If something had happened to alter this it were best not known.

'Well, good night then, Nanny.'

'Good night, Mr Leyton.'

He waited with his hand on the switch until her footsteps changed and he knew she had reached the top of the stairs. He let the darkness fall over him, momentarily.

'Are we,' he asked, under his breath, 'to go on for ever cursing the darkness of ignorance and oppression and fear in which five-sixths of our population labour, or are we,' his hand moved to the adjoining switch which illuminated, though dimly as conscience, the upper landing, 'to light a candle of hope?'

His feet were on the stairs.

In his own room he stripped his tie and looked at himself in the long mirror, which was tipped back between its own two legs, a skeleton watcher of the skies.

There he appeared. There he appraised himself. A neat man small enough to be dapper were it not for the dark shadow on the jowls though he shaved so very closely and often twice a day. Putting on weight and balding too. He bent close to his reflection, stroked his face this side, then that, and stood back to eye with Mr Stranger's sharp and serious eye the man in the shirt who had brains, he informed his neighbour, his ignorant shadow, brains. He'll go far, he promised, and began to recall his future. But no, although nothing could stop him now, it was bad to anticipate too much. Nothing ever happened the way one hoped, so it was best not to hope too vividly for the moments of triumph. With a stiffness, for a man who undertakes power is gilded with specialness, he opened the bathroom door, and saw the light under the other door across the room. So she was still awake. His willowy wife – the neighbour might admire. Should he, or should he not? That bathroom had once been a veritable Hellespont, but nowadays Hero lit her lamp only to read by. He made his decision. He would not proclaim – his news was too important for that – but *mention* what he had achieved this day. He was by no means sure how important her reception of it was to him.

He assured himself he had no desire to impress her. And yet, at the same time, he dearly wished her to be overawed. Hot and cold, he turned on the taps. He wrenched open the little door of the cupboard, rammed it home again.

'Is that you?' she called. She seldom said his name to him.

'Co-ming dear,' he cooed, dove-deep, ironic. He would take his time, he told himself, fumbling the toothpaste tube, dropping the brush.

But the door opened and there she leant against the jamb, a blue thing clutched to her shoulders.

'I had a visitor this afternoon,' she told him. Had she waited up to tell, he wondered. He rinsed noisily, stirred the brush recklessly in the fast emptying tumbler.

'Really?' He seized a towel and was very busy. 'Let me guess. Venus and Minerva? And hell-driver Freddy fresh flagged from the track?'

'Noo.'

'No? Have they stopped descending here on Saturdays? Is there no longer any need for me to flee into public life?'

'Well, yes, they were here. But it's not them I mean. Someone else came too. Uninvited.'

'The suspense is killing me.'

He went on drying his hands, finger by finger.

'What happened at your meeting?'

'I got the nomination.'

He looked into the mirror and bared his teeth. Show all to thine enemy but thine heart.

'Well, congratulations.'

'So who was the deus ex machina, other than Freddy?'

'A young man.'

'How romantic. Anyone I know?'

'You met him but you wouldn't remember.'

As he was cramming the towel over the rail she moved back into her room. And he, though he knew the dangers, left the no-man's-land of the bathroom and followed. It seemed that, after all, the significance needed stressing.

'I –' he began.

'It is really quite pleasant,' she said, laying her peignoir over the footrail and sitting on the edge of her bed, 'to know that I still have my attractions.' With a swing of white satin she was in bed and gathering up linen and wool to her breast.

He strolled to the window. He'd deal with this first.

'And what occasioned the visit?'

'He,' she leant back on her pillows and looked up into a high corner, 'just admires me.' And in case that made him of insufficient importance, she added, 'He's going to Spain. To fight Mr Franco.'

Rayfel Leyton looked out silently into the darkness. White crumbs were scattered on the sky. Because of something difficult to handle, this was the first moment for some hours that he had felt uncertainty. Then he put his hands in his pockets, clinked coins and said, in a drowsy way, 'I take it he has no desire to engage the fellow single-handed?' But he knew it was lame. There was something he had to forgive himself for. 'Is he an idealist, or does he just like fighting?' he asked, wanting something to clash his disillusionment against. If he had the cub himself here now – 'You fire ahead, my boy. Prudence is the hard-earned prerogative of maturity.'

'As far as I could make out he's going in order to annoy his father,' she supplied.

Rayfel laughed with relief. He'd always appreciated his wife's astringency. At certain times more than at others.

'Now, now,' he admonished her though, 'if we can't be kind let's be tactful. You're to be the wife of an MP you know. Next election – or even before if old Roux drops dead which is not improbable.'

'Ah yes! Well, I've been expecting it for some time. How nice. Isn't it what I married you for?'

Ever since he had settled for the sidebar after so much academic distinction he had promised her a greater scope for his vocal attributes on the stage of national politics.

'Surely not.'

'What then?'

'Why, for my modesty.'

'Oh that too. Naturally. Will I have to be an Indefatigable Worker for the Party, and entertain ageing political bores, and kiss the soggy babies of the People?'

'Why, yes, my dear. Your character uniquely fits you for the role. Wasn't that why I married *you*?'

'I thought you married me for my money.'

'Oh no, my dear. You're entirely wrong. How could you say such a thing? I marry you for your money!'

'What then?'

'Why, I – I married you for love. And I *loved* you for your money.'

He laughed delightedly. She made no reply.

'Lovely night,' he said, 'look at the stars.'

Anyone would think he had put them there. He was probably invulnerable now that he was getting what he wanted.

'Good night, my dear,' he called.

He shut both doors between them.

Freda fell asleep regretting the mole, and in her dreams she abolished it.

*

Nanny Binny stood in her long white cotton nightdress (which was open at the throat), pulling the pins out of the high tight bun of her hair while she gazed down mournfully at the metal bird on its wooden eggs. She shook her head, so that pins scattered, picked up the brush and asked herself (or

Alan Jesus who half opened one eye), 'What is it made 'im like that I wonder? I remember now the time,' she frowned and leant forward, straining to see without her specs past the leather-backed clothes brush, and photographs of other children and other dogs on the chest of drawers to her own reflection in the hanging glass, ''e went into 'is mother's bedroom and took 'er scissors from 'er drawer and cut up 'er fox into little bits. 'Undreds of little bits. Lining and all. And the eyes pulled out. Ruined it was. But that was one thing. Mischief. What I'd never 'ave believed was that 'e was cruel. Whatever could 'ave made 'im like that? I always thought 'e liked animals. Then 'e goes and cuts off the 'ead of that poor little stray cat though I never could make out what it was all about. Upset 'imself over it too. You would 'ave thought there'd be an end of it. But no.'

She laid down the brush, fetched the scissors and held them under the bedside light again. No doubt about it. Fur was sticking to those blades and what stuck it was blood. Her tongue clicked. Well, she'd made up her mind, and she'd stick to it. She wouldn't tell a soul. If it was anyone's fault, if anyone had led him astray it must be her, and it was up to her to put him back on the straight and narrow. Unless it was that Willy had put ideas in his head. She'd keep an eye on that brute. And with Simon there was only one way. More care, more watching over. She would spare no pains. He was more her boy than ever. And late as it was she ran water into the vast basin and set to with soap and scrubbing-brush, and afterwards with her little whetting stone, determination giving more power to her elbow, and increasing the energy with which she herself could wield the blades.

2

HEROES

Simon expected no less of Willy than that he should be a murderer.

Nanny Binny expected less but bad enough and had warned Simon off that boy, just let her catch him hanging round him again.

But spring had deepened into summer, and seeds sown, there was much to be done. In the afternoons, after school, Simon found his chances to help Willy mow and rake, and to watch him juggle with the little white bones.

'Have you ever seen a dead person?' Simon asked Willy.

'These is dead man, Mosser Simon.'

'Did, did, did, did you kill him yourself, Willy?'

'They more clever than live man, Mosser Simon.'

'And, and, and, and –'

'One day they grow tall, tall and they live man again.'

'My sister says they can't.'

'You tell no one nothing for these bones, Mosser Simon. No one she knows nothing for these bones. Only me, me, Mosser Simon. You tell no one nothing for these bones.'

Simon wouldn't.

'Si-maaan. Come on in now. Where are you? Do you hear me?'

Nanny Binny had always, until quite recently, preferred to keep Simon in the garden: not just because that was where he would rather be (rooted in shadow or galvanic in sunlight or listening to weeding Willy's tales of that thin man's marvellous other life, filled with hunting and many kinds of animals, the like of which he modelled in Simon's plasticine, so all were a cold and pallid grey mottled with blue and streaked with red); but also because the out of doors was safer not only for him but from him.

Simon was a danger to almost everything. Nothing on him ever stayed stiff. New shoes grew old on his feet within an hour, and his clothes unravelled and tore. His cuffs were home to dirt. (And when he opened his hands, you could see how grime had turned into flights of tiny, distant birds in the creases of his palms.) In the past Nanny Binny had always to be reprimanding him; though because of the saving maxim that boys will be boys she had seldom got really cross. 'Out with you,' she'd say. 'And don't go through the gate and don't get up to more mischief than you can 'elp.'

But lately, unaccountably, Nanny's sternly loving law of tell-him-right-but-let-him-be had changed. Now it was say-little-but-keep-him-by.

'No, Simon I've already told you once. There'll be no running wild in the garden without me there to keep an eye on you. And that's that.'

'Well, you come out too then.'

'I can't do that until I've got all the big trunks packed. Now you be a good boy and sit and read a nice book until I'm ready then we'll go for a good long walk. There now.'

She fitted the tray into the trunk she was busy with. Underwear, sandshoes and the new woollen bathing suits underneath, now the cotton sun hats went on top and Josephine's liberty-silks for afternoons. For it was the time of the biggest disturbance of the year, of preparing to go away to the seaside, when things were utterly though reverently displaced, packed up and sent ahead or locked away in cupboards. Which made Nanny Binny quick-tempered.

But this alone could not account for her keeping Simon there. Especially at these times Simon had always been barred out.

'Where'll we walk to?'

'To the Zoo if you like.'

Simon did like the Zoo. Both of them did. They'd tell the time by the flower-clock, drink from the fountains, and keep off the grass – unless a peacock sauntered into sight trailing his feathers, stately enough until Simon came pounding in his seven-league boots and sent him scurrying among the trees.

Josephine liked the polar bears, in their pit with giant blocks of ice. (Nanny Binny, who had almost as much respect for animals as she had for God and the King of England, always said when it was very hot, 'Think of those poor polar bears in the Zoo.') And she liked the Chinese duck with their precisely outlined markings, and the way the water moved, like a frown, and the reflections like windy flags. And the kangaroo, so narrow above, so broad below. How Simon used to laugh at the kangaroo.

But he could hardly be coaxed away from the cages where the lions paced, and the panthers, jaguars, cheetahs, the hyenas, the leopard and the lynx. And he liked the enormous blown-up parrot cage with concrete rocks in the middle as high as a hill, where the vultures clung – ragged old geezers with naked scraggy necks.

'Poof, they're nasty looking things,' Nanny would say, for there were one or two exceptions among animals.

But Simon would bare his teeth and gargle his most revolting laugh deep down in his throat.

Often they would sit on a cannon, planted at a point of vantage, to eat ice cream and drink lemonade. From here they could see, at the end of one of the wide avenues across which unperturbed peacocks trailed from shadow into sunlight and back into shadow, the thickset arc de triomphe known as the Monument, though in commemoration of what nobody seemed to know. Even more of a puzzle was the sculptural device with which it was crowned. On the top of an inarguable ball which Mother said was the world and Nanny Binny as firmly pronounced an onion, a possibly human-type figure was balanced, its conceivable head bowed, its upper portions otherwise obscured either by asymmetrical wings or a bulging tangle of ragged draperies. And whereas Mother (driving with Josephine past the Zoo on the way to the market garden of a Saturday morning, this knob of a thing bobbing on the treetops) would identify it as Victory, Nanny Binny (sitting on the green slats of an otherwise bird-like chair) maintained that it was Patience.

Thus and thus were the visits to the Zoo. And then, on their last visit, the children had witnessed a feeding which they hadn't seen anything like before. Into the soundproof cages of the pythons, cobras, mambas and boa constrictors (which lived, singly or paired, in miniature wildernesses, each with its concrete igloo, its bare, forked 'tree') the keepers pushed live guinea pigs. Simon and Josephine watched one of the little creatures tearing up and down on its very short legs, pressing against the glass as it frantically tried to find a way out, and they saw quite distinctly that it was weeping real tears which ran down its face and stained its hairy cheeks. So it must have known what its fate was to be, and realised quickly that it was trapped: and it must have known its enemy, the black snake, though never before confronted. The predator did not move for several seconds after its supper had been put in the cage and began the desperate beat. It was neatly wound beside its tree, a shining hose. It slid out at leisure, the flat head coming from the midst of its coils, advanced over its own outer rim, and paused to flicker awhile at the passing pig.

At last it went further, gave itself more play, curved its neck in an arc, opened its jaws amazingly wide so that the fangs showed full and clear, and placed its mouth like a portal arched with scales in the path of its victim. The guinea pig, perhaps blinded by tears, or perhaps eager for the end as a terror final at least, or perhaps crazed by fear, or perhaps carried by its own impetus faster than realisation, ran into it, and was swallowed whole, head first. Josephine, giddy and with clammy hands, turned away, and even the grass turned red. But Simon gripped the top of the iron rails, mounted the rungs and craned towards the glass, his eyes fixed on the lump in the snake's body.

'Is, is, is it still alive? Hey? Does it know it's in there? Hey? When will it be dead? Will it die very slowly? Hey? What will it die of? Will it be suffocated or, or, or just didge-didge-didge-ested to death, hey?'

Nanny Binny had been conversing with a macaw, but had come up in time to see the poor living innocent disappear down the reptile.

'Good gracious me,' she said. 'That wasn't a sight for you children to be gawking at. That snake was very cruel and nasty, d'you 'ear me Simon? Very cruel and nasty. They shouldn't allow it with children 'ere and all. Get down now at once. Come along. If you 'urry up like a good boy we'll get a tram back and you can buy the tickets.'

'Can we go and watch the snakes?' Simon asked now.

Nanny Binny's mind was on the care of the crowns of hats. 'If you're a good boy,' she said, which was more than he had expected.

'And the lions?'

'And the lions.'

'And the big baboon with the blue bum?'

'If you're good,' crooned Nanny, her hands so busy with their smoothing that her own feelings lay still.

'Willy made me a baboon out of plasticine.'

'Oh blow that Willy,' said Nanny, tissue paper falling from its cupola. 'E's no business wasting 'is time with you children. 'E's got 'is work to do. And don't you swear like that.' Rustle, rustle.

'The postman's come,' said Josephine, chiefly to stop Nanny's anger. She was leaning out of Nanny's window which overlooked the drive but had the mine dumps screened by the oaks. 'Frances is going to the box to fetch the letters.'

'And it's not the right thing for you to spend your time 'anging round the natives. You've got to grow up to be a gentleman.'

Funny, thought Josephine, when Nanny Binny said the word 'native' she made it sound so like 'naked'.

'That Willy,' Nanny Binny had frowned, deciding to be particular.

'Mother's just driven in,' said Josephine, at the window.

'She's been 'aving 'er 'air done,' said Nanny.

Josephine watched her mother walk, from the car to the front door. When she looked round, Nanny was folding silk and Simon was gone.

''Ullo,' said Nanny, 'where's 'e got to then?'

'I'll go and see,' said Josephine.

*

The afternoon opened its jaws.

Coming in, Mrs Leyton could see nothing for a few moments but the dancing red spots that the white glare turned into. Then her hand went to the envelopes on the hall table, her eyes to the mirror above it. Her skin looked glassy, her nose too big, her hair varnished. A thin red line was pressed into her forehead. Her earlobes were pink. The house upheld its tidied, polished, dusted silence despite the treason of a clock, a fly, a child's voice calling faintly, and the distant ringing of the commonplaces by aluminium on the kitchen sink.

She felt awful. The earth was flat, and all upon it little and dry and dreary. The only thing that stopped her feeling dejected past endurance was the thought of the change for which they would be setting out day after tomorrow. Oh how she needed to get away. The thought of the sea came close to reviving her. All the same, this was one of the moments of philosophy, the fly buzzing within, irremovable flecks catching the sunlight, blemishing the glassy surface of her being. Was this all that the long past had brought her to? Was this her life? The fly settled on the fanlight and the buzzing stopped, became intermittent. She reviewed it all at a glance: the weeks, the routine, the banal little tasks, which unnecessarily – since there was Frances the cook, Sixpence the houseboy, Willy the garden boy, a weekly washerwoman, and of course Nanny Binny – she performed, since it seemed there was a space at the top from where a superior eye should be kept.

On Mondays she telephoned the big weekly order to the grocer. She could hear his voice in her ear as she thought of it, the silly little man with his speech defect, stopping the buzz-buzz with 'Wosebank Gwocerwies'. And the scrabble for small change to pay the washerwoman. Tuesday. Wednesday, tennis with Maisie and the rest of the 'girls'. Thursday, Frances's day off, so she and Rayfel had always gone out to dinner on Thursdays in one of those restaurants with the ceremony of the Ritz and the food of an English boarding house: though lately, Rayfel having his meetings, so many meetings, what did they find to talk about, she had a Nanny Binny omelette thin as a pancake and exactly folded all on her own of a Thursday evening, and more and more days were becoming omelette days too. But Lord, what evenings she spent when the occasions for wives came round. In a buzz of inanities even the mind was trapped. Where was she? Fridays. Friday, ordering the fish for dinner, because although Nanny Binny was not a Catholic she took it for granted; and the hairdresser. Saturday fetching the vegetables from the Portuguese Market Garden and home to the smell of baking and later Aunt Lydia's abrasive voice, Frederick's complacency, and Jenny's impossible mixture of sentimentality and dreary prosaic thorough good sense. Sunday, Rayfel in his cream-coloured sports jacket and talc-white chin which he felt tenderly in a cupped hand as he walked up and down the terrace in the sunshine, phrasing the future. What else? She had to face it, face it, her life was a stupid and empty thing. The occasional party; clothes-buy-ing; birthdays and anniversaries – the dull, private and only festivals; the annual holiday; and now and then, twice in fact in the last ten years, the venture into the civilisation of Europe, which for all the glamour of its nouns crystallised into a cluster of hotels, theatres, opera houses and galleries through which she strolled wondering what was the proper attitude to adopt, what the right emotions to feel, what the right thoughts to think. Europe could never repeat that first surprise it had given her with its rich evidence of ultimate dust and perfect levelling. But it might, one day, give up a buried treasure, of people, stimulating people (though faceless), such as she sometimes arranged about her lounge when she was alone; people with responsive sensitivities, who were quick to understand, quick to appreciate, who never misheard, were never dull, and in whose company one could remain at all times perfectly at ease. If she never found such people her wit would become ingrown and painful, and her talents shrivel away. So she did not lose faith in Europe; and although so far no one had lived up to her expectations of cosmopolites, she delivered every letter of introduction.

And then the scenery in Europe was well arranged, easy to admire. Not only was it small and well-worked, but it was amply described in so many books. It had every stamp of approval, and it was friendly.

But here she was in this raw country, among these people, in this house. Trapped.

Now as always, after such moments, she became busy and bustling as the fly. She gathered the letters in her hand, shuffled through them impatiently and one by one laid down the bills, circulars, envelopes addressed to Rayfel, and here was a big square white one with 'Mrs Freda Leyton' printed on it in large, irregular capitals, and in the corner foreign stamps. Spanish stamps. Her face felt differently, in the mirror glanced more mercifully.

She took the letter into her cool blue lounge and sat at the walnut bureau under the window to read it. She used her forefinger as a paperknife under the flap of the envelope, but it was a hasty and unusually clumsy instrument this time, and it tore the stamps. She wondered if she should regret them as she took out the folded piece of lined paper torn from a notebook. The writing, she noticed, slanted across the page and the words were a mixture of capitals and script, of care and scrawl, the first pages better arranged than the last, on which the pen had moved shakily.

Dear Mrs Leyton,
I am in a kind of hospital in Madrid. I have very little Spanish and have been able to converse only with an English footballer (a fellow idealist!) whom they kindly put in the next bed. But today he has gone and died, lady. So now my need to talk to someone brings me to you. Once more. Again I have something heavy to say. It lies on my chest like a tombstone. I can positively feel the weight of it. It makes it difficult

for me to breathe. I don't know if I'll manage the off-loading any better than the last time – but this time, if you'll believe me, I know what I'm talking about. I couldn't say it to my English friend. I couldn't tell him (who lost a leg three weeks before his life) that one can't die for a cause, that the only cause served by death is the cause of dying. And I couldn't say to my mother – to whom I have just written a cheerful friendly letter about the weather, the food, the scenery, and what news of the war I have gleaned from a week-old English newspaper – I am heartily sorry for coming to Spain. And how abject I am, confessing my wrong-headedness to you. Could you have warned me? But of course no one profits from the experience of another – except the one-in-three, the wedding guest? Well you are the only witness at my marriage to remorse. Strange that I should meet the bride abroad. I was destined for an academic life. But my life being academic I was so ignorant. I thought Real Life was passing me by, that Real Life was the life of the body, the active life. Well, the body's death is real too. Look into my glittering eye while I tell you that no one should take up arms except to defend himself or his own. The bell was not tolling for me, Freda. I just had to go and climb on the deadwaggon. Was it conscience that misled me? Well, conscience can be bloody stupid and ill-informed. I have been stupid almost unto death, Freda. Playing at games with pain and nightmares. I thought that to live I would have to climb down from the high white cloudy world of pretence, of theoretical living, down into the dark spawning mud of reality – amoral, frightening, incomprehensible, disorderly, uncontrollable, inarticulate, uninterpreted. But now I know, Freda, now I know, that neither in cuckooland nor among the mudlarks but between the two at human height where the mind and the body are equal intermediaries between visionary impotence and plasmic stupidity is the place for a man to strive in, where imagination and conscience and open-mindedness might protect him and others from self-destruction above and savagery below. Oh my erstwhile beasts of fantasy, my alien chimeras, my rose-coloured reveries, my castles – and my wars – in Spain! I'll stop writing now. I'll try again later.

I am in a fever. Everything is bright and distinct and exciting. The nurse's moustache a passing cloud. Yet a priest followed by a boy in a lace surplice looks quite spectral. The shafts of the late sun X-ray them, splay them out like cards as they pass between me and the window across this hall where I am lying. I must be mad. No priest would dare to come in here. They – we – would castrate him and burn him, as we have done before. Dust steams in the sunlight, and now there's a quiver in it like invisible flame – it's the incense. It both gladdens and soothes me. Incense? It's the fumes of my own heat. I could be won by it so easily now into Godlove. I need a woman. The nurse reminds me too much of my father. I wish you were here, Freda. Godlove reconciles men all too easily to the blood and the cruelty and the pain and all the other stenches that incense usurps. Love, love – what a haze. Dear Freda – did you think me an awful fool when I sat there in your house expounding the value of life? And if so, can you feel for me now? You should have told me, Freda, what you felt about me, even if I hadn't listened to you. At least I couldn't then have complained (as I do, against every blessed writer I have ever read) that nobody warned me, a fool, who lacked even the beginnings of understanding. Perhaps you were telling me in your own way, only I was deaf and blind. I seem to see you more clearly now than I did then. Dark hair, but skin so pale you'd seem like porcelain beside these Latin women. I've even dreamt about you. Two nights ago I saw you dancing in your orange shoes, and I came towards you, but you rose in the air and flew away. I tried to follow you but I couldn't rise more than a few feet above the ground, and then I fell into a pit. Goodbye Freda. Perhaps you will write to me? I expect no pretence of emotion from you. I know that you are unsentimental. And clearer sighted than most. Let me laugh at the people of the Golden City as you see them. Salud.

Benedick

Mrs Leyton folded the letter in its creases, fitted it back inside the envelope and pressed the torn bits into a partial neatness.

'Benedick,' she mused. 'A Tudor name. So English. Sir Benedick.' And parts of the letter were beautifully *put*, after all. A surprise.

'But I haven't got any orange shoes,' she said.

*

'Si-maaaaan?'

'Hush,' came his voice from the deep shade.

'Come out and let's play.'

'Go away, I'm watching something.'

Josephine wandered back towards the house. Without him beside her the garden was a strange land full of daunting silences.

'Well,' called Nanny, leaning from the Nursery window, her face wreathed in ivy, 'where is 'e?'

'Under the pergola.'

'Not interfering with that Willy I 'ope?'

'No, he's all alone.'

'As long as 'e's 'appy. It's getting too late for the Zoo now anyway. You wait there. I'm coming down to get the peas for dinner.'

Nanny had always had business in the garden. She cut the flowers for the vases, and was the personal attendant of the pelargoniums and arums in the big pots on the veranda. But lately she had taken more interest in the kitchen garden. Now, moving between the pea-vines with her bowl, she glanced up frequently and looked towards the row of outbuildings stretching from the edge of the drive, from which they were hidden by the big oaks, to the side fence. Behind the brown doors were the rooms of Frances, Sixpence and Willy, the laundry, and storerooms. Once when Josephine had passed Willy's door and it had been ajar she had seen a bed raised high on bricks, and she had felt a cold coming off the concrete floor; and the room was dark and very small with one high small window covered with wire.

Nanny's head was bent and her hands at work when Josephine saw the door of the washroom opening. The washerwoman came out, walked along the stony path to Willy's door, and went in.

'But,' she said, 'today isn't Monday'

'No,' said Nanny, 'did you think it was then?'

'But the washerwoman only comes on Monday'

'Well she's not 'ere today, is she?'

'I saw her go into Willy's room.'

Nanny Binny straightened. The keys made a rumpus at once. She balanced the basin on her hip and stood there staring at the brown door.

'Ah-ha,' she said.

She stood quite still, chewing on nothing. Josephine looked for pods on her own. She was not afraid with Nanny.

'And oo's that now?' said Nanny.

Josephine rose to see.

Through the gate and along the path towards Willy's door came a man of the same yellow colour as Frances. He wore a yellow jacket and tie, and grey trousers and yellow shoes, and a small straw hat with a yellow band. He opened the door and went in.

'Drink,' said Nanny. 'I always thought 'e was brewing. 'Ere, 'old the peas. I'm going to see your mother about this.'

The keys applauded as she went.

*

So it had come then, the great love? Was it a great love, this of the ardent young man? If so, whatever would she do with him when he hove back into view! Whatever should she do with him now?

There was of course the chance that he would not come back. Perhaps he was dying even now. In which case she probably ought to protest an affection for him. A man can be allowed to outlive unrequited love, but not to die in it – not at least by a woman who knew the value of love, who had read it and heard it with as much response as she had read it and heard it all her life.

Freda enjoyed poetry less now than she used to, but read a good many novels and biographies, and found the pleasure of listening to music almost inexhaustible. On clear days like this, the sky several indefinite blues across which so pleasantly and sadly time carried the white events of passing clouds, the jacaranda branches barely stirring, the birds droning or creaking peacefully along with a mower, a roller, an aeroplane, she liked Debussy, Schumann, Saint-Saens. On wet days when the drip plunged heavily from the eaves and every leaf of ivy was hung with water drops, she liked the chamber music of Schubert, the piano music of Beethoven. On cold days, symphonies. At night, strings. Never opera, seldom oratorio. She did not care much for the human voice. But pure music, profound emotional experience ready processed to be felt, stored and felt again at will, while one lay on a sky-blue couch, on air itself, neither hot nor cold, in almost a physical limbo, gentled one through youth and joy, put one through regret, pains, storms, holocausts, even through deaths, and raised one to participate in a calm, luminous triumph, perhaps even in a transfiguration. Lying with her eyes closed, flowers, stars, wind, sea and other recommended but challenging items were delivered into her power, and she and the composer were one in spirit; his the expression, but hers equally the inspiration drawn from the same source, though he had happened upon it first.

So Freda had grown wise and mellow on art.

But this was a secret.

And secretly she had even felt that one day she was to write, not music alas, but poetry at least. She remembered how, at that party of Maisie's she had almost confessed to the young man, perhaps because he himself had seemed so vulnerable, so unprotected, that she wrote, or had a great intention to write, poetry. He might have had reason to fall in love with her then. Perhaps in fact he had sensed the what, the warmth in her. Whatever, whatever should she do with him now?

If she were to write a love-letter – very subdued, very controlled of course – and it were to be discovered after his death, no one would blame her for having pretended something comfortable to a dying man. To Rayfel she could say, well, something like, 'Comforts for the troops dear – extra irony rations.' Oh not that she was tender of Rayfel's feelings, only that she could not lose face before him, and ostensibly they shared, Rayfel and she, a scepticism about love. Always had. And yet, she remembered, in the early days of their marriage she had waited for signs of feeling in him that would prove his scepticism to be an armour. And a feeling had been lurking in there of course, but for a long time she had failed to identify it because it wasn't what she had expected. Vanity was its name. Egotism. Whereas her own armour, she was certain now (being caught up in a combination of strings, brass and percussion) protected a passion. A passion which nothing in her suburban, provincial, humdrum 'outer' life had yet been worthy of. A passion which justified her scorn, her leisure: though in no eyes but her own, since no one knew, so that she was for ever being misjudged. Who would she care to inform? Not a soul she could think of. Yet if only the young man had understood and *then* loved her!

Perhaps there was still time to improve the quality of his infatuation. Always before only the pale lyricism of dissatisfaction had shone through, and usually even then been cooled into doggerel by her impatient breath: but there must be some other way, to let a flicker of fire reach out through that metal casing of her own?

She read the letter again.

But why should he not? she thought. Why not love me for the image he has of me? Wrongly coloured rather than wrongly shaped. The truth, if not all of the truth.

There came a knock at her door.

'Oh, who is it?'

There was a rule about not disturbing her.

'Mrs Leyton? Mrs Leyton? I 'ave to speak to you.'

'Well, come in. What is it?'

Nanny stood, determined, in the doorway.

'Mrs Leyton, I'm sorry to 'ave to bring tales to you, but I've been watching the boys' rooms for some time now and

I'm sure they're brewing. That Willy's got someone in 'is room now. You don't want strange natives 'anging about. It's not safe.'

'What do you want me to do, Nanny?'

'If we telephone the police they'll come and look. They know what to look for.'

'I don't want to have to find a new garden boy just as we're going away. And besides, just because Willy's got a visitor it doesn't mean he's brewing anything.'

'We'll be away and the 'ouse will be empty. If there are a lot of drunkards 'anging about the 'ouse there's bound to be trouble. You won't 'ave to get a new boy. They'll fine 'im, that's all. And you can get a good boy to take 'is place when we get back.'

'What makes you think he's brewing?'

'Yeast 'as been taken from the kitchen. And there are always such a lot of strange natives 'anging about. There's a yellow creature there now, and the washerwoman oo as no business 'ere of a Friday. I wouldn't be surprised if they wasn't 'aving a horgy.'

'I think we should ask him first.'

''E won't tell the truth. They never tell the truth.'

'Well we could warn him this time.'

'If you go near them when they've been drinking Mrs Leyton you're asking for it. And you can't say as nobody 'as warned you.'

'Oh very well, Nanny, if you think it's the only thing to do, phone the police. Only please don't let them bother me.'

*

Nanny took the basin from Josephine, and carried on with her watching. She said nothing. Josephine pulled at pods, sometimes wrenching the vines from their wires, and dropped the green envelopes into Nanny's bowl, but Nanny, champing a little, did not seem to notice.

As Josephine came round the corner of the top row, near the wall, a big thorn caught at her sleeve, tore the cotton and the skin. As she craned over her own shoulder to see the wound, there was a bang on Willy's door, voices in the room grew loud.

'What did I say,' said Nanny, 'a drinking horgy.' She shifted the bowl to the other arm, champed harder, and looked towards the gate.

With precise synchronisation, two policemen came in at the gate and Willy came out of his door. He was without his apron. One arm was held across his eyes, and his other hand clung to the little brass doorknob. He leant against the door and let out a queer high-pitched squeal, and another, and another, all on the same note, all the same length, all broken off suddenly as though he had to gasp for air in between.

'There now,' said Nanny Binny, 'look at that. Look at that. Just look at 'im. Now what's 'e been and done. Now 'e's for it. Now 'e's asked for it. There, now they've come for 'im.' And she clicked her tongue. She didn't move forward. Josephine stood there with her, and they both looked on as the two men with all their buttons strode on, unhurriedly, towards Willy.

'Well I don't know I'm sure. 'E asked for it, didn't 'e, Oh dear,' said Nanny.

They heard the fly-screen of the kitchen door bang behind them. Frances, seeing Willy and the policemen, began to shout, 'Ma'am, ma'am,' turned and ran back towards the door, one hand pressed to her bosom to keep it still. Josephine, near the end of the pea-row, watched her. The screen banged again.

The policemen reached Willy's door, and Nanny Binny could wait no longer, no longer hope that if she stood still nothing else would move. Pain always cried to her personally, so she set down the bowl and ran, and Josephine too, who would rather have gone no closer, but was caught in the running like a deer.

'Now what's the matter with you?' Nanny called gruffly, gripping Willy's shoulder.

Willy squealed a longer squeal, let go of the knob and sank on his knees in the dust. Both forearms in their tattered striped sleeves leant on his lap and covered his face. His ankles, jutting out of the yellowing canvas of sandshoes looked particularly thin and bare and chafed and sad, with no socks.

'Willy, Willy,' called Nanny, bending over him, looking sterner than ever before.

'Mahnd Misses, excuse me,' said one of the policemen. 'Is this the boy they phahned about?'

'What is the matter with you Willy?' Nanny called. 'Are you drunk or are you ill? Now you stop that noise and tell us or we can't do anything to 'elp you can we?'

Willy had stopped squealing. He seemed to roll further forward so that his forehead and the prongs from his cheeks almost touched the earth with its half-buried stones.

'Ow, *Misses*,' he groaned.

The other policeman, an older one with a piece of sticking plaster on one of the folds of his neck, walked slowly round Willy's crouched form and into the room behind him. (What, Josephine wondered, were the yellow man and the washerwoman doing in there? The room was too small to hide in.)

'Hey, Porsons,' he was heard to call.

'Pooza hey?' Porsons expected. 'Ya got the evidence?'

'Better come and tike a squizz,' advised the big one.

Porsons obeyed. Josephine could see nothing but darkness in Willy's room. But she heard one of the policemen whistle long and low.

Meanwhile Nanny had knelt down in front of Willy, the keys sounding an alarm.

'Willy,' she pleaded, 'tell me what it's all about quickly before they come back. If you're 'urt we'll get a doctor –'

'Misses –' Willy groaned out again, but the two men returned.

'If Ah could use the phahn. Misses, Ah've got to call the sty-shin.'

'No no,' said Nanny, standing up. Her hands were shaking. 'It's quite all right. You don't 'ave to trouble. There must 'ave been a mistake. You can go now. I'll see to 'im. We've got no complaint.'

'Ah'm sorry Misses but Ah'm afraid it's serious. There's been bleddy murder gaing on around here, if you'll excuse the expression.'

*

And what if (Freda thought) this were the moment that had always been in store for her; the moment when The Event was to begin, the second movement of her life in which the inexorable occurs?

How long, after all, she asked herself, not noticing the persistent pointless buzz of the gramophone trailing like a long thread from the end of what should have been a closing resolution, how long could that faith of 'some day …' linger on into adulthood? The damsel-dream; of the handsome gallant, since what possibilities other than he were there? It was hard to say, though she had looked for them, had studied many of the recorded roles which life had to offer. Yet none of those men and women of vision whose eventful worlds were packed on her shelves had been able to demonstrate that here and here in her own life were beauty and value, nor show her a direction. Indeed for her particular combination of facts there was neither precedent nor analogy recorded. If only there were, somehow her life would have more validity; with a chart she might be living it better. She didn't seem to fit into any of the labelled cases, however capacious: not the religion one, not the nation one, not the country one, not even the language one or the culture one: for her religion was no more than a brand-name; her ancestry a – a *rumour*; her country, this one fenced acre; her culture this roomful; and even her language was only a kind of loan.

As though to move out of the searchlight of her own thoughts, she got up and walked beside the bookshelves that filled one side of her cool dim room. The gold letters shone out from the spines. And there was no escape from her own illumination. She had tried her best to find mirrors in books. Here she had read of a lady who had just such eyes as she, and there of another who shared her preference for blue. There was one a Jewess, but in an age when she could also be a queen. There was one who lived and played the piano on a far frontier, but she was dumb and died young. And though Freda Leyton had long admired, and resolved that in similar circumstances she would behave just like the calm brave intelligent women who were often as tall as she, yet they remained beyond her emulation, distinguished by adversities of which she had no hope. In this real life what adversities did come along were always degrading. And besides *they* so often had compensations which were equally beyond her grasp – castles, mansions, estates, beauty, at the very least dedicated listeners who never failed to understand their meaning, never missed a subtlety, never misheard. How she was wasted in this provincial town among these smug and soulless people. It was no less than a cross. Doomed to be nailed every Monday by 'Wosebank Gwocerwies'.

My parts, she explained, to a small white head of Byron, came in separate boxes, labelled, but without instructions for assembly. What's more, it seems to me that they belong to quite different construction sets.

Well, but what if now something well documented, universally familiar, were to happen to her: a drama of love? A drama of love! Oh dear but what a to-do. She became aware of the gramophone's irritating noise and turned the knob sharply. (It was getting loose, something would fall apart one of these days.) And returning to the couch she decided that she actually envied those people whose experiences were all lived through, done with, tidily recorded and made all the greater for that, and compactly stored away in books.

She had raised her feet on to the cushions when another interruption came, no timid knock but Frances blustering, 'Ma'am the pleece –'

'I know, Frances, I know. Let them carry on with their work, let me carry on with mine, and you have some to carry on with too, haven't you? You could make the tea. It's a little early but I'd very much like a cup of tea.'

'Yes, Ma'am.'

'Oh, and Frances.'

'Yes, Ma'am?'

'You could offer a cup to the policemen if there aren't too many of them.'

*

But Frances did not make tea.

Outside in the sunshine Frances drew up beside the large policeman. Her apron and cap were very stiff and correct, and looking down at Willy she was all starch.

There was a silence, but for Willy's moans.

'If you dahn't believe us ma'am, you can see for yourself.'

'No,' said Nanny. For it wasn't the crime she doubted, but its cause. She hesitated. She looked at the man's uniform.

'Well – If you're sure – Frances, show the constable where the telephone is.' And her head shook, and her suddenly useless hands.

Frances passed on the order to Sixpence who was just arriving.

Then Nanny remembered how children must be protected. 'Off to the Nursery with you. You read a nice book until I come.'

Josephine went round behind the others and stood watching.

Everyone waited. But for the low rough sound of Willy's pain there was a stillness. It was like, Josephine thought, the silence that comes when the refrigerator switches itself off, and only when it stops you realise what a noise it had been making, how it had been getting louder and louder as though it were going to burst, how you had been afraid without knowing it, and silence is a relief and a shock together.

*

Freda drew a piece of hand-made blue paper towards her.

Dear, or My dear?

My dear Benedick, comma.

Something about his state of health. Concern. Come back to that later. Confirm his impression of clear-sightedness and so on.

'We ladies on the whole keep clear of subversive policies such as love, imagination, open-mindedness, tolerance, especially love, except as a password into marriage. Don't be deceived by our niceness, which we cultivate to the point of utter insipidity. Nor by the fact that we all hold the right opinions. We are very much on the side of the right, but only provided it costs us none of our comfort – as you so *rightly* saw.'

Yes, that would do. That could stand. And as the next words occurred she flushed with excitement and wrote quickly:

'Oh we'd rather have the kiddies than the kudos,
We'd rather have a Buick than a brain;
But while we drive the blacks
With a sjambok to their backs
We hope the Bolshies win the war in Spain.'

Good. Fine. Now a few words of gratitude, a suggestion of guardedness, deliberate restraint, the reason for which could be left to a reader's hopes or suspicions. One dare not give clear cause for expectation.

A little bell tolled.

Oh to *have* loved, to *have* suffered, to have won through to peace – or triumph; at any rate to have won through to one's third movement, not by skirting the second, but through the proper course to gain the full rewards of resolution and fulfilment.

'Porsons here, sir,' said a loud voice in the passage.

Because in fact to come into harbour without having made a perilous voyage, to reach calm waters without there having been a storm, to have life drift on as it always has towards nothing but old age and from nothing much at all.

'Ja sir, we got him, sir. Ja, with the waggon, sir,'

would be dreadful.

'– to chorge him with murder, sir.'

'Dreadful,' Freda said aloud, to the lucky ladies who were folded like butterflies between the covers on the shelves.

'Ah think sa, sir. He is hurt, sir. Right, sir.'

Again the bell tolled.

'Terrible. Unthinkable.'

But where was the tea?

She pressed and pressed the electric bell set in the wall above her sofa, but no one came. She would have to go and see.

There was no one in the kitchen. Out she went into the assaulting glare of the garden. Were they still fussing about in the boys' rooms?

'Oh God,' said Mrs Leyton. 'What is it now Nanny?'

Nanny did not even look at her, but Porsons explained. In his dreadful accent.

'You mean the other two are *dead?* Do you mean that Willy killed them?'

'Bath of them, Misses. That's what drink mikes them do. We've phahned for the embulance and everything. Smit'll wait here till they come and Ah'll tike this one in. Hey Smit, lock the door hey and give me a hand with this one to the waggon.'

'We've always treated them like human beings,' Mrs Leyton remembered, looking prejudice in the eye. All Afrikaners were prejudiced. And all policemen were Afrikaners.

'You corn't be too soft with them,' said Porsons.

One on either side the two men bent down over Willy. Josephine crept forward and watched them tug quite gently at Willy's arms and part them so that Willy's head stuck forward without support or cover. At the exposure Josephine and others cried out. It was enough to wilt starch.

'Good God,' said Mrs Leyton.

Not only was Willy's face laid open in several gaping pink and black wounds, but both his eye-hollows were dark and sticky bogs. There was blood on his sleeves and his shirt front, and blood, they saw now, looking down, in the dust and on the edges of stones.

Smit took out his handkerchief and bound it round the poor head.

'You can't take him like that,' said Nanny. 'Put 'im on 'is bed and I'll do what I can until the doctor comes.'

'Dahn't worry, Misses. We'll get a doctor to him. He'll ga to the hospital orfterwards but first he's got to come with us sa we can chorge him.'

A crowd was growing. Houseboys in white suits, and garden boys in blue aprons, and maids in green overalls and little winged caps were gathering round, drawn to the one crystal of event in the great still afternoon. They gave way as Smit and Porsons carried their charge, gently enough though his feet dragged, towards the gate. After a moment's silence everyone began talking. Nanny was protesting still. They had come under the oak trees when from who knew where a bolt descended, big Constable Smit staggered, and the fist of Simon, who had landed on top of the man, discovered how sticking plaster, if struck and struck, would, like a bell push, cause a noise in another place. Smit cried his cry. He drew Willy down with him as he went on his knees, but let go in order to grope for the wild, thudding merciless thing which was hammering his tender spot. Porsons too let go to come to the other's aid, while Simon, busy as he was, yelled, 'Run, Willy, run,' but Willy fell prone on the gravel, which made Simon, though evading the grasping hands, slither down the mighty back of the law to which he had been clinging like an outsize monkey, and stand and look, and Smit and Porsons also stood still a moment, while a yellow trickle ran under the dark arch of Smit's collar. Alan Jesus, who had appeared with Simon, was barking joyously round the sporting Willy.

'Is he dead?' said somebody, sucking air through teeth, an insatiate of thrills.

'Na man. He's just bluffing. Get up you,' Porsons ordered, prodding the prostrate man in the ribs with the nub of his boot.

Willy rolled over and moaned, arms over his face again. Alan Jesus licked the blood on his chin.

'We said get *up*.'

Smit drew back his navy-blue leg. His toe was an iron and stubby hook, but he was moving his weight back on to it when a large grey stone in Simon's hand glinted once from the quartz in it and struck, not thrown, but hammered surely home on the lowest fly-button of the flexing Smit, who grunted and brought his knees together.

'Si-maan!' moaned his mother.

But Nanny Binny who was standing there with shaking head and trembling hands, and who had taught obedience, said not one word to halt the acts of Simon's fury.

'Hold him,' Smit ordered, his face red. And Sixpence, whose fears were in the right place, took hold of the boy. But Simon was docile in his grasp, and watched without a word the two men resettle their caps, raise Willy between them and start towards the gate. Smit looked back at Mrs Leyton.

'You must watch that kid, hey. He'll be a joov'nile d'linquent if you dahn't watch out. Just a word of warning, hey?'

'I want you to let me know what happens,' she said, to confine the man to his sphere.

'Yes, ma'am.'

And Mrs Leyton hurried back to the house. But everyone else went on to the gate to see Willy stowed in the waggon.

''E needs a doctor,' Nanny persisted, going right up to the door. Smit clanged it shut and locked it. She went round to Porsons in his front seat and knocked on his window. It jerked down. Porsons said, 'Dahn't worry Misses, he'll be looked orfter lahk a by-bee.'

The black van moved forward, leaving Nanny Binny standing in the middle of the road. The narrow slit high up along the waggon's side was filled in with bars round which, here and there, black hands were gripped, like strange beads on an abacus. Josephine counted the hands and wondered if any were Willy's.

'I thought I told you to go back in the 'ouse, and where is Simon? Go on, go about your business all of you.'

Josephine withdrew among the oaks, hoping to find him. The crowd dispersed. Smit took up his post outside the closed door, his face glowing in the refulgence that now bloomed on the houses and gardens of the well-kept world. And Nanny Binny, passing back through the kitchen garden, stared at the bowl of pods that stood in the sand between the pea-rows, but left it there, her hands straying to the wild and idle tendrils of the vines and tightening them about the wires as though every reaching filament of nature could be brought into the discipline of love.

*

'Here!'

For once *Simon* had been looking for *her.*

'You've got to come with, and, and, and do something.'

'We can't go out the gate.'

'Come on. This way.'

Although the wall was high on the garden side it was quite low on the side of the pavement, except where it rose to become the back wall of the outbuildings. Where Simon stopped among the blackjacks and tall grasses with red feathery tops, there was a window at the height of his knees.

'I'm too big,' he said. 'You've got to go in for me. Look, it opens.'

'What do you want me to go in for?'

'The bones.'

'I can't go in there Simon. I can't. They said they were both dead. They said that Willy had killed them both.'

'Who? Who? Who'd they say he'd killed?'

'The washerwoman and the yellow man.'

He looked at her face.

'Aaaaa!' he said. 'He didn't. Did he?'

'They say he did.'

He bared his teeth, opened his mouth wide and laughed his horrible put-on laugh. Then he was solemn again; again

90

stared uncomprehendingly at his sister's white face and unfamiliar frightened eyes.

'I'll go,' he said. 'Just, just, just come and help me with this.'

'Oh please don't – they'll find you. You won't be able to get out again. They'll take you away.'

He lifted the window hinged as a flap. Its wire was fixed on the inside, to the casement itself, not the frame, over the broken dusty glass. He tried to see into the dark below, lying on his side and holding up the window with one arm.

'If you won't help me then you must go away,' he said.

'All right. I'll hold it for you.'

He lay on his stomach and snaked backwards into the dark hole while she stood to the side holding the window up with both hands. He grunted as he squeezed his shoulders through. She heard something rip. But at last only his fingers were to be seen clinging to the frame. They left go. There was no sound of falling or of feet hitting a floor. He must have landed on the bed, or stepped down on to a table or a chair. How in that small room could he avoid bumping into furniture – or things. She let the window gently down. It brightened, and lifting it again she saw that the electric bulb hanging from the middle of the ceiling was lit. She turned her head away, let the weight fall from her hands and bang against the frame. She didn't want to see in there. She wanted to run away, but stayed for an age, watching the tiny grass insects, which moved all together like darting and hovering clouds, shimmer over the pavement grass, the sunlight harden on the empty street where not even a garden boy stood at a gate or a single black woman with a baby on her back sat in the shade of the plane trees. Whatever was happening in the world was happening down in the earth, out of sight. She would not think of what Simon was doing down there.

Hardly breathing, she waited: for revelation, which often started pleasure, could equally discover pain. And perhaps when she had seen to the rock of her own death she had not after all fathomed the depths, nor even begun to explore them. Things might swim up in unpredictable shapes.

'Psssst. Pssst.' It was Simon hissing for her attention.

She lifted the window but would not stoop to look.

'Hold it,' he whispered. 'I'm coming up.'

His arms and then his head came through.

'You'll have to pull me,' he said breathlessly.

'What are you standing on?'

'I'm standing on the man and he's on the bed.'

'I can't pull and hold the window.'

'Sit down. No with your feet against the wall. Bend your knees. Hold the window up as high as you can. Now I'm going to grab your legs.'

'It's no good. We can't. My arms are breaking.'

'Hold it!' he commanded, his face contorting with strain. His cheek pressed to her shins, and grunting, he got a knee up on to the narrow sill; then he fell sideways into the grass and dust.

'Quickly,' she called, 'come out of the way, I have to let go.' She did not know how she had held it so long.

He kicked and slithered along the ground, and the window went down.

When he stood up she saw that his clothes were in tatters and that grime was mixed with blood in patches on him – he had scratched his arms, knees. His own blood of course. Of course.

She sat pressing her aching arms to her body, rocking backwards and forwards and looking up at him in fear.

'They, they, they –' he began.

But she didn't want to hear about them. In time she would have to know, not yet. But she asked, 'Did you find the bones? Have you got them?'

'No,' he said. 'Damn 'n' blast. I forgot about the bones. But look at this, hey.'

He put his hand behind his back and when he brought it forward again it held a gory knife with a long, slightly curved blade and a yellow handle.

*

Freda did not finish her letter to the young man. 'One evening,' she thought, homing to the haven of the lounge and seeing the rectangle of blue on the bureau; 'perhaps one evening,' she thought, and she read through that verse again with pride and pleasure; 'one evening when I'm sitting on the balcony outside my hotel room and watching the sea, I'll know what to say.'

She folded the sheet she had written on and put it into the torn envelope along with his, and carried it up to her room.

'But if I were really in love with him,' she pondered, 'mightn't Rayfel be very annoyed indeed?'

This was a new idea. She stood quite still with one hand on the rail at the bottom of her bed, her eyes fixed on a Monet print above her dressing table which she admired for being so extremely smudgy that all manner of things could be made out in it other than those the painter had intended, and looked at the possibilities which the idea presented. What, after all, did she have to oppose to his vanity? Some day she'd know. Some day her opportunity would come. Some day she might even accomplish his overthrow.

On her bed lay nightdresses and peignoirs in a rainbow of colours. There were the chiffons that she seldom wore because they bunched up into small hard knots under one's body as one slept But she always took them to hotels. They looked lovely all together in a drawer. She'd had them for simply ages – since before Josephine was born. Maisie Gould had been with her when she bought them. That was when Maisie had told her that she actually liked sex.

She drew aside the curtains of her dressing table, revealing a pair of small doors, and with the key taken from a glass box with a silver lid that stood before the centre mirror, she unlocked the doors and on the bottom of the empty cupboard laid – the love-letter. That cupboard had always been empty, locked and empty. Now she locked it again on its secret contents, and put the key back in its box with the hairslides, safety pins, paper clips, and an earring screw that had lost its raison dêtre (whether diamond or glass). She straightened the box between its parentheses of the narrow curved clothes brush and the paddle-shaped hairbrush, and then the tinkle of the four o'clock bell called her down to tea at last, which she would take alone in the blue lounge. And being unwilling to think any more of matters which had frightened her so, she put Mendelssohn on the gramophone and took Thackeray from the shelf.

*

'Quick. Now.'

Josephine had watched through the window of the lounge until she had seen her mother return. Then, with Simon hidden in the hydrangeas beside the kitchen door she peered through the wire of the screen and saw Frances out of the kitchen with the tray for the 'Nursery tea' which would be set in the dining room.

At her word Simon hurried through the kitchen and up the stairs. There was great danger on the landing. At any moment Nanny Binny might appear. But he reached the bathroom safely and locked the door. He set about the business of scrubbing himself, while his sister went for clothes. Nanny Binny was not in the Nursery, nor in her own room. Josephine had got the clean things safely to Simon, and his torn and bloody garments bundled in her own arms before she heard Nanny's voice calling from below, with a slight hoarseness, 'Si-maaan. Josepheene. Tea-time.'

She turned on the landing. Where was a hiding place?

Over the hills and far away. And was that Nanny's foot-step on the stairs? She went through the nearest door, to hide behind it if necessary. Her mother's room. She remembered the little doors.

The key was easy to find. It was pressing against the glass, the long little body with a fin-tail at one end and an O at the other. The cupboard was empty but for an old letter lying on the bottom. Old letters lay about in all sorts of places, she had seen before now. She stuffed the shirt and trousers and socks into the small space, locked the door and took the key away with her. The two children met at the top of the stairs and went down to tea together.

'There you are at last,' said Nanny Binny. 'And 'owever did you go and do that. Blood all over.'

But it was Josephine she was talking to. Her arm, her sleeve. The thin dash and the row of dots began to sting as she noticed them. And Nanny Binny said nothing about Simon being dressed in his grey flannel best or his hands and face and knees being almost clean. Perhaps she expected it now that the source of his delinquency was removed, but was in doubt as to its value.

Later, warned to keep away from the outbuildings where 'men were busy', and having no desire to go there anyway, Simon and Josephine, together, wandered off down the garden, crossed the tennis court and came to the weedy, rickety, neglected pergola, with its creepers, morning glory, black-eyed susan, jasmine and golden shower, so tangled that it became a dim tunnel, and a cave of darkness at its far end. Josephine stopped under the morning glories of the first arch – they were already folded, white and purple stumps and no trumpets. There she delivered to him the key of the hiding place. He went on alone with it. She waited until darkness had spread across the garden, but when a bat flapped out, close to her face, she fled to the safety of the lighted house. In, in, *in*. Praying: walls, doors, windows, floors, hold me, keep me.

*

The long scream blew back in the wind. But Simon was quiet, and his quietness, like the land through which they passed, was a step beyond the present safety of her actual life. Her ghost was out there too, but travelled, a transparency, swiftly and serenely over the lumpy earth, undeterred by batting telegraph poles. She could know, she would go, but now her thoughts were bound towards an immense delta of personal happiness, and so she would keep them. The train was a sealed tube, a travelling safe furnished with delights, which tore through alternate desert and darkness to the sea. Soot gathered on the window ledge (though the windows were firmly shut). She sat on hot green leather and ate pieces of chicken and the damp sandwiches they'd brought in a basket. But by the evening of the first day the bread was beginning to dry and most of the chicken was eaten, and she and Simon followed their father and mother, Nanny Binny coming behind, to the saloon. How lovely its polished wooden columns were, the white cloths, the gleaming cutlery. Its African name – whatever it was it always began with Um – was written in a semicircle of gold above the doors at either end. The lights on the walls were inverted chalices of smoky glass. The cruets clover-shaped, holding the solid bells of the pepper and salt, and the metal egg with its clanging top and a window for a spoon, in which sometimes there was mustard. Vinaigrettes had their cut-glass bottles of pale gold and amber liquids. Flat napkins on the china plates had each its springbok. And clipped against the wall under the narrow mirror between the windows, the wine list wreathed with leaves and tendrils and bunches of

96

grapes, and the menu, with everything written in French and Afrikaans: consomme – sop; poisson – vis; legumes au saison – groente. And the real grapes which came in a basket were larger than any that were ever to be found at either end of this journey: green and round, or long and yellow with little strokes of amber on the flesh beneath the skin, or black-red with a deep shine in every one.

At night, as she lay between sheets that smelt of laundered steel, others in waiting walked by on lonely platforms. The spaces on all sides were very quiet, she knew. How fearful to be left all alone at night in the vast emptiness of the veld. Though Simon had once told her that he would like as much as anything to lie down to sleep in the desert with no one about, and all, all, all, all the stars above him. And he would. But now he lay near her, the train carrying them both through darkness and distance, which she held in her mind and was the ruling spirit of. It was a dangerous joy, because when she slept she might find herself lost in her own country. But as long as she lay awake she indulged herself with the pleasure of playing out sheer Africa in her mind. And one day she might traverse it and find out its details. Signs are not always to be read, but the coloured bulbs under glass domes on the ceiling could have been dry flowers or dead bright birds.

When the green blinds were barely lighted from the other side, there came a rattling of metal on metal, a steward's knock with his crank-key on the finger-slot of the door, and without waiting to hear a 'come in' the man slid the door back with a sound of dragging air, and all dressed in white and light and shiny buttons stuck his cropped head through the door – Nanny Binny pressing the sheets to her throat – and shouted, 'Morning, tea or coffee, more tee of koffie?' And when he had gone the blinds were raised, and the pale gold of nowhere, which the train had achieved, was flowing by.

At breakfast time the children went to the saloon with Nanny Binny only, for Mother and Father had their breakfasts in their respective coupés. And now the cruets sparked off little suns. The fried eggs looked as thick and glazed as the plate they lay upon; it was no more conceivable that they had ever been in a shell than that the slightly blackened tomato-half had ever hung on a stalk.

Later the sun travelled beside them on the green leather seats, and they played snakes and ladders while outside the Karoo with its casual hills slid by, the near bushes at speed, the distant more slowly. Reaching the top row by throwing a six, and knowing that disaster with its snake head lay between her and victory, Josephine held her breath and turned to watch a dusty peppercorn, a miraculous willow near a water tank with its nasty dangling elephant trunk, slide past on journeys of their own. Or stop beside the train. And children came running under the windows, calling 'Penny, penny,' while the train throbbed and hissed. So many, from those five huts, on all sides of which the flat spaces stretched. Josephine could imagine how they waited for the train to creep out of its mouse-hole on the horizon. Their excitement would grow as its self-important speed and noise grew. And if it didn't stop, but only slowed, they would gaze up at the faces behind square after square of glass, passing by: those shut out scanning those shut in. And when the train had gone out of sight, what an immeasurable victory silence must regain. What were those huts like inside? No picture came to mind. They must be very cold in the winter. One day she'd look inside them.

Mrs Leyton came into their compartment and loosely bundled the dry bread and half-picked chicken bones in greased paper and string, opened the window for this one important act, leant out with the parcel and dropped it. It burst in the dust, but the children, big and small, ran to it and plucked up whatever their hands could touch. Jostling one another and shouting, they started to eat, dust and all, on the spot. The thin young girls with smaller brothers and sisters pickaback handed pieces of food over their shoulders. They talked to each other in their clicking language. One child, with a round belly but knobbly thighs and shoulders, arrived too late to gather up even the paper or the string. He stood watching the lucky ones. He was naked but for a necklace.

Mrs Leyton came away from the window, forgetting to shut it, and went in search of iced water. Simon leant out in her place and stretched his arms towards the child who stood watching. The child, thinking he was being offered something, ran forward a step or two and then stopped, seeing the hands open and empty.

'Give me,' Simon called, his fingers thrumming the air, 'give me,' and he tapped his own throat with a forefinger.

The child stared at Simon, but as the train jerked he fumbled at the wire round his neck, unwound the necklace as he ran beside the train, and then, stretching up, put the necklace (which was his safety) into the hungry hands.

Simon pulled himself in – he had been hanging out from the hips – and turning fell with his arms across the table, knocking the red and yellow counters, and the green, for Nanny had been playing too, into undetermined squares. The necklace lay across his palms – fragments of bone, some split, sharp, yellowish, some almost a ball and white-bright as alabaster, and also what could have been a few dog teeth. One by one he pulled them off and stowed them away in his pocket. The wire too, squeezed into a lump. When Mr Leyton came in, rubbing his hands, he found his son shaking a die vigorously in its cup.

'Hot, wouldn't you say?'

Rayfel Leyton had long ago decided that one must say what one wished regardless of one's audience. He held that this saved him from bitterness, proved his generosity, and gave opportunity to the general to discover who amongst them might have a taste for caviare. As for children, he did not believe in them. He did not look at his son or daughter, but out at the turning land. 'We'll get some ice cream at the next station. If it is a station.' He laughed. The children gazed at a bristly slope, a smooth round glistening mountainhead.

'Do you see those two sheep out there?' their father asked.

They looked out and saw a great number of sheep.

'Do you know what the one is saying to the other?'

They waited. Father always joked with them on journeys, rubbing his hands in a jollier way than usual. They knew it was the journey and not they making him jaunty.

'Well I'll tell you what they're saying. I happen to know. The one on the right, you see him? There – now? Well, he's saying to the one on the left, "Funny, I keep thinking it's Tuesday".

He laughed. Then he bent his head close to his daughter.

'Don't you see the joke?' Because he enjoyed sounds of having been heard.

'Yes,' said Josephine.

'What can it matter to a sheep in the middle of the Karoo whether it's Tuesday or any other day?' he stooped to explain.

Father, Josephine thought, had an awful knowledge. But she must go on with the game, to pretend she did not feel it, and to please him.

'If they could talk then it would matter to them,' she said.

'Why's that?'

'They'd need to know the days of the week if they could talk.'

'In the middle of the Karoo?'

'Well, people in the middle of the Karoo need to know the days of the week.'

'Well, well, you're going to be a debater like your father, hey?' he said, reaching for her cheek. He chuckled, and again she accepted the hurt and the feeling of ugliness on the one side of her face. But he, catching sight of himself in the mirror between the windows, let go to feel his own cheeks with both his hands. She seldom looked up as high as his head. She wondered if he admired anyone as much as himself. Did he look up to anyone, as she to him and Mother, as Nanny Binny to God and the King of England, or as Simon had to Willy? Had he ever wanted to keep with someone, as she did with Simon? She had heard him speak with great respect of a number of dead persons, someone by the name of Burke, a pair called Addison and Steele who stuck together as kith and kin, and a Doctor Johnson who was often but not always in the company of the two, like an older brother to a pair of twins. But was there anyone alive?

Mr Leyton heaved on the door and left. He had not looked at his son. Simon, he had concluded, some time ago, despite his wife's concurrence, was not only no great brain, but would grow up to be a lout if steps weren't taken. What steps were yet to be decided. Such as had already been attempted had not proved efficacious.

He shut the door firmly behind him.

Soon they were rounding mountain after mountain, and descending, and far off and down between the feet of mountains, they glimpsed the first green valley. Simon, daring the soot as Nanny was gone to the saloon for her cup of tea, leant out and sang a loud tuneless song that toned with all the discords of the train and the sliced rocks, and the tunnels and the passes through which the train was bounding now, merrily, easy on the home run, into, at last, the widest of the green vine-valleys (and the fence made of railway sleepers was one long ladder that carried you on, row after row) towards the Atlantic shore. The mountains pivoted now, and Simon's anger or regret was wound up on the great spinning reel of the land, the wind rushed past his head, the sun burned upon it, and there, far out but lustrous, spread the sea.

'Hey, can you smell it, the, the, the, the sea, can you smell it? And and, and, and look how it, how it, how it – glitters.'

He went floundering about the corridor, imperilling trays on steward's hands.

'Whoo, out of the way with you,' said Nanny Binny cheerfully, putting him aside as she came back towards the compartment. She shut the window, lifted her black coat off its hook, brushed it with her leather-backed brush, and sighed, smiled, sighed, smiled. After all, 'e was a real boy. Listen to 'im. Like to deafen them all.

He was out of her sight when he stopped at an open window and was quiet again. He wanted to reach out, to touch and hold. Failing that, he brought a handful of bones up from his pockets, stretched out into the bright wind and he too dropped the pieces, but one by one, into the furious dust.

*

With a ripping and a snapping his hands tore out the half-moon and the bulging, serrated stars.

And in the middle of the box Josephine placed the sea-egg, the little green minaret studded with pearls.

It was the day after the South-Easter had been blowing, and the tideline was trimmed with stinging bluebottles like narrow cellophane bags full to bursting with pale blue ink. Josephine, carrying the box, carefully stepped over them. But Simon, running, trod with his bare feet on a whole long row, popping them all, and without being stung. They were left as little bits of broken skin with long navy-blue threads. Nothing flowed out of them. Simon ran on down the strand, round the heaps of rock, to where people were gathered in front of the bathing booths of St James. There Nanny Binny always set up her outpost with a brown umbrella, towels, lotions, books and knitting, hats, plasters, spare bathing suits, vests, shirts and knickers, Marie biscuits and a coil of rope which she never explained, on the smooth strip of sand beside the 'pool', a wedge of safe sea walled on three sides. As the water rocked down the sides of the wall you could see the green hair which grew from it poxed with water snails, and the strips of seaweed ribbon, shiny as oilskin. Outside the wall were heaps and fields of rock, with hollows of sea clear and full of colour at low tide, boiling and dreadful when the waves broke over them.

As Simon built his castle other boys, pink and white and browned, were drawn to watch it grow. It was high and wide but without architecture, without skill, with no care for detail or finish, no neat shape of inverted bucket or print of spade. Some of the boys shifted their weight from foot to foot, bent out their knee bones, flexed their fingers at their sides, longing to get their careful hands to the job. But they didn't dare, any more than they would have dared the height and extent that he did. His walls circled families, took in bathing booths, erected barricades between bathers and their pool which they'd have to skirt or leap or smash through. Most of them went round. A lady smiled at the boys who stood doing nothing and asked them why they didn't build in a more convenient place. They all turned their heads and looked at Simon, who stared at the questioner without insolence, interest or apology until she turned away.

'Shells,' he yelled, without looking at them, but expecting their obedience. 'Shells for here and here and here and all along there!'

And all the little boys, fat, thin, thick-haired, shaven-headed, hatted and bared, long-costumed and trunked, peeling and pale and tanned (and the one in spectacles called Benny who accosted new acquaintances with, 'I'm barmitzvah. Are you barmitzvah?'), jumped to it, ran off down the beach, among the rocks, searching in the bays and the rock-pools where the anemones lay spreading their colours and millions of shells were stored by the tides. Handfuls, hatfuls of shells they brought, and Simon allowed them to do the planting, along his walls, upon his turrets. He stood with his hands on his hips, taller and broader than any of them, his yellow head a sun in their midst, and watched as they squatted, working, chattering, quarrelling, putting the final touches to his kingdom. Some took much care over the task: one shy little boy (with noticeable eyelashes, and called Simon by his grey-haired mother who was camped on the beach near Nanny), put flags of seaweed on a watchtower, and a starfish raised like a trophy on a stick. Simon the Great waited until the last of the shells and weeds were in place, the last boy settled back on his haunches to admire his own handiwork and the general effect, and then he pounced. First rising in the air with a gurgling cry, he fell hard and furiously upon the nearest mound, set round with its graded shells, and his hands, arms, legs, feet, even his face pressed away, flattened, ruined it all. He grimaced, growled, threw handfuls of sand, so that mere flesh and blood scattered in fear for its eyes. The boys looked shocked for a moment of disbelief, then they all fell upon the heaps of sand and shell, threw it to the winds, every one wild, with a wild noise. All sprawled and shot their fury about. All but the shy boy who stood there and laughed.

When Simon ran into the sea the rest followed. Those who could not swim went at least as far as they dared, leaping, caterwauling, like a raiding tribe, then floundering back to their depth, from where they'd watch the enviable swimmers reach the far back wall of the pool and stand there perilously, facing the oncoming waves that seethed among the outer rocks and hurled themselves against the wall – at high tide gushing right over it, sweeping boys here and there into the bobbing water of the pool – then dragged back like paws, and sank, gurgling between the rocks.

One afternoon, Josephine, sitting beside Nanny on the beach (Nanny with her straw head bent over knitting and newspaper, her striped dress well below her knees but her bunions uncovered to the healing sun), saw the shy boy, the other Simon, who couldn't swim, walk on the wall at high tide right to the end, the danger spot. He stood there a moment beside the others who dared, and was swept off, out the other way in the backwash, out among the treacherous jagged rocks which she knew were there. And so quickly afterwards that Josephine (but for her faith) might have supposed that he too had been carried off, her Simon plunged clumsily after the other, down out of sight. She sat craning but quiet, with a cry like a wad in her throat. Unable to move she fixed her eyes on a bandy young man in maroon trunks who stood, untroubled by wave and backwash, gazing down into the churn where the two boys must be floundering.

The young man put his fists on his hips. He didn't see any reason to help, or else he was a coward. He went on watching, though. If there was anything to watch. If the calamity had not already happened, and both unconscious bodies been swept far out into the Indian Ocean.

In fact Simon had reached the boy before the waves could either slam him against the rocks or drown him in the bubbling depths between. He got him by the hair, and as a new wave came, gripped one of the serrated spurs which threatened like a shark's fin, pressed his body to the razor-edged shells stuck over the bulk of the rock, and kept hold. Though the current pulled at the boy it did not prise him away. And before the backwash could gain its impetus he had with three strong kicks reached the wall and flung himself half over it, his one hand curling over the inside edge, the other still clinging to the hair of the rising, sinking boy, the rocking water stropping his thighs on submerged crags. The hands of the other boys and the young man stretched out and he relinquished his charge to them. Ignoring more hands which asked for him, Simon the Brave himself, he hauled himself flat on the wall and lay there fetching his breath awhile, feeling victory in his body, though breaker and backwash rocked him still, and the surf below roared like a hungry beast in an arena.

Some marched the rescued boy, when he had done with his gasping, back round the wall to his mother, with the greatest care.

She was sunning her back and had seen nothing.

'Will you be all right now?' they asked him, and when he nodded they, the tough ones, strode back to the place of danger.

Simon looked at his ignorant mother who had sat up at this.

'Why?' she asked. 'Did something happen?'

'Naa!' he said, turning away, wanting nothing of her though he shivered, though his face stung inside, and his chest ached.

The other boys could not leave Big Simon now. Waiting for him to get up they stayed upon the wall, daringly, as the waves still sprang, but stronger for the company they kept and steeled by their witness of the fresh heroic deed. They shouted, 'Hell, man, gee, that was close!' Benny jumped into the pool to bring his face near Simon's and asked, 'Weren't you scared? Are you hurt?' Simon made no answer. But when he was ready he rose, stretched in unnecessary preparation for one of those sprawly dives of his, and – made every boy there his vassal for ever (though each might forget who or what it was had cast him in the lifetime role of subject, worshipper, follower at least, and though he would in time confuse this boy with any number of gods, causes or golden calves).

Josephine too saw the scrapings on Simon's chest and legs and the watery smears of blood, yellow and red. She gasped first, and then cried out, but her cry was stolen and magnified by an electric train which rounded the headland and wailed with pleasure as it started round the curve of the bay.

Withdrawn by something from the entangling rows of print and wool, Nanny Binny looked up, blinked in the glare, and saw a thin old man with a long white beard plod down the beach to the pool's edge and wade out into the heaving water.

'Why,' said Nanny, 'there goes Bernard Shaw.'

'Who's Bernard Shaw?' asked Josephine, glad that Nanny was distracted for the moment.

'I can't rightly say,' said Nanny. 'I've seen 'is picture in the paper though. I think 'e's a book-writer. Anyway, 'e's somebody your Father thinks 'ighly of.'

Somebody Father thought highly of! Josephine, full of wonder, looked at Bernard Shaw floating on his back, his beard on his striped chest, his eyes shut against the sun, and after a while wading out and strolling up the beach on legs made out of plasticine.

*

Mrs Leyton in a pink peignoir, with a thrusting aside of curtains, dismissed the insidious temptations of dreams, and after wrestling a moment more, but with a brass knob, flung back the wings of the balcony door and stepped out into the sea-loud bugle-bright morning, to find her husband already there, issued from the next room, fastening his tie and following, since his chin was raised, the sweep of a gull.

'Whatever got you up so early?' she enquired, sinking into wicker and chintz and winding silks and muslins about her into quite a cocoon.

'I'm going in to town.'

'On a morning like this? For God's sake why?'

'Hofmeyr's speaking in the House. I'd like to hear what he's got to say. A valkyrie. Screams like a valkyrie, that bird.'

'Is he a good speaker?'

'He's no Burke.' He thrust his chin a little higher, felt the shape of the knot with his fingers. 'But he has a sound grip on Economics.'

'But you have a sounder. Mr Burke.'

'He does his job well.'

'But you'd do it better.'

'When I am a Minister I shall do better. It won't be Economics for me of course. Justice more likely, even Foreign Affairs.'

'You've got a long way to go.'

'I'll get there.'

'It's all you care about, isn't it?'

'I have never pretended to be without ambition.'

'And in the pursuit of your ambition you have no time for side issues.'

'What side issues? I'm not aware of neglecting any of my responsibilities.'

'Me.'

'Oh, get along with you! You don't want a puppy of a husband dancing round your feet do you?'

He was in a good mood. It was a lovely morning. He was looking upward, forward, away.

'I don't want to be of no account at all to the man I married.'

'Sh. There's someone walking under us.'

'Then do your duty and stamp.'

'Isn't that Maisie Gould? She must have arrived last night.'

Freda hurried to the balustrade. Below, long-shadowed, beach-pyjamaed, a woman crossed the paved terrace towards the steps.

'Maisieee!'

Maisie turned, shielded her eyes and waved.

'Good gracious! Hello! Shall I see you later? Are you going to the beach?'

Through a door on the other side of the terrace three men came out. Of course Eric Gould would be here on holiday too. None of the three men was Eric Gould. Freda did not care for him. He had a ladylike voice.

'I'm not sure. I'll see you later anyway.'

Maisie descended between spaced pots of red and purple fuchsia. The men glanced up. The vantage of the balcony was vindicated once again.

'She heard,' Rayfel accused.

'So what? And how do you know anyway?'

Freda returned to her chair.

'She pretended to be too surprised.'

'If she'd lingered awhile she'd have heard something far more interesting.'

Freda looked far out across the bay to Hottentot's Holland which was only a denser blue, but no more material than the sky.

'Oh yes?' He stepped into his room.

His wife waited until he came out again, shrugging on his pin-stripe jacket. It set him apart, a fat dark assertive peregrine of wool in a chiffon day.

She said thoughtfully, 'I might leave you. I mean *actually*. I have already left you in another way. I have' – her voice remembered London comedies, the casualness – 'transferred my tolerant affection to another man.'

'You aren't serious are you?'

'Never more so.'

'Then we'd better go inside and talk about it.'

'I'm quite happy here thank you.'

'You want to make a public spectacle of yourself do you?'

'I want to stay out here so you won't fly into a temper and make a public broadcast.'

'Well let's have it. Who is this fellow? But I must tell you now. I can't afford the indulgence of a divorce at this stage.'

'And must I sacrifice myself, my whole life, my only chance of happiness to your career?'

This time she spoke with feeling. And at once regretted it. She had had him floundering among the reeds. Why had she let him up for air?

'As bad as that is it?' he asked, while considering the next move.

'Yes.' Sharply defiant. Let him dare to scoff. But she looked down at the strip of intricately patterned carpet which failed to cover much of the hard red polished floor.

'How long has this been going on?' He didn't believe her, but he wouldn't say that her claim was a fiction. That would be to acknowledge an alien, individual need.

'I don't know. I only know that I'm a woman and I'm not old or ugly yet and I deserve some happiness out of life. With you I have no *scope*. Your world is not mine. I'm not prepared to make a martyr of myself so that you can feel important. My ambition might not be as grand as yours, but it's a simple human one and it's just as necessary to me as yours is to you.' Her voice shook. If the case were as she stated it, how sad it would be! But truly moved by her role, she had no time even to nod at a passing irony. The balcony had become a stage, the hotel was made of cardboard, and she could rely upon him to tease out the drifts of airborne, rainbow phrases just as she did. And still she would have the advantage, for out here his love of the limelight was less than his fear of jeopardy.

But a gull screamed, and a little train came crying round a headland. The hotel was not cardboard. There *were* realities.

'Aren't you being a bit melodramatic?' He called down softly, having, for once, the advantage of height.

Her eyes traced rapidly the interweaving of curling golden boughs, climbed the steps of faded blue medallions, and landed amongst the stripes of long grass. She had no idea where it would all lead to. But she was ready with what she hoped was venom.

'I hate you,' she said, in a matter of fact and measured tone, getting to the heart of the pattern. It was a faded blue diamond there in the centre.

'I see. Now don't say anything for a moment. Nanny Binny and the children have just come out. Morning, morning.'

'Where's Mother?' She heard Simon's voice. Half covering her eyes as though against the glare she went to the balustrade and waved her free hand.

'I wanttogoandsurffff,' Simon's voice rose and broke and foamed.

Last year Freda had taken them with her to Muizenberg to surf while Nanny Binny had been unaccountably struck down for a day by the sun. Once or twice each year Freda hired a surfboard and entrusted herself to the waves. After all, this was the safest of coasts.

She went to Muizenberg only for the surfing. It was a horrible place, crowded with vulgar, loud, ugly people whose grammar was worse than her Aunt Lydia's. They came down every year from their tasteless houses in Johannesburg, fat women with red lips, moustaches and diamonds, and fat men with wet lips and flashy cars who stood about in indecent bathing trunks talking at the tops of their voices about money and business. They had spoilt whiny children. They spread their gorged flesh everywhere over the beach which they had ruined with a hideous pavilion and concrete promenades. Gross, gregarious, philistine *Jews*!

'Why has he got long trousers on, Nanny? It's going to be a scorcher.'

''E got ever so burnt yesterday and 'e got all itchy and 'e scratched 'imself – 'Nanny white-lied for her boy's sake. He'd never hear the end of it if they found out about his accident. They'd blame her too, but that would not trouble her. She would deserve it.

'Use plenty of ointment,' Mrs Leyton advised, and waved again to hurry them both on with their buckets and spades to the beach where they were safest until lunchtime.

But Simon persisted.

'When will you take me then?'

'Later.'

'When?'

'Hush.'

'When?'

'This afternoon. Now off you go. Have a good time. Don't forget the ointment.'

She leant there. She called out. She watched them descend. A complicated winding of white cords fastened Josephine's blue sundress at the back. Nanny's linen hat went last. Emotion – she had dipped deep into the pot, it was thick on her fingers – must be tried on everything. My children, she thought, not summoning back Josephine's vacuous face, nor Simon's ostentation, but just allowing their existence to back the word with a mood of reality, as music in a film supports photography with a more tremulous chiaroscuro. There had been other times too when The Children had been, though irreducibly physical, yet without identity, replaceable as actors in a part, or as the first, supplantable children of Job.

'I've got to go,' Rayfel said.

How sharp were the lights on the water.

'We'll talk about all this later,' he added, lazily.

'Goodbye,' she said. 'Enjoy yourself,' she added on a rising note, drawing in breath, taking courage, prior to resignation to her fate, her life, her children. But it had sounded sardonic.

'Thank you, but I can assure you I shall.'

He was gone, and she sighed at the view, not noticing that the sea was so still that the mountains were reflected in it. Could it not be his vanity, she hoped, that made him unable to countenance the possibility of her adulterous love? His career, his career, what did she care if he attained sceptre and orb, if he stifled all the world with his Justice, cut off the ruddy sun with his dark bulk, what did she care. But was she really unhappy, was her unhappiness going to be hard to endure? She went into the dark room with spots in her eyes – they broke into galaxies before they died – and groped for the bell that hung above the bed. Nellie, the coloured maid without any front teeth, would smile at her, and bring her hot tea, and press her ice-blue linen in time for lunch.

*

Maisie invited Freda to sit with her and Eric at lunch, but Freda declined, saying she had a book, little appetite and a slight headache. So she sat alone at her table next to the window and read: "'No, thank Heaven … The blood of that noble heart does not stain my sword! In its last hour it was faithful to thee, Beatrix Esmond. Vain and cruel woman! Kneel and thank the awful Heaven which awards life and death, and chastises pride, that the noble Hamilton died true to thee …'"

This afternoon she would finish that letter, if she could find it. She might have brought his with her since she'd intended to tell Rayfel anyway. The sea looked rough. A haze on the mountains. Where was she – the noble Hamilton.

'Beatrix's mother looked at Esmond and ran towards her daughter with a pale face and open heart and hands, all kindness and pity. But Beatrix passed her by, nor would she have any of the medicaments of the spiritual physician. "I am best in my own room by myself," she said. Her eyes were quite dry; nor did Esmond ever see them otherwise, save once, in respect of that grief …'

'I'll have the roast beef,' Mr Gould's ridiculous voice rhymed unforgivably. Why were there no people in her world like Beatrix and Esmond – or say Thackeray, or Tennyson, or Debussy, or – there was fat Dr Hodgkiss sucking up soup through tubular lips behind her. A breeze swayed the fuchsias.

It takes a bad climate to produce a good literature. And good music. It was too hot, too bright, too benign, too wide a world this for the doings of people to seem worth re-cording. And with a gentle jolly breeze, what chance of symphonies?

But banjo and drum and tambourine came jogging down the main road towards the hotel and in through the gates. In satin suits of sunflower-yellow with big blue buttons and blue-striped hats came a band of Malays, both men and boys singing the months of the year in an over-and-over tune that compelled Mrs Leyton to abandon her dessert and flee from her window, while others in the dining room, clutching their napkins, came up to the glass to peer, or went through the doors right out on to the terrace, summoned by the music, the joke music, with smiles on their faces for the folksiness, the colour, the much too big waistcoat on the tall thin man, the wheeling children, the insignificant words. The tinplate of the air became a festive tympanum, on which the sun condescended to dance, celebrating their good humour.

Embarrassed Mrs Leyton hardly paused in her flight as she cried above the racket, 'Any letters?'

'Er, yes, Mrs Leyton.'

So she had to stop. The hand of the lady clerk strayed before the catacombs, while Mrs Leyton's tapped. Life, cluttered with clerks and things.

'IN CASE OF FIRE BREAK GLASS', she was directed by a brass plate on a red box beside the door. How would that help, she wondered.

The handwriting on the envelope was unfamiliar; the postmark, Port Elizabeth. There was a cousin in Port Elizabeth but he never wrote. She started up the dark stairs (it was only one flight to her room – she never took the lift unless it was actually open and waiting), laid her book on the sill of the first small landing's stained-glass window, and read by its light.

Dear Mrs Leyton,

I have to tell you that six days ago I received news that my beloved son Benedick Alfred died in a hospital in Madrid, Spain, of pneumonia contracted in the course of his duties as a soldier. In one of his letters he asked me to let you know if anything should happen to him. My delay in carrying out his wishes is due to the shock I received which made it difficult for me to think of anything but the loss of my young, brave, brilliant and only son. I am afraid no one will ever be able to persuade me that his death was anything but a waste.

I am still in bed and I have had two specialists in, but I'm not the complaining sort, Mrs Leyton. I flatter myself that Benedick got some of his virtues from me. I take it you knew him well and that you were fond of him. Of course anyone who knew him and understood him must have been fond of him, if you'll pardon a mother's pride. If you would write to me and tell me something of his life in Johannesburg during those last months before he went off to that terrible cruel country (I have always thought of it as a terrible cruel country, with the Inquisition, and the Armada, and the bullfights) if you would tell me what sort of things he did, what he liked to talk about, where he went, who he saw, anything at all, I'd be glad. I always knew he was different from other young men. I can assure you, Mrs Leyton, the flesh cannot be heir to a greater shock than I have sustained by the news of his death. You might say I have been inoculated against shock, if you understand me. So please do not hesitate to tell me anything that you know to be the truth about my son. I am his mother, and he could do no wrong in my eyes – except destroying himself which no one could stop him from doing. I keep telling myself that at least he died with a faith. He had something he considered worth dying for, and that's more luck than most people ever have. Most of us I'm afraid go to the grave without any illusions.

Hoping to hear from you,
Yours sincerely,
Elsa Colley

Freda folded the letter and carried it on upwards to her room. *Henry Esmond* remained lodged on the sill, forgotten, though not in every way, by its reader.

*

Out of the doors and on to the terrace issued men with panamas and bare-backed women, until they were crowded at the balustrade. Wives nudged their husbands, stretched out sun-browned arms with jangling bracelets, threw down copper and silver coins. Their children danced to the music, showing off in mockery on the terrace, or with growing conviction down among the performers. Simon, who had led the rush from the children's dining room (in which at his age he had no right to be), had hold of a tambourine and was bashing it without regard for the general rhythm or the crown of his own head, and as he pranced about on the gravel he stirred up more dust than all the rest of the dancers together, and his feet scattered coins under parked automobiles whence even the littlest of the Malays failed to retrieve them all.

The tambourine was repossessed by a tall acrobat who bent backwards almost to the ground then rose again shaking all over from ankles to cymbals, so that his satin rippled like water. Meanwhile others struck tunes from the wires of banjos. Simon remembered he had been promised another joy; told Nanny he was going with Mother to Muizenberg, and thundered indoors, up the stairs and down the passage to his mother's room. He seized the doorknob with both hands and twisted it this way and that. It was locked.

'Who is it?' she called.

'It's me. Are you coming? Hey? I-I-I-I-I-I'm ready. To go. I-I-I-I-I've finished my lunch and everything.'

'Simon? What are you talking about? Go where?'

'To the waves. To sur-ur-urfff.'

'Good gracious. Certainly not. And for goodness sake stop rattling that door.'

'You promised. You said you'd take me this afternoon to, to, to, to surf. I want to do the standing up kind.'

He let go the knob and put both hands on the panels of the door, hearing through it the silence, and through that the tunka-tunka-jingle from below.

'You promised. This morning you said this afternoon. It's this afternoon and I'm ready,' he shouted into the wood and right through to the silence, which came bleeding out.

A door across the passage split from its jamb.

'A little less noise please,' begged someone wearing red and white checked slippers, determined to stop what it could, if not the beat and tin of the band which came right up, though strained by the wadding and tuft which pack up the worldly from the world.

The boy took a clue of wire from his pocket, thrust it in the lock and jiggled it about. He'd break in and fetch her. But the wire only pushed out the key on the other side. So he waited, forehead and hands pressed to his mother's fastened door. The other across the passage had closed. He had never stood so still, so long. Then a key turned, he stepped back, the important door was thrown wide, the throb of the music stopped and there was faint applause. She stood in the doorway in her blue dress. Her eyes shone and she seemed to be smiling.

'Simon,' she whispered, 'you must try to understand. Something has *happened*. Something very sad. I can't go out this afternoon. Do you understand?'

Even he must understand now.

'What's happened that's very sad? Hey?'

'Someone – a dear friend of Mother's has died.' (Oh God, but talking to Simon was like talking to someone who spoke a different language – or none at all. Could he possibly understand what it might mean to her if a dear friend had died?)

'Is that why you're whispering?' he asked.

She should have known he couldn't.

'Hush! People are resting.'

'But why can't we go to the waves and surf? Hey?'

'I've told you once already, no! Run along now and don't come and disturb me again.' Her own whisper gave way to plaint, and if he went on rattling she'd take no notice and to blazes with the people who were resting. (Resting! And these were, quite possibly, in Europe, though news takes time to travel, the – the dies irae.)

'Who's gone and died?'

'No one you know. Now run along. Off with you. And don't make too much noise,' she added hoarsely (since she wasn't absolutely certain yet).

The door closed, the key turned. She undressed and put on a nightdress of chiffon, managing to ignore the importunity, the growing racket in the passage.

'Hey!' he shouted. 'I want to surf! What's people dying got to do with it? Hey!' His banging and the other banging outside and below, started again.

And the door behind Simon opened again.

'Little boy,' said the person in the slippers who at any rate was still alive and was also, it now appeared, wearing a hairnet, 'if you don't stop making all this noise I shall have to complain to the management.'

Simon, putting his hands in his pockets, looked hard at the face-flesh.

'Are you a man or a woman?' he asked.

The door shut quickly. The boy, wild, but raised a captive, ran down the passage from medallion to medallion, then flew down the stairs to the halfway landing. He took up a book that was lying on a window sill and placed it carefully on the roof of the lift, in a little mahogany howdah on its peak, where it would ride up and down for ever in the fancy iron shaft on its carriage of glass and polished wood.

*

Boys were on the beach, building small castles, splashing in the pool. They did not miss him when he came out among them; everywhere among the rest who lay on sand or rock, or strolled or ran or bathed, the heads of boys turned to him. He stood looking out to sea, and slowly they gathered, pretending at first to be just coming there, anyway, to dig, to splash, or just to stand, like he did. But soon there were so many of them there that they stopped pretending, and stood looking at him, waiting. He wouldn't let them down. Simon the Less sat cross-legged at his side, building a tunnel in the damp sand. Two smaller boys continued to laugh and shout and squabble in the pool, tugging at a pipe of seaweed. But the silence of the crowd made them stop and look shame-faced, biting their lips and shrugging their shoulders at each other as though they had been reprimanded by a grown-up. Then they too just stood and waited. They saw him raise one shoulder, put a hand behind his back and bring out his knife. It drew from them a low moan of pleasure. The only fear was in the eyes of the smaller Simon, who looked up, looked down, and with one light blow flattened his tunnel.

'Right,' said Simon, turning the knife in his fist so that its blade was pressed up against the inside of his arm. They made a path for him and he started off. They trusted that he was going towards something, and they followed, except for his namesake, who got up but remained standing there looking after them.

The sun, going down, lanced at them as they streamed after their armed leader. The margins of the sea marked by the retreating tide were like the underlapping pages of an open book. The top page was the sea itself, the next, of which a wide piece showed, was glistening yet, and there the footprints quickly fattened and filled. On the next and narrower piece the sand was smoother and firmer and their path remained distinct. Much higher on the beach, and out of the book, they had to labour over the soft humpy piles where every dent was a valley of shadow. The humps be-came dunes, and the boys plunged from ridges into giant hollows where grasses grew, sparse, upright as wart-hairs or clustered and coarse in shaded pits.

Simon made straight for a city of white boulders, as if he had himself appointed this as a meeting place, as if it had been at his injunction that the current had borne here, to the base of the tallest rock, a big smooth seal. It lay in a shallow pool on a scree of pebbles. The tiny pool had a grandiose gateway on its seaward side, a high white arch of stone formed by a natural lintel bridging a pair of monoliths. Or it could have been seen as an entrance into the sky itself, and the pool a bright, semicircular doorstep. Or an altar. And here the seal lay and panted, its head stretched forward with the bristles, its eyelids drooping almost all the way down over the eyes and then slowly opening very wide again perfectly in time with the swell and fall of the sea's quiet breath.

The boys climbed on to granite ledges round about the pool to stare down at what at first moved them to delight and pity.

'Aaaah! Shame!'

Their cries were uttered one after another, same sound, same tone, the cries of birds of a species. They were of a species of shining merciful boys; lion-hearted; of the Round Table.

'He's swum all the way from Seal Island.'

'He'll rest and then he'll swim back.'

'Ja, he'll be all right.'

'But what will he eat? I mean if he lies here for days and days,' said Benny, standing well back on the beach. Though of the kind, he was both weaker and shriller.

But Simon, who was something else, bigger, with a horrible guttural noise of his own, silenced them. And the ugly laughter was not real, because he wasn't even smiling as he straddled the fat sheeny body and looked down at it, one fist on his hip, the other rising with the blade pointing down. And only then did the flock understand what the consummation was to be. Assaulting the sand itself had never really been enough. White rock, white sand, white sea, white sky framed knife and body together in their sight. Their lives, all things which they could see and sense, were pale, lacked colour. Everything was dead marble, waiting. Their feelings prepared themselves for the bursting of something strong and sore and distinct as the bursting of a sour plum in the mouth. They drew in breath. Braced themselves stiffly. And the first shock of realisation changed quickly to desire, and desire rose to overcome pain, and pity, and guilt.

Benny alone was content without blood. He was standing behind Simon and did not see the knife. His fear was at first of the animal, and for himself; but when he saw that Simon was not to be attacked he crept up and squatted a little distance from the creature's head. Fear and indifference were alternately signalled by those eyes as they opened, closed: or so Benny read the argument, being a boy willing and able to deal with a theory of need. It was frightened, he reasoned, and, or, exhausted, and, or, hungry, and, or, sick. Rest and food would probably set it working again. All would be endearingly well, even for this little grey fact in the great Economy. He might not have felt the same way about a shark, but this thing had charm, chiefly in its eyelashes.

The boys above kept their eyes on the knife. But Simon lowered it to his side.

'Aaah!' said the boys, on a new note.

'Kill him,' cried one, and then they all cried, 'kill him, kill him!' Benny looked up, startled. He moved out of the way as Simon backed and took his place at the seal's head, squatting and looking into the two bright globes in which the life surfaced and receded. The boys were clamouring, leaning forward on their perches, waving their arms at him, straining their voices to impress their wills. 'Kill him, kill him.' Yet not one of them would have dared, and Simon, Benny was grateful to know, would never do what they told him to. Thank God it was he who had the knife and not them, and of course he'd never hurt such a nice thing. Just looking couldn't kill.

Simon did not listen to the boys. He didn't even hear them. But it was between the eyes he chose to drive the blade with slow, controlled strength.

Some of the boys, when the hasp touched the flesh, moaned into limp silence like the failing soundtrack of a broken film. Some saw nothing and went on crying for slaughter, until Benny, who had not believed what he was seeing for several seconds, screamed. Simon wrenched out the knife as the seal honked and heaved and floundered, and then he rose and stabbed with superfluous, panicking force, speed, random aim into the blubber of the body which soon had so many mouths that blood was its only protest and it lay motionless. Until, either because the blood deepened the pool in which it lay, or because the sea swelled under it, it went drifting out of Simon's reach, its eyes fixed wide and sightless, but with terror in them still. It was carried straight on through the arch of granite and down the middle of a bright road. Very soon rags of blood were littering the ocean as far as the horizon, and even hanging in the sky. The seal itself was nothing but a dead, black, contracted heart. Benny, the barmitzvah boy, stood stiff and quiet, his mouth stretched, his eyes half closed, looking at what the goy had done. Only a goy could have done that. The others almost slouched under a heavy calm, their eyes and thoughts resting on the kill. One sighed deeply, his shoulders rising almost to his ears, then dropping peacefully. For all of them, though not for Simon, lust was appeased, and something broken that was broken for ever, something they would look back upon for a long time with contempt now that they had won new dignity.

But Simon had purpose.

He called out, 'Get it. I want it back here. Get it. Go on. Get it.'

They were sluggish, and he had splashed in (sandshoes, long grey flannel trousers and all) and had even launched out in the deeper water with his clumsy crawl before the others moved. They all did eventually, except Benny. After all, they were his men. They dared less than he, but belonged to him. Some leapt down into the pool, some edged their way with care, using their hands, their fatter bums; some followed him all the way out into the ocean; others only as far as the great arch beyond which the unbroken stretch of ocean seemed too dangerous; and the rest, except Benny who stood on the pebbles, with his spectacles opaque as tinfoil, went at least so far as to let the bloody water at the edge of the pool cover and hide their feet.

The seal was brought back, and under Simon's directions they carried it, everyone taking his turn in groups of four or five, back along the wet beach beside a tideless sea. It was difficult to hold but their fingers grew accustomed to dipping into meat.

*

Mr Rayfel Leyton was considering, with more than a little sense of frustration, as he drove home in a rattly hired Buick after enduring a long hot day in the House and a good many speeches the best of which did not come within shooting distance of his own educated thinking and polished phraseology, that here he was, well past his political puberty, and not yet having made his maiden speech.

But his thoughts were shifted as he came within view of the Constantia mountains, and the thought of the valley and its wines, since he was thirsty, made him consider other means to gratification. And then he was forced to admit to himself that this was indubitably the most spectacular sunset he had ever, as far as he could remember, exclaimed upon before. Sky and sea so sanguine. But the vlei orange, gold – because of the mud no doubt. And though the sun itself was out of sight (so that of course the heart of the splendour could be assessed only from the southern margins of the Atlantic bays on the other side of the Peninsula), this eastern stain was affecting enough. Which proved, he urged, the Buick melting in the light which even reddened the road, that he wasn't as his wife had so often insisted, a heartless man totally devoid of emotion. Of course he kept his emotions in the right place. And of course she would not leave him. Nor sabotage his climbing of the ladder. He was going to be a man of considerable importance. The day was not far off when she would look at him in a different way, and he would, he decided, almost dazzled by the crimson glare, not be ungracious.

Later he talked a great deal at dinner. His wife (who had put on no rouge) was silent, perhaps because of remorse, and an atoning attentiveness to his theme. He had lunched with five Members. That fool Legrange maintaining in the teeth of all evidence that Germany would not go to war.

It wasn't until they had reached the lounge and were comfortable with coffee that she found her opportunity.

'– a young man I knew who went to fight in Spain. I had news today that he was dead.'

Her head on one side, her eyes on the moving surface of the coffee as she stirred the spoon (a small Excalibur) round and round the little cup, thinking, she would have him endure her endurance, from now on, without mercy. She did not see their friends the Goulds advancing down the long room between the columns.

'I was very fond of him,' she pressed, as he sipped his coffee to fill in the pause between the chapters of his narrative.

Her 'very' had been unintentional, but now that it was out she heard how it lessened the fondness, a plain statement of which might after all have made it too particular, enough to startle the wrong questions out, and the matter was not to be opened for inspection.

Rayfel was polite. Restored this evening to invulnerability (though a veteran of the sunset), he was good enough to converse, and asked, 'Was that the chap who went to annoy his father?'

A flattering blow. That he should remember her mots, and at the same time remind her that he knew the truth. Touché, he thought, and to his own satisfaction drove the blade right to the heart of youthful folly.

She lifted coffee in the air with her spoon and let it fall back into the cup; would seem to be thoughtfully, soberly withdrawn. Let him crow. She could wait.

But conversation must go forward. The Goulds, Rayfel noticed, had stopped at another table but had not sat down. They would be upon them in a moment, and pleasant easy chatter must be under way.

'What is the father's reaction now, do you know? I should think that if the risk of his son's death annoyed him, the event would infuriate him. And as the son is no longer in a position to derive the least satisfaction from his own achievement, what morals we may draw from the contemplation of the ironies of life, death and human relations! But the last laugh will be on that idiot Legrange.' He raised his voice with the last words, for here was Eric to whom he would tell his tale again.

'I don't think a young man's death,' Freda began, not seeing Eric who had come up behind her chair, 'is a subject for –'

'Who's dead?' a high-pitched voice interrupted.

'Good evening, Eric,' said Freda, not looking round. She bent forward and reached for her cup.

Eric prowled for a chair.

'Who's dead, did you say?' he asked again.

'Some young man that Freda knew,' Rayfel said, in a tormenting tone of innocence. 'What was his name my dear?'

She continued to sip her coffee but her hand shook very slightly. She would have liked to slap him, with a truth if there'd been one to hand, or at least with another revelation. But there was nothing for it, she must reply, and her tone must not be too special.

'Bene-dick Coll-ey,' she enunciated, so that there need be no repetition, and because spelling is less personal than naming.

'Good gracious, is he dead? When did this happen?' Eric carolled, shriller than ever with surprise and public concern.

'What's that? Who's dead?' asked Maisie, arranging her fringed wrap over the back of a three-legged chair, and chinking her bag with its dangling jet beads on to the glass-topped table. She sat awkwardly, and looked from Freda to Eric.

'That Colley boy, what's his name, Benedict did you say Freda?'

'Do you mean Elsa Colley's boy?' Maisie gasped, regret beginning on her forehead.

Freda was ageing in the depths of the sofa.

'I wouldn't know,' said Rayfel. 'Do you know, Freda?'

'Yes, that's quite right. As a matter of fact we met him at your house –' Keeping her voice crisp, hard, she tried to bring Benedick's face before her once more. And she succeeded. Strange she had never realised that he was the image of Lord Byron.

'Oh I hardly knew the boy,' Maisie was saying, 'but I remember I'd promised Elsa –. She and I were at school together. How on earth did he die, a mere boy like that?'

'He got pneumonia,' Freda murmured, de profundis.

'What? In midsummer? In Port Elizabeth? However did he manage that?'

'He wasn't in Port Elizabeth. He was in Spain.'

'Spain? Whatever was he doing there? Isn't there a war on in Spain?'

'Yes, he went there to fight in the war. He contracted pneumonia – in the course of his duties as a soldier.' Freda's voice implied that she knew the details, but preferred to be brief. And it surely was her reputation rather than her words or tone which made Eric add, as though on cue, 'Or so we who knew him will maintain to our last breath!'

Freda was struck, struck while she was down! It took her some moments to recover. She searched for help, and saw that the good soul Maisie was shifting in her chair and looking most uncomfortable.

'How dreadful for poor Elsa! And for Martin too of course. Such a waste! And it's not even as if they had the compensation of thinking of his death as a sacrifice. I mean, it's not as if he'd been killed in battle. *Pneumonia*. It's such a pointless death, isn't it? Good Lord, one can die of it at home.'

Upon which Maisie got up and moved to a more comfortable chair. At once she looked happier, under the fronds of an Edwardian potted palm on a high stand.

'Which lot was he fighting for?' asked Eric, tugging at the knees of his trousers since he too was an active sort of chap.

'The Government of course,' said Freda, managing to rise with grace. She gathered up her crimson bag and shawl and then looked down at Eric.

'It may interest you to know that I am extremely upset about all this, I don't think it's a laughing matter, and the young man was very kind and sweet to me too. Now if you'll forgive me I'll go up to bed.'

She turned away without a glance at Rayfel's face. And with her head high she walked between the fat columns down through the centre of the lounge, her route de triomphe, and out through the gilded arch. Perhaps she had overdone it, but Oh he'd asked for it, Rayfel had.

'I didn't know she knew the family at all!' said Maisie.

'She's just a bit touchy tonight. I don't think it was anything we said that upset her,' Rayfel reassured her.

'She did seem a bit depressed today,' said Maisie. 'She wouldn't even join us for lunch.'

'But she was the first to say something well sort of – humorous, I mean, not malicious or anything really, just sort of humorous about it, wasn't she?' Eric looked from one to the other of his allies, mystified. 'It doesn't mean that you don't *feel* anything.'

'I had lunch in the House today –' Rayfel began.

'Well, whatever the consequences, they will just have to come,' Freda thought, mounting stiffly in the lift, into which she had stepped with so much resignation it might have been a tumbril. Yet she was unable to assess the extent of her commitment. She only knew that she felt tempered, more than a little proud that she had endured, and strong enough to face whatever might come to try her in bedroom or lounge. Tall and straight she marched down the passage, the lift sinking away behind her like the past. For things would be different now, she told herself firmly, opening her door. Her bedside light was on, but her bed not turned down. It did not even look as if it had been made properly, but as though the cover had been pulled up over the rumple. Had she left it like that after her lie-down this afternoon? And why had Nellie not turned it down as usual? The chiffon of the earlier hours lay over a chair. She undressed, put on the preferable satin, and bent close to her face in the wardrobe mirror. She looked delicate indeed in the soft light. One shade the more one ray the less had half impaired that nameless grace. She went slowly, gracefully to the bedside, pulled back the cover, gasped and turned cold. Somebody hideous, bloated, wounded, bloody, with whiskers sharp as needles, somebody earless and hairless was outrageously lying there looking at her.

'What are you doing? What do you want?' she shouted after a few moments. Was it he? Was it he, materialised here in her bed by her own conjuring?

The eyes did not blink, nor the face move.

She ran to the door, opened it, looked out into the passage.

'Nellie, Nellie,' she called softly into the empty distances, not loudly in case doors should open and she be seen in her nightdress. She went back round the bed, trying not to glance at its incredible occupant, and pressed the bell until Nellie should come. She heard the distant trilling in the hinterland, and that she herself was whimpering.

Neither Nellie nor anyone else came.

Why did no one ever answer bells?

Mrs Leyton pulled a peach-coloured wrap from behind the door, clutched it about her like a cloak, and hurried down the passage to Nanny Binny's room. Mistaking the door she burst in upon a man and a woman standing side by side in evening dress looking into the mirrors on a wardrobe's doors, simultaneously removing hairnets from their iron-grey hair. The two faces in the mirror looked at her expressionlessly. She made no apology, but slammed the door and ran on. By the time she found Nanny she was crying. Nanny Binny put her to sleep with a pill and a hot-water bottle in her own bed and would allow no one to disturb her with questions, while she herself (having gone bravely to investigate the intruder) organised the removal of the body and the remaking of Mrs Leyton's bed from mattress to quilt.

But no one could have made her say she liked it.

And the next morning she finally delivered herself over to the devil past all saving, for love's sake. She did not say, of course, that she'd supposed him to be with his mother. She had quickly seen the truth and chosen what seemed the wisest expedient. She insisted that he, Simon, could not possibly have done such a thing without anyone knowing it for 'e 'ad been all afternoon with a 'ole lot of other boys and several other Nannies 'ad been kept waiting down in the dining room but all the boys 'ad come down at last clean and tidy except that Simon was already in 'is nice grey trousers and it was true 'e'd got them wet but then all the others 'ad gone into the sea and 'e 'adn't 'ad 'is costume with 'im and you can't blame a boy for wanting to join in. And no, she knew for certain that 'e didn't 'ave a knife, and anyway the penknives that boys 'ave could never do such a thing. It must 'ave been those Coons done it for a practical joke, though it wasn't her idea of a joke, or of singing and dancing either for that matter.

Black lies.

Too late she saw that the first time had done as much as the seventieth time could do, that the first blow is the destroying blow. He was lost and damned, but so was she. She would not leave go of him. They were lost and damned together.

But such a fine stalwart lad. So strong and plucky. 'E'd made no fuss when 'e'd fallen among those dreadful rocks the other day. And look at 'im now, teaching that other little boy called Simon 'ow to swim. I could lend 'im the rope to 'old 'im up with, she thought. Then she hastily added aloud, 'Knit one, purl one, knit two together,' to help her shut out the fear that flashed before her mind.

3
JUSTICE

Mrs Foster's Infant and Preparatory School was built against a stony koppie on which pine trees thickened towards the summit, and in the weedy needly crevices of which there were said to be snakes.

The suburb ringed the hill, clasped it with claws of walls and fences. But the hump of it, though divided by title deed between the Tudor cottage, the Cape Dutch house, the Spanish hacienda and the rest, was in fact unfenced, untended and unfrequented except by the unpossessing, who blazed it with tins and scarred it with ash. The rare proprietor on a conscientious tour of his property found proof enough that trespassers had camped, eaten and more where he, whose right it was, would seldom venture. Dirty, careless creatures! why did they have to leave such litter behind them? And once the widowed Mrs Foster herself discovered (on a solitary expedition equipped with pith helmet, Wellingtons and a heavy stick) a newborn baby, several days dead, lying between two boulders under a thin scattering of brown pine-needles. A strong-minded woman, she didn't faint or scream. She simply sent for the police and begged them to see that the mother who had done this dreadful thing be whipped within an inch, within an *inch*.

Mrs Foster was well known as a humanitarian, and as a militantly liberal educationist. She had had her no-nonsense, yellow-washed, red-tin-roofed school built on a square of red earth dug out from the hillside. The neighbours, who made a special point of architecture, called it an eyesore. The first rule, and Mrs Foster believed that rules were the ground on which justice was built, was that no pupil should set foot on the hill. All but one of them were too afraid, not so much of punishment as of the place itself. The one who was not afraid went in search of snakes, though he found only lizards which darted and stopped dead still on the rocks, paddled over his hands, and lay, when he put them inside his shirt, with throbbing throats against his belly. He did not carry them away from their runs and crevices. All the other children knew that he went up there among the trees, and wondered at him, and asked him questions which he never answered. But none, not even the envious, gave him away.

One morning Josephine, at hopscotch in the girls' corner, saw him come out from among the trees through a clump of shadows and tall grass, stand in the sun on the edge of the escarpment – where no eye of authority could have missed him with his yellow head had it been looking – and drop ten feet on to the red dust.

'My brother,' she boasted to the two she was hopping against, 'knows everything about animals. He even knows about their insides.'

The two were sure this was so. But Hannalore Schultz, who had her hair cut like a boy's and wore socks to her knees and who never played with anyone but just stood and looked on, or sat and looked on ('Hannalore Schultz, will you pay attention!' the teachers all cried for even they saw that she was hopeless), said in the round, clear, uncompromising way she had, 'He's too big to wear those short trousers. And he is too big for a primary school. He can't be so very clever or he would have proceeded by now to a secondary school.'

Josephine knew perfectly well why Hannalore Schultz said this. Hannalore Schultz wore truth itself as an armour.

Another day the three players had hardly finished marking out the circles and squares for their game when the bell clanged and Miss Pereira, the youngest teacher, called, 'Into the hall everyone', and they all were lined up each in his place as for morning prayers.

Mrs Foster called the register.

'Simon Leyton ? Where is Simon Leyton ? He was here this morning!'

Josephine wanted to call out a saving lie – 'He's gone to be excused' perhaps – but couldn't in that big silence stretching behind her, and Mrs Foster looking so set on an answer.

But before anyone went in search he pounded in, found his place and stood stiffly to attention, his rumpled socks full of blackjacks and something grey and nameless lodged in his brazen hair.

'Where have you been, Simon Leyton?'

'Up on the koppie,' he shouted in an equally resonant, clear and ominous tone, so that while some of the children gasped at his daring, others sniggered at his insolence.

'I will see you in my office after this assembly,' Mrs Foster said. And now,' she went on, more resonantly yet, but with anger turned to triumph on an instant, 'today, children, is a great and important day for us all. On this day, in London, in England, our new King and Queen are being crowned. It is their Coronation Day –' And as the big state carriage of her speech found its comfortable trotting speed and travelled along with Their Majesties smiling from every window, Mrs Foster began to sway. Young pretty Miss Pereira walked between the rows putting little Union Jacks in the children's grasps. 'Now wave your flags, children,' Mrs Foster trumpeted, 'and we'll give three cheers. Hip hip –' and the flags waved, and Mrs Foster swayed like a great balloon on a pair of cardboard feet. Every child was given a thick china mug with King George and Queen Elizabeth looking out from an elaborate drapery of bunting and oak leaves. They stood stiffly while Miss Pereira banged the piano's bass in chords so terrifying that all knew the awesomeness of imperial power, but they awoke into the enlightened and tender dawn of 'God Save The King'. The children prayed that he be victorious, glorious, and no sooner was the King done than Miss Pereira launched into 'Die Stem', that other anthem for which a few knew the right sounds and made them, while those who did not kept their mouths open and their voices going, so that acoustically at least it was a highly successful occasion, and when it was all over everyone felt that he had done breathless right by his country and his king.

But Josephine, as she went off to the Afrikaans lesson, was afraid that the new reign was starting off dangerously. She sent her thoughts with Simon to Mrs Foster's study, but could not keep with him. Meneer Kruger, the Afrikaans master, was always grumpy, and today he was grumpier than ever. He was big and bald and clean as a new round india rubber. He wore a pale grey suit and a pearl in his tie. And several times during every lesson he would shout, in English and Afrikaans, 'Work, children, work. Do not sit and dream. We have a land to build.'

*

Mrs Leyton got up from the piano. She seldom attempted to make music herself nowadays, having such a grand collection of gramophone records. And today the effort was really too much. Even in her usually cool room the heat was great. It was a personal assault. Stifling, ridiculous, unseasonable weather. Why, it was late autumn if not already officially winter. Great clouds were coming together and there was that prickling in the air that boded an electric storm. But the rain must come too. The tension was unbearable. There was a weird light on the garden.

The air that seeped in through an open window seemed hotter than air trapped indoors. Since glass afforded protection, she was about to ring for Sixpence to shut the window, and to bring iced water, when she remembered that she had made resolutions. The event by which she had been a little further set apart from her fellows, which had saddened and distinguished, had also bettered. She had seriously considered whether she ought not, whether everyone ought not, to earn her own living. But what would she do with the money she had? She couldn't very well just give it away. She had children to think of. Then she had thought about doing the sort of voluntary work that several of her friends and her Aunt Jenny had lately taken up, those 'soup kitchens' whose very name she had often said in such a way as to make people blink in the steam. But she just knew she couldn't stand for hours and hours. She got dizzy. And as for housework, it had everything against it. Too revolutionary for one thing: she would seem to others to be intending only to shock, and besides she couldn't put her servants out of their perfectly good jobs which they needed. Furthermore, she had no idea how to cook, was certain she had no talent for it, and hated to get her hands dirty. So that she must bear with her ease and comfort, peculiarly martyred by them in a way that no one else could ever understand. It was part of her secret sorrow this. But what little she could do, she would. She came down to breakfast instead of having the tray carried up. She remained patient under the impact of 'Wosebank Gwocerwies'. And she would fetch her own iced water.

She stepped into the passage as the telephone rang.

'I would have sent a note,' said Mrs Foster, 'but I thought a talk might be a good thing. He's not an easy boy, Mrs er,

Mrs Leyton. The fact is' (Oh don't come at me with facts, Freda thought) 'I have to tell you that he's not easy. Charming yes, honest yes, a strong and sturdy lad certainly, a delightful boy in many ways, Mrs Leyton, but easy, no. I've only given him a warning this time. But if he does it again, Mrs Leyton, I shall have no choice. So perhaps you would have a word with him and make sure that he really understands. Rules exist for their own good, that's what one has to drive home and drive home. If anything happened to your child on the koppie it is I who would get the blame, from you, from your husband, would I not, Mrs Leyton?'

'Oh, but I'd never –' Mrs Leyton felt compelled to return her warrant for such candour.

'And I've told them and I've told the parents, and I say it again, it's dangerous up there. The school has taken its precautions and more than that it cannot do. It must be up to the children themselves – particularly the older children – and your boy is the oldest child in the school, Mrs Leyton – I can't impress it strongly enough. I mean, just think what a little foolhardiness and showing off – and that's all it is, Mrs Leyton, believe me, I know that and you know that, it's nothing more than the sort of mischief that children get up to, and we expect them to get up to it, we expect it, and far be it from me to try and put reins on a boy who wants to try what he can do and I – I – but the point is, and this is where I want your cooperation, Mrs – Mrs Leyton, no child has any business going where there are quite possibly snakes, and poisonous snakes, let me make no bones, Mrs Leyton, no bones. And secondly where I know for sure that gangs of skollie boys and their kaffir girls meet, and make fires, and quite apart from any actual danger carry on quite disgustingly I shouldn't be surprised. So *may* I count on you for this, Mrs Leyton ? Good, good. Then I hope we'll hear no more about it.'

Headmistresses were people whom Mrs Leyton found it impossible to be cool with. She forgot about her iced water and returned to the lounge hotter than ever.

The heat *and* Simon!

She sank on to her blue sofa.

Simon and the weather. Simon and this damned country. It was as hot now as that spring she had walked in her garden smelling England among the wallflowers, feeling giddy, and wondering whether it was a poem coming on, and it had not been a poem, but Simon. And when she knew, she had awaited – Oh a slender and delicate boy, already held in a series of future still projections close to his mother in attitudes of loving understanding. But the child given, the son born, was a lusty greedy twelve-pounder. Freda had been able to do nothing but mourn the irreparable, and substitute Nanny Binny for the undeliverable embrace.

Yes, both the children had been disappointing. There was so much more to them than one had ever been given to expect. Especially of Simon there was more noise, more clamour, more demand, more squirming, more weight, more size, more activity, and (even of Josephine) more sheer *presence*. And Josephine would not be pretty. Her skin was so dark. She was a smudgy child. And the way she stood and stared.

Then not only had Simon failed to turn out the perceptive, articulate creature through whom all his mother's gifts would come to full flowering, not only was he not her masterpiece, but so alien, so, as the years went by, increasingly alien, that had he not been born in this very house she might have fancied some terrible mistake had been made.

All body. That's what he'd been from the start. Twelve pounds would hardly be fair to a kaffir woman. And he'd yelled exceedingly from the first, a born destroyer of peace. He could even choke up the out of doors with clamour.

This goddam country. The heat continued to prickle, and the strange light stayed on the garden. There was a flash of lightning. Oh if only it would rain. She had a headache now, but she'd better get up and shut that window. One day, she feared, Simon would flatten all barriers, break open every sealed-up thing, break glass, and wood, and bring bricks and mortar toppling, tear out the very heart of every secret, and expose it to dust and sun and trampling feet.

But now, as thunder rumbled, she felt so in need of protection, reassurance, that she remembered what she had for a little while forgotten. She walked through the storm-dark house and up the stairs, on a pilgrimage to a source, from which she would bring strength back. She needed to remind herself that *he* really had said that he loved her. Strange that she had not needed to before now. Perhaps she was stronger than she had let herself imagine.

She was sure she had put the key back in its box. Or had she put it somewhere else for special safety? She frowned as she searched, her head aching, and the thunder going on and on almost without pause. She shook and rattled and even kicked at the doors with her long polished shoe. She might, she thought, borrow Nanny Binny's strident bunch and try the likely ones.

'Look, look, look I can climb the ivy –'

His voice. So there he was, home from school. She couldn't, she just couldn't talk to him now. Couldn't talk to him. Wasn't he Rayfel's son too? And didn't he always leave it to her to deal with Simon? Almost always. This time he'd have to. If this piece of news from Mrs Foster didn't work on that indifference of his, Mrs Foster herself would be put on to him to tell him a thing or two about his son. Perhaps he'd listen to that old battleaxe. For one thing, she was one of his prospective constituents, and an influential one, wasn't she?

Determined to challenge obduracy where she might, she again seized the knobs of the little doors and shook them and shook them. But the fact she was after remained securely hidden.

At seven o'clock the storm blew up. First the wind, carrying clouds of dust from somewhere (from the mines, Nanny Binny said), rattled the windowpanes, brought night early. Then the deluge, which after a while, as the thunder receded and the lightning changed to flashes in the valleys of the cloud, lessened to a metronomic drumming and tapping and dripping.

But Mr Rayfel Leyton LlD, Attorney-at-Law, was not a man to be bullied, blackmailed, tempted, bribed or browbeaten.

He heard his wife out. He listened calmly to her repetition of Mrs Foster's cautions and threats, her insistence that his own indifference and unwillingness to see what he didn't want to see was the chief cause of matters growing worse (he had allowed her to rouse him with this once before), and her own view that Simon was not just naughty, but actually, somehow actually, fundamentally *bad,* though God knew it was a terrible truth for a mother to have to face.

After which he spoke up, but the carving knife which he wielded with a dexterity he was proud of did not hesitate in its easy sliding motion under the thinnest of slices of roast beef out of the hummocks of which freshets of blood welled and trickled.

'Come now. Let us not exaggerate. Justice demands perspective. When you say "bad" what exactly do you mean?'

And he lifted the slice with its grades of colour from brown through pink to most royal red on to the glossy white of Spode.

'I mean bad. Look.' She stared down at her plate and tried to describe what was not there. 'There's something *missing* about the boy. He has no – Oh what is it – *imagination.* I mean for one thing he's not afraid of anything. There's no rule no authority or anything that the boy respects. If someone has no fear at all he can't have an imagination, can he? I mean surely if one can visualise the consequences of doing wrong, one hesitates to do it. But – it's not only that. You know, sometimes I think, I really think, that your son is little more than a complete *idiot.* I mean it. He should have gone on to a high school at least a year ago, but his writing's illegible, his spelling's atrocious and according to his last report he hasn't even been able to learn his tables. He's never come anything but bottom of his class. He had only one Quite Good and that was for basketball of all things. Oh and he got a Good for handwork once when he'd been doing nothing but sawing up blocks of wood, and there was something about a cow made out of plasticine. But I'm sure he couldn't have done it himself. He'll end up as a labourer if he's lucky. The way he's going.'

She waited. But he helped himself to pickles and said nothing. The quiet voice she had kept lately irritated him. Now as she watched the pickles tears came into her eyes.

'He is your son, you know. You must see that what he does will reflect on you, one day, won't it? Now in all fairness, isn't it time you took some interest in the way that child's growing up?'

Gently she pressed her temples with her fingertips.

Whether it was her gesture, her voice or her weary appeal, implying a lifetime of patient martyrdom (where had her humour gone, her cattiness that had saved them from having to be solemn about one another?), or whether it was, as he knew she would choose to believe, the need to deal with their son, irritation tightened his lips now, urged him to fling down the knife and lift up his voice. But instead he started carefully to carve another slice, and said, in the manner of a kindly uncle to suppliant child, 'What would you have me do then?'

She sighed. And he smiled for his little victory.

'Perhaps he needs a good hiding. I don't know. I can't struggle with it any more by myself.'

'What remedies have you attempted that have failed?' he enquired, still calmly, pressing his advantage.

'All I know is,' she insisted, suddenly impatient with carping and becoming purposeful, though not loudly enough to disturb her sorrow, 'that the boy needs a strong hand, and if you can't perform the duties of a father, then boarding school's the only answer.' There. She was neither too tired nor too pained to protect her own, whatever worm was gnawing at her heart.

Ah. Now. Now he could be righteously angry. If he, the good provider, the head of the family, a man of importance, were accused of failing in his duties, what coals of fire were it not his right to heap?

But stop. (Aha, that time he'd nearly lost, nearly been tricked.) What she wanted was that he should show that he cared for her opinion of him. And he did not care. He did not care that she should pretend to think, or even that she should truly think, that he in this or that was failing or had failed. The judgements by which he should stand or fall were not to be sought in the domestic sphere. And further than that (since he was not blind, nor defective in memory, nor insensible of innuendo) he did not care whether she pretended to love, imagined she loved, or indeed truly loved any real or fictitious, dead or alive, young idiot. If she would cling to this adolescent sentimentality, if she would behave as a child, he would treat her as a child; not harshly, but firmly; not arbitrarily, but justly.

The storm kept Simon awake, which nothing had ever done before at night. He went to the window and opened it wide. He admired what he saw and heard, but how would it feel?

He took off his pyjamas, spilling them on the floor, and climbed out and down the ivy. Through the dry side window of the dining room bay he saw his mother sitting at the table, and his father with a white napkin tucked in the top of his waistcoat and spread across his chest. There were candles on the table, their flames so very still while out here the wind bent the poplars and streamed out the tops of the gums, and the rain quenched everything but its own white flash and lightning in the furthest cloud.

From his mother's ears hung two raindrops on gold threads. They would never fall.

The lawn was a swamp, the orchard a rain forest. The rain was no longer cold on his body.

Mr Leyton having considered his verdict, laid down the knife and its companion fork on either side the beef and its circling boulders of potatoes.

'Physical violence,' he instructed, achieving neither a debating chamber nor a courtroom tone but, rather surprisingly to himself, the hoary pontification of the Old Testament, 'is the courage of the weak, but the imprudence of the wise. It is the first resort of the fool, the last of a reasonable man.'

In addition to which, Mr Leyton had not forgotten that on a previous occasion, when he had been conscripted by his wife's hysterical fury to deal with their son for having cut up her fox fur ('The horror – there's nothing to be done – it's gone too far now – it's too late,' Freda had grieved for a world past mending), Simon had laughed at him: not with the forced laugh of insolence and daring, but the way one just does laugh at something funny. The boy had refused to bend over or even stand still. He had already then been too strong and too agile to be held by one hand while the other was exercised with the stick, so the father had found himself dancing about his study, reaching over furniture, striking chair backs, books, a bowl of dahlias, the very whistling air, but hardly at all the person of the offender, though soon in spluttering fury he would have hit the boy anywhere, his head, his face; could have gone on until his arm ached in satisfaction, but it got none. It would not move swiftly, would deal no power, continued, as in a nightmare, insufficient to his will. And the boy kept turning to confront him, from the other side of the desk, a table, a chair, the room; to look into his eyes not only with laughter but with a delight in his face as though expecting his father to enjoy the joke with him. But the father had been able only to glare the more, and shout. By God he could have burst with frustration. Simon escaped through a window but put in his head with a Cheshire-cat leer on it. That was a taunt, that time, no doubt about it. Mr Leyton lashed right at the mouth, but the boy was gone, across the lawn, across the tennis court, into the wilderness of the garden. Turning from the window Mr Leyton had snapped the stick in two and flung the pieces to the carpet. 'I'll kill that kid,' his voice had squeaked: but when he looked up, he had been soothed. For in the glass that fronted an etching of Temple Bar in Dr Johnson's time, he saw his own face, huge and transparent, the Zeitgeist of the Age of Reason.

'What then?' Mrs Leyton persisted.

'There is no such thing as a bad child.' The time had certainly come for such a precept. For now Simon had grown. How he had grown. Even Mr Leyton, who did not look, had noticed it. 'If Simon is disturbed, a trifle abnormal in some respects, then someone who understands and has experience of the emotional difficulties of children must be called in. If one has a raging temperature one calls a doctor. If one has –'

'A raging son one calls –'

'A sore mind one calls a psychiatrist.'

'– him abnormal.'

'Nowadays there is no longer a stigma attached to seeking the assistance of an alienist.'

'But he's not mad, he's just maddening. Do you want some gravy?'

'One does not refer to "madness" any more. The diseases of the mind have been categorised. Certain treatments have been found highly effective. They also say that –'

'The mustard please. No, not the horseradish, the mustard.'

'– that, that, where was I, that neurosis is an entirely different condition of mental disturbance from psychosis. They say that the neurotic is as far removed from insanity as the sane. It's a fast-developing field of scientific discovery. But the law is hopelessly out of date. I had a case the other day – Whatever is the matter?'

'The matter? Dear Jesus! I don't believe you've even listened to me.'

'Are you really so upset about him?'

'Good God. And that surprises you. No. It's too much. I can't –'

She pushed her plate away and covered her face with her hands.

Mr Leyton tore the napkin from his belly, rose, flung the thing down on the seat of his chair and gripped its back as though that were his self-control.

'What? What is too much? Is your life so hard? Are you overworked, impoverished, friendless, driven from morning to night, ill, deprived, oppressed?'

'You don't even try to understand.'

'No, I'm too insensitive. And since I so lack insight into the workings of the adolescent self-pitying mind, perhaps you'd be good enough to enlighten me as to the nature and cause of your unendurable sorrows.'

The rhythm and flow of his speech carried him off down the room. Invisible eyes always watched when he spoke. Had he looked towards the windows over which the curtains for some reason had not been drawn, he would have seen his own ghost looking in eagerly, and candleflame unquenched by the rain. Nothing of substance.

'Don't you care if I'm unhappy?' she enquired, as though this were a new and incredible possibility.

He turned and stood.

'Listen. I'll put it in words of one syllable –'

But whatever attempt he was to make at such simplicity and clarity was not to be heard. Voices were calling everywhere, in the house, out in the rain, down the chimney, 'Si-maaaaaan? Si-maaaaaan?'

Simon? They had lost him. Nanny Binny said she had tucked him in bed and five minutes later he had gone. Frances and Sixpence were helping her search the house.

'The nursery window,' Nanny said, 'was open.'

She took them up to look. And at the moment when Mr Leyton looked out, a prolonged flicker of sheet-lightning revealed his son prancing among raindrops on the tennis court, naked as a savage.

*

An unfamiliar head cropped up among the arums and pelargoniums on the veranda. A red neck, wrinkly and bristly, thoroughly clippered but not too recently. The hair was the colour and hardness of the toffee on a toffee apple. Curious, though expecting to be sent away, Josephine mounted the steps to her mother and the guest. Each sat on a creaking cane chair from which the cane unwound at corners to reveal its skeleton. The woman, however – for it was a woman – was thick, thick-legged, so broad she filled the chair though she narrowed like a tower towards the top, a small cropped head, a pair of large uncovered ears. She was smoking a cigarette and she had an untidy moustache.

'One cannot hope to unravel the conscious mind like a bandage,' she was saying. 'Or go grovelling through an attic to find a missing front-door handle. One must *startle*' – she paused to pick a fragment of tobacco from the tip of her tongue – 'the fox from its lair. Or the wild boar as the case may be. In this case, you seem to think, it would more likely be the wild boar. So to answer your question, Mrs Leyton, no, I am not a Freudian.'

'Well, we were actually told by Mrs er – what's her name, the friend of Mrs Gould whose nephew you treated –?'

'Hausmann.'

'Mrs Hausmann, of course. When I telephoned her to get your number because all that Mrs Gould knew was that Mrs Hausmann's nephew had been helped but she couldn't tell me much more, so that's when I telephoned Mrs Hausmann, well she did mention that you were very *eclectic* in your methods.'

'Not so much eclectic no. Unorthodox certainly. But I must make it quite clear, Mrs Leyton, quite clear from the beginning, that if you put your child in my hands for treatment' (she was singing) 'I will brook no interference, none at all, Mrs Leyton, once I have decided on what is right, the parents must have enough confidence in me to start with, and once in my hands there they must leave them until I say that the treatment is completed. My methods have been found *most* effective, Mrs Leyton' (now she was snapping), 'with what are called *naughty* children. Often, you know, personality disturbances, or what parents call naughtiness, have a physical cause, and I investigate the state of their physical health as well as probing their minds. As a matter of fact I have several publications to my credit. So, far from being a Freudian, Mrs Leyton, one might say I am a *Weissian.*'

Her lips closed and stretched into a smile, her head jerked to one side and she leant back to look up at Josephine.

'How fascinating,' said Mrs Leyton. 'This is my daughter Josephine. A very different cup of tea. If anything too much the other way, if you see what I mean. Josephine, this is Dr Weiss. Say good afternoon to Dr Weiss.'

'Tell me something, Josephine,' Dr Weiss invited her.

'You want to put out your arms and seize me with your hands,' Josephine could tell, but she did not say anything.

Dr Weiss swung straight in her chair and informed Mrs Leyton, 'Most people try to win the confidence of children by asking them questions. But children prefer to tell you things.'

Again she pressed herself into a corner, and pushing on a chair arm with a heartiness that made it creak and creak in rhythm with her words, as the cane slackened, and the very bones groaned, she called, 'I am sure that there are lots and lots of interesting things that Josephine could tell me if she would. Mmmmm?'

But Josephine would not be gripped and if the hands on the ends of the arms had reached out, they would have found no flesh but melting wax.

'About your school, your playmates, your favourite food, your favourite colour or what you will do when you grow up?'

'And then you'd like to put me in your pocket,' thought Josephine, and pressed her teeth into her lower lip and gazed with that stolid almost moronic look which her mother found particularly irritating and helped her divine that there was nothing *in* the child. And Dr Emma Weiss, who prospected into flesh but had never discovered soul, felt in the girl, as in all children, a void. A void that must be filled, with fear if necessary.

'Nothing?' she cried out.

Josephine mercifully shook her head.

Mrs Leyton too came to the rescue. 'Now run along and send Simon here,' she said. 'It is his turn to talk to Dr Weiss now.'

Josephine found him helping Alpheus, the new fat gardener, to rake leaves into a pile for a bonfire.

'You must let me light it, hey?' said Simon.

'Yes, Baas,' said the new boy, smiling.

Simon kept his head bent and gave abrupt orders. He would not look Alpheus in the eye. But he spent as much time with him, almost, as he had with Willy, undeterred by Nanny.

'Look,' he said when he saw Josephine. He showed her a very small frog, hardly bigger than a tadpole.

'Put it away,' said Josephine. 'I don't want to touch it.'

He put it down his shirt front.

'Mother wants you on the veranda. She wants you to talk to a woman. The woman will ask you to tell her something.'

'No,' said Simon.

'She looks,' said Josephine, bending light round tree trunks and hedges, 'like a kangaroo. And she has a moustache.'

'All right,' said Simon, and flung his rake on the pile. 'Don't light it till I'm back,' he called.

'Hello Simon. My name is Dr Weiss. Can you say that?' She had not expected anyone so big. She had expected a boy. This was hardly a boy. And his hair was unexpected too. Was it actually crackling? No, that was the chair.

He did not answer and Mrs Leyton said nothing to prompt him. Emma Weiss knew this was a test. She called, 'Simon –'

'Do you want me to tell you something?' he shouted, louder than she.

'Why yes, *please* do,' she said, turning to Mrs Leyton and this time parting her lips on a smile that showed her teeth, where triumph was written in letters of gold.

Flatly, and in a lower tone he said, 'Your knickers are showing.'

'Oh. Oh I see. Do you think that is rude?'

Mrs Leyton frowned. She had hoped that not too much of that would be necessary. After all the mind was – well, right at the top. With the mind there was no need to – touch. This woman especially. There had been something about her which had made it impossible to entertain her in-doors. Even when she'd talked about *art,* she'd made it sound – impure.

Simon looked at Dr Weiss's knickers which she did not try to hide, and took the frog out of his shirt.

'What is it you have there?'

The tiny creature leapt to the ground.

Dr Weiss uttered a guttural noise of disgust.

'Take it away at once,' Mrs Leyton ordered, tucking her legs back under her chair. 'I loathe them,' she said, and squirmed.

Dr Weiss, out of revulsion and fear, rather than to oblige, stamped galvanically, hammering the frog with her thick cork heel. The mess remained there, except what stuck to her heel.

Mrs Leyton got up.

'Will you come and visit me in my little home?' Dr Weiss asked Simon, who was looking down at the squashed frog. 'You will bring him soon to visit me, won't you Mummy?' she called to Mrs Leyton.

'By all means,' Mrs Leyton called back. 'What a lovely idea. When do you suggest?'

'Tomorrow. How about tomorrow?'

'What a good idea.'

'I'll see you tomorrow then, Simon?'

He looked at her as she rose on her thick legs. His eye measured her strength. 'All right,' he said.

*

'It's got to be wetted to stay flat, and I've got to cut those filthy talons of yours, because you're going to see this Dr Wise though the dear Lord knows why.'

And no one else. But Simon was sat in the car in his new long grey flannel trousers and with hair still so wet that the furrows of the comb were noticeable, before his hands grew hot again or Nanny Binny's Lord had noticed His mistake.

Under the railway bridge and into town they drove, with Simon in one of his rare stillnesses that seemed to generate heat.

'Come on, get out.'

Mrs Leyton put her hand in his back as they climbed the steps. Now all hesitations were gone and she couldn't get him there quickly enough.

'You must listen to Dr Weiss,' she said, scanning the tiny windows at the side of the entrance hall for the five letters that spelt relief. 'You want to grow up to be a decent, civilised human being.' They advanced into the lift. 'Don't you?' And she pressed the button. 'Don't you?' As nothing happened she pressed again. The gates slid shut and locked them in. But it began to rise, the lift, and she was pleased, rising and rising in the narrow shaft, through light, dark, light, dark. 'Or do you want to grow up to be a useless creature whom everybody laughs at? Now is the time to make up your mind. Well?' The lift paused and settled, the gate slid open. Out they stepped, and on past doors and doormats, the boy almost as tall as his tall mother, down a dark closed passage at the end of which behind her door the leering Doctor stood on her legs and waited.

Her bell was the zinging kind, a passing wasp.

The door opened upon a smell of cooking carrots and Jeyes Fluid, and the Doctor in an unbuttoned white coat.

'Ach, Simy,' she glinted, 'do come in, this way, Mrs Leyton, this is my little den.'

Oh yes, thought Mrs Leyton. Of course. The cabbalistic leather couch. The touch of enlightened salaried suburbia in the copy of an Epstein on the desk, surely an Epstein, the rigid upright man with praying hands, the kneeling girls on either side, their hair sweeping in skeins over his archetypal feet. No. She didn't like it. There was something – Wagnerian, over-earnest, yet – what would the word be – motor-car-mascot about that man, and everyone's hair looking as though it had been *raked* –

'No need at all for you to wait,' said Dr Weiss, taking over. 'He's a big enough boy to find his own way home. I'll tell him the number of the tram and where to get it. Look Simy my boy,' and she pulled aside a corner of the clacking Venetian blind and beckoned him over (so that he could smell her armpit), 'the tram terminus is over there – you see – all the trams waiting, all the lines crossing? – just give him enough for his fare, Mrs Leyton.'

'Be careful – 'Mrs Leyton called back, but did not think of what. She felt so light, going off down the passage, down in the lift, she had pressed the right button, and she was free. Free to choose who and what should vex her, in her loneliness.

*

Dr Emma Weiss was known to get results. Boys who went to her wild and insolent came home tamer after every visit, and quite soon so very tame and obedient that parents could spare themselves the expense of her exorbitant fees. Some of the little boys would take to bed-wetting and screaming in the night, but this, Dr Weiss would explain, was not her department, and she'd recommend time, or another doctor.

After one visit boys would become anxious about the next. They'd be delivered again, protesting and sweating, into her marsupial hands, the door would be firmly shut on their mothers, and the horror inevitably begun. They'd become quiet once help was past.

'Shall I lift you up Denis, or Peter, or Neville?'

'Yes,' they'd scarcely whisper, but feeling the necessity of opening their mouths and speaking, perhaps to force a look of normality on the event.

They would sit on the edge of the high couch trembling visibly, and she would lay her hands on the jelly of their thighs just under their trouser-legs, and say, 'Now you know what's got to be done, don't you? You've been a naughty boy and we've got to find just where the naughtiness is hiding.'

She'd lay them down – even strap them if they resisted, press her hands side by side on their bodies lower and lower, and at a certain moment undo buttons, lay open and reveal their shame.

'There now,' she'd say. 'I can see that you're a very, very wicked little boy. You wouldn't like your Mummy and Daddy to know about that, would you?'

'No,' the child would beg, tears of penance or despair filling his eyes.

'Well then neither you nor I will tell them anything about it shall we?'

'No.'

'Well come along now and we'll see what we can do to make you a proper good little boy.'

From behind the door she'd unhook a rubber apron of liver-red. Tying this about her she'd be off out of sight down the passage, and through the wall they'd hear preparations that clinked and hissed. On her return she would strip them of every vestige of pride from the waist down, and bear them to the place of treatment, of torture, of, as they'd know after the first time, ablution and purification. She carried them if they were not too large, one hand thrust beneath, from behind, enwrapping their parts profane, to the bathroom, which was fuller of pipes and white enamel than any they could ever have entered. There were gurgles and sucking noises, and occasional squeals. Light was sharpened on hard bright mirror surfaces. They felt weak with fear. Ah, what was this dame going to use to rid them of the shame which had grown in dark and secret too long ago to remember? The hot water steamed and the cold misted the taps as she washed and washed her hands. There was a row of rubber bulbs on a glass shelf. They had piercing horns fixed to them, not sharp, but some as thick as a finger. The boy would ask no questions. Prone and still across the great cushion of her lap he'd lie.

And as well as her knowing everything, now he would have to endure the awful feeling in his belly. And on the cold white china afterwards, while she stood and watched and heard and smelt, his evil precious strength came spurting out of him; and after that, on the sitz bath – the witch's soapy hands sliding down and through and up and over and in – he knew that the forces of retribution were come upon him, had put a spell upon his body, that there was no resisting, and no help anywhere.

But never never before had Emma Weiss been confronted by a boy who, though so young, was tall as she, with such shoulders and such hair, who bore himself already as a conqueror, and who, to crown it all, was here, for her, and imminently touchable.

Or was he? From the moment she had first seen him, a bulk against the sun with a flicker of gold about his head, she had known of course that he was no Denis or Peter or Neville. Not only was he not to be carried about, but she was almost certain that his knowledge was at least equal to hers; knowledge of the body which body alone could have. She sat down behind her desk and looked at him, tapping a pencil on a thumbnail. Tic-tic-tic-tic. There he stood, spreading open the front of his jacket and setting his fists on the belt about his hips. The folds of the white shirt told the concave of the belly where the flesh would be creased as he bent a little forward. Then the shirt bulged a little over the top of the trousers. The button of the throat had come undone, the tie was loose and crooked. Muscles showed at the neck. The stance should have been elegant, but wasn't. There was a clumsiness about the lad, a touch of the bull, for all that he had no stoutness, no swell of flesh. It was this that spoilt any resemblance his features might have given him to those Apollos which Emma Weiss had, in fact, never much cared for, having preferred the great foreheads, bony noses and lank limbs of the northern heroes, though they had come no nearer her attainment for all her preference. But yes, that mouth was Phidias. Epstein would never have been hot or drunk enough to fashion such a mouth. Epstein, she suddenly thought, was a failure. Failure – it pulled inwards to her centre with a jerk. She stopped tapping, laid down the pencil and curled up her fingers into fists. She gurgled in her depths, and a drain in another room agreed, 'glug, glug' quite slowly, with a hungry, unachieving sound.

He'd stand there no longer. He walked towards the couch and leant against it, hands in pockets.

'Simy?' she said, reaching for her pencil and turning it slowly in her hands, scrutinising it. 'Do you mind me calling you Simy?'

'I don't mind. I don't mind what anyone calls me,' he said. 'Sit down, Simy.'

He looked at the chair on his side of the desk, then he half sat on the couch. Again there was a pause. She laid down the pencil, took a cigarette from a silver box and put it back again. Traffic noises below in the street. The clanging of trams. She got up and adjusted the blind. The softer light itself seemed to muffle the noises, put them at a distance.

She let go the cords, strode round the desk, bumped her groin against a corner, and stood in front of him.

'Well now,' she said, rubbing together those hands that served their profession. But they were moist, and could not be allowed to touch him anyway, so they went into the stiff white pockets of her coat. His eyes were laughing at her; not just amused, but laughing. Oh my God, I am so ugly, she felt, and was aware of nothing but the hair on her upper lip, the dandruff on her scalp, the mucus in her nose.

'Simy,' she said, hoarsely.

He looked at her face, lay back on the couch, stretched out, bent one leg up almost to his chest (his shoelaces dangling), and with chin thrust up, eyes squeezed shut, he laughed until every drawn breath was a trumpeting fanfare for Emma Weiss's kismet. Her undoing.

*

There were several new feelings to be had from it, Simon found. For stabbing into flesh was not all. Nor were the revelations of hill and creek and marsh and dune, gully and crevice, thicket and crater, grotto and gorge, all. After exploring came subjugating, and with no weapons but what were his by nature. Every afternoon when school was over, for nearly a fortnight, he went full of laughter and excitement to the Doctor's. 'Ach *zo*, ach *zo*,' she would grunt, and whenever she had been touched to the quick, to what in her dreams she thought of as the very Bauhaus of her being, she cried out, 'You have killed me, you have killlled me, ohww!', the last sound being a kind of whistle like that of a receding train. He preferred it when she accepted his government, and soon his exploitation, in silence, or at least with no more referential sounds than those the body talked of its own accord. But Emperor of the Leather Couch though he was, and hurry though he might to begin and to depart at the end of each sally, he could not prevent or avoid the repulsive obscenities of her tongue – 'I love, love, love, love, love you,' and 'my darling, my cruel boy, my *god*.' (Which last was the worst of all.)

*

At home nobody questioned him about the Treatment. Not even Nanny who had been told not to, and anyway had an opinion. For a week Mrs Leyton was satisfied with the way things were ordered, no voice in the garden, and the days succeeding one another neat as graves. Then she got a letter.

'I have now,' Dr Weiss had written, 'completed my preliminary investigations, and have come to the conclusion, you will be pleased to hear, that, in my opinion, no treatment is necessary. Far from being abnormal, paradoxical as it may sound, he is, without going into technicalities, abnormally normal. It seems that the boy is deriving some pleasure and benefit from his visits to me, and I am delighted for them to continue. But as I cannot claim to be administering to him professionally, there is no charge.'

For the first time in her life Emma Weiss was doing the only thing which really was its own reward.

But now Freda knew her to be an impostor.

On the day which brought this letter, Rayfel Leyton, having something vital to do at a desk, drove home early. He entered the house by the kitchen door and prayed to rubber

157

and wool to keep him safe as he stepped down the passage towards his study. But for once the door of the lounge was open, and Freda was looking over the back of the sofa towards the door.

'You're early,' she said (accusingly, it seemed to him).

'I've got something I must see to –' he murmured (he hoped not apologetically).

'Just one moment. There's something I want to tell you. Come here and read this.'

From between the pages of a book she pulled out a folded paper. He frowned as he took it but opened it without haste.

'Well,' he said heartily, spreading his arms and pushing forward his santaclaus front, 'there you are then. What good news. There's nothing for you to worry about. This is extremely reassuring I must say. And how nice to have dealings with an honest man.'

'Dr Weiss is a woman.'

'Well,' he laughed, 'even women are not spoilt by honesty.'

Freda drew in her lips, to suppress an anger before expressing it. But he had to hurry. Later, later, they would talk of it. He shut himself in, sat down at his desk and drew paper and pen towards him. But the room was warm, the heat of the midday winter sun was increased by the glass through which it struck printing six squares of lighter green on the dark green carpet, and he slumped a little and brooded for a few minutes on the side issue of his son. Simon was not really a child any more. The boy was growing a yard a month. Normal? Normality was of no importance. Brilliance was what counted. In a fleeting image he saw what brilliance looked like. It had little hair and that of a dark colour, it tied its shoelaces and though not towering inclined to a judicious corpulence. How in God's name had Simon turned out to be as he was? They say they grow bigger and blonder in the New World, but surely not in a generation. Had the child not been born in this very house he might suspect a mistake. Or a cuckoo, if he believed Freda capable of amorous adventure with the body; which he did not: any more than with the heart (whatever she might affect, and he find politic to notice). Well, perhaps some foremother took a Cossack for a lover, willingly or unwillingly, and thus a Nemesite gene was set on the road, the long, long road to the green pastures. Was the time now come for the iniquities to be visited?

But that was a dark imponderable question. His task at present was to cast light where he could. He blew a fleck of dust from the paper before him and wrote in big black letters the title of his article for a new, cautiously left-wing political weekly: 'The Extension of the Franchise among the Bantu'.

Rayfel Leyton planned to be a powerful liberal influence in a dignified sort of way. He hoped to overawe rather than to rouse. He set down his heavy sentences with that object, feeling them rumble in his chest. When he had amassed six dense equal paragraphs, he sat back to resonate them aloud with deep enjoyment.

A butterfly flew against the windowpane. He was distracted. One of the six squares trembled. Was there a flaw? He changed 'rule of law' to 'nomocracy', 'poverty' to 'impecuniosity'. Now there was no ripple in the darkness.

He prided himself, Rayfel Leyton did, on never needing to consult a dictionary, on not possessing a thesaurus or an encyclopaedia. And when he was to speak, he never prepared more than a point of view and a few epigrammatic phrases beforehand. True fluency, he always said, was not premeditated; but once one was committing oneself to paper, a little polishing was permissible. And ink might irrigate his reputation. Still, he preferred speaking to writing, for then others took down what he said, and he much preferred to be overheard rather than listened to. Communication was not his intention. Law had drawn him at first by its sheer prolixity, but after a while its pleonasm, fussiness and imprecision had lost it his interest. It was an unmalleable, imperious style. A deceptive beauty he had longed to master, but found he could only serve. He had learned early in life that words had power of a different sort. Long ago at his school in Doornfontein little, lithe, fair enemies had mocked him for their sport until one day he had said that he had 'found out the truth about them', and when they had forced him to tell what it was, he had confided that they were 'feculent excrescences and pustules on the face of humanity'. And as though he had pronounced a curse in a sorcerer's tongue, they left him alone thereafter in superstitious dread. Also he could recall the day that his clever, cold, Yiddish-speaking mother had looked at him, her only child, for the first time with interest and pride, respect, almost fear, when he interrupted a conversation to say at the age of eleven (and after seven years of her own fumbling with the English language), that 'dialectical materialism was a triangular wheel for sentimentally educated bourgeois dupes and simpletons to try and push uphill, but if it would keep them preoccupied while the redistribution of the world's wealth was effected, let them push.' Nobody guessed that he had learned the sentence off by heart in order to storm her defences.

Yes. Words were weapons. Words were shields. His speeches were magic screens of glass through which he might look out, but which he made opaque to others: and they reflected back to them all matters that concerned their common welfare as such complicated, serpentine, long-worded affairs, that they could only be too glad to leave them to him who could manage such monsters.

Now once more he read, a trifle louder, his concluding sentence; which exactly, concisely, gracefully summed up his argument, yet did not lessen the opacity of his case. 'Thus it would be soundest policy to govern haste with prudence, and to temper mercy with justice.'

He would have preferred 'precipitation', but left 'haste', for the sake of the flutter of the phrase.

*

Every day Emma Weiss powdered her feet, did her exercises, and when it was close to his hour of arrival, poured eau de Cologne down the front of her blouse.

She had a new, submissive tone. He was by no means tender. He never said anything, except once he told her to shut up when she was murmuring some endearment, and sometimes he would laugh that irksome laugh. Yesterday – she hated to recall, but did upon a Thursday afternoon – when she had been lying limp and drained of all but breath, he got up suddenly from between her big raised thighs, seized her feet and dragged her right off the slippery wet leather of the couch on to the floor. She had been half stunned, and her back still ached. She had whimpered and moaned like a little hurt darling, while he had staggered and flopped about the room holding his ribs and laughing that laugh of his. Such Schadenfreude! How she worshipped him.

She licked a forefinger, passed it over her scant eyebrows. She looked at her watch. He was late. She went to arrange the hand-made chocolates from the Viennese confectionery in the silver dish on her desk. The first time he had eaten the lot, and though he hadn't touched them since, you never knew. One had a piece of candied violet, one had a little silver ball. The round ones were covered with tiny chocolate chips, and the marzipan were of irregular shape, pudgy and dusty. But she must resist. She was keeping an eye on her figure. (That shape which surrounded her own pulsing, hungry void which he so deliciously packed with his hard flesh.) Ach, Simy, I am the luckiest woman on earth. Ach, Simy, my circumcised Apollo!

Still he did not come.

You never knew.

She raised the Venetian blind and stood looking down at the street. The trams came rocking in and stood and went, but none of them carried him. The sun went down behind the cooling-towers, and the blustery winter evening enclosed the city in an old loneliness. She was a friendless woman in an empty foreign land. Was it possible he no longer wanted her? Perhaps he was ill. What him? Perhaps he had to go somewhere else. With his mother. With his mother? Perhaps he's just had enough of me for a while. For a while? Ach, Simy, I *love* you. But you do not love me. Perhaps you hate me. If only you'll come I'll let you hurt me, as much as you like. I have a strap, I have a stick, I have some little instruments. You can hurt me, you can punish me. I hate myself. I loathe myself, thought Emma Weiss. Emma Weiss. Emma Weiss the Weissian. Didn't she *deserve* love as much as anyone else did? Ach Gott, Emma Weiss.

Si-maaaaaaaan!

She devoured all the chocolates, and when she felt calmer she made a plan.

*

In the bright swift gusty midday Simon vaulted the wooden gate and started up the road behind Nanny Binny and Josephine, who set off, with heads lowered to the grit, up the road from the school and its frantic disgorgement. The wind tore at the cries of the boys and girls and left them in tatters. The children's hands were curled in wool. Their thoughts too, curled for safe carriage. The wild air spread its arms and rushed at them. All windows were shut, all doors barred. Great trees along the top of the ridge bowed down. But only Simon's head was raised to see them. He did not huddle. He wore no gloves. Josephine looked round for him, stopped to let him reach her side, but he was dawdling. The little leaves on the evergreen hedgerows shivered, and she turned again after Nanny. The grey knot at the back of Nanny Binny's head pushed her hat forward on to her forehead where her hand had to retain it. Her neck with its two long cords looked ready for a blow, stretched as they were between the wisps of blowing hair and the collar of her black coat, so that Josephine felt sorry for it, and loved Nanny the more.

Nanny Binny and Josephine rounded a corner. But Simon stopped to search a patch of coarse grass (which the wind swept aside for him, whipping off blackjacks and hurling them into the fertile gardens round about) for those stones, some white and not to be confused with the sunbleached turds, and some pink, and some ochreous, with which you could draw on walls and pavements and blue slate. Not that Simon drew, but he liked to mar smoothness.

A car stopped against the kerb beside him, but he did not look up until it hooted. There, mouthing, was the hectic face of Emma Weiss. She leant over, and the door on his side flew open, batting the air so violently it seemed in danger of flying off altogether from its canvas hinges. He went a little closer.

'Get in. Just for a moment.'

He got in and shut the door with a whack that made its yellowing celluloid window wobble. A smell of breath and dust and oil. He looked at her face. Not that he hadn't seen enough and more than enough of it, but it was quite a funny one.

She looked ahead through the real glass of the windscreen. But she knew she couldn't keep him waiting long. Her lips parted stickily; a white gum almost kept them together.

'I just wanted to say something to you Simon. It won't take long. I haven't been able to think of anything else since you left.'

He stopped listening. Along the main road ahead cars flashed by. Every few seconds her humble little carriage was seized and shaken, as by an importunate dog.

'So I beg you to come tomorrow afternoon. You won't be sorry I promise you.'

Simon opened the door but the hound knocked it from his grasp, put teeth in the boy's sleeve and pulled at him.

'Will you come? Simon, Liebchen, will you come?' She pleaded, putting her hand on his other arm.

'Okay,' he said, and was gone, off round the corner, leaving her to wrestle for her door with the jealous wind, which could have won had it not quickly tired of the sport and lain down in the sun to snooze.

*

One day more, and Simon again climbed the koppie behind the school.

The cries of the playground stopped reaching him as soon as he attained the wild height above the cleared, used earth. In a soughing stronghold he stood still and mocked the lament of a Piet-my-vrou which he could make out beyond the black lines of the branches and the smudges of the needle clumps. Or the bird was mocking him. The rustling of nearer birds and the riffling of finches' wings he almost felt upon his shoulders, in his chest. He lifted his spread hands and the sun shot long spears between his fingers, through the stockade of trees, but they disintegrated into a light dust which settled on the fallen brown needles or shelved on the wooden petals of the cones. He himself, though it would have taken other eyes to see it, cast a shadow, two shadows, even more, on the dust in the air, and was himself only a denser shadow as he walked into the light. As he came near the edge of the wood a nest of needles in a near fork caught fire, reflecting Simon's own head, on which the sun pressed with not yet sentimental warmth. But then the dust pouring through the air on either side of him, his head becoming the exact colour of the light, his body a shifting shadow of no distinct outline, he was nearly lost, nearly broken up altogether into the elements of wood and earth and light and air. Ah, but there he was. No figment this. He came running out into the white light of the hill, with a sound like burning twigs, and never was anything more solid, not even the big old stones with their black shadows at their feet.

Noiselessly he paced through the grass, stopped upon a slope of white rock, lay flat upon it and pushed his way to its crest. Peering over, he hoped to surprise one of those creatures which are supple as rock is solid. And there was one. A real beauty, long and flat, gangrenous gold, sickled to gain purchase on one side by effort of its horny hands and levering knees. On either side its blunt head, above the curved ends of its stretched, black-banded mouth, an extuberant eye was lipped between equal lids. In a flash its body swerved the other way, its baby limbs strove, and it made for a narrow grassy hole of darkness between two squares of mottled quartz. But a black shoe with trailing strings and a collar of grey wool came down beside it. A hand scooped it up, a blind and mouthless finger stroked its neck. Then down inside the shirt it went.

The boy set off again, for this was a day for hunting, over a scrabbly slope of broken stone, starting small avalanches behind him. Across a plateau near the crest of the hill he approached a little tower of tall tablet rocks leaning together. He stopped dead, because a shadow on a corner was swelling along the ground. Slowly, jerkily, it grew. Some large, weird, terrible beast had woken after an age-long sleep in the earth and was lumbering now out of its rocky doorway into daylight; a thing unknown anywhere else in the world, a strange, lonely, lost, light-blinded, clumsy, warty, scaly, leathery, hairy creature which he would pounce upon and capture. He had his knife with him, but he would rather not use it on such a prize. He swelled with expectation and strength, and the skin of his arms and legs prepared itself for the contact it would have with scale or bristle or fell. It lengthened, it came on, and Simon with his practised beast noise, war cry, hunter's halloo, but primitive gargling, leapt and seized and bore down the magnificent monster, which had a rubbery feel, and cried out with a human voice. He left go, rolled over, sat up, and saw what he had tackled and brought down.

Mrs Foster sat, her legs stretched out in front – china doll legs, the upper parts all bag – and watched her pith helmet roll down the hill. When it was out of sight she stood up, dusted and straightened her clothes, and said, 'Come with me, my boy.' She passed him on her rubber soles, plunged heels into the fall of little stones, and strode on through the grass, at every stride flicking the corner of her skirt with a thin cane.

When they reached the edge of the wood Simon put his hand into his shirt to take out the King of Lizards and set him free in his kingdom. But he changed his mind. As he would probably never again come up here he'd take the King along with him.

He did not trouble to collect his books from his desk or even his overcoat from its peg. He pulled back a brown wing of the front door, letting the sunlight look inside at green paint and floorboards. As he followed the path to the gate for the first, last and only time, Meneer Kruger, who had often rapped his knuckles with a ruler or pulled out small hairs from his temples, implored through an open dormer, 'Werk, moenie sit en droom nie, ons het 'n land om op te bou!'

When he reached the main road Simon did not turn towards home, but crumpling the letter in his pocket (which told why he was no longer welcome to attend Mrs Foster's Infant and Preparatory School), he crossed the tramlines and boarded a tram. When they read the letter, his mother might cry and his father would splutter. It was a to-do that he preferred to postpone. So he rode into town on the back balcony at the top of the tram, swaying to the jolly rhythm, encouraged by the rude and warlike bell, and watching Mrs Foster's School sink into the past. Only once the King stirred, began to climb the wall of flesh, but was thrust back and lay again in its pouch, awaiting light or doom.

Simon had caught the first tram that came along. Only when he reached the town did he consider that he should have travelled the other way. If he had gone to a distant, end-of-the-line terminus and then walked on he might have got far away by evening, and been able to walk alone in the great space of the veld. But here he was, in his father's city. In Dr Weiss's city. It was time she was done with. Feeling behind to make sure his knife was there, he made towards his prey.

She opened the door and sound and smell rushed out, the sound of the recovering cistern, the smell of ageing smoked female skin on which old scent has spoilt, and of floor polish. She was clutching a kimono across her chest. Her hair stood up uncombed about her face.

'Ach, Simon. I didn't expect you so early.'

She led the way. Hauled on cords with one hand until the slats changed noon to twilight. As she turned towards him she let go her gown (there was a most fierce dragon embroidered on it), and her expectable dingles were to be glimpsed with their crops of hair.

'Simy, darling –' she said, leaning against the desk and looking down at the floor. 'I'm going to come straight to the point and be quite frank with you,' she said, but there was a frog in her throat, and she paused to clear it, at the same time scratching her head vigorously, so that a fine snowdrift fell on the fiery night of her gown. 'I – I'm a very unhappy woman.' She looked up, blinking, at the planet Saturn, made of green glass, hanging from the centre of the ceiling with rings of chrome. She pressed her lips out, as though she were blowing it a kiss. They were white and scaly but for a rim and a ray or two of dragon pink. She opened the gown wide, then folded it again side over side across the duck-bills of her chest, and went and sat behind her desk, and whirled her chair about on a swivelling screw until she faced the view of the blind, and it was the dragon who spoke to Simon. 'I've had a hard life,' it said. 'But of course I don't expect you to understand what that means. And I don't want to bore you with all that. Come and sit down and let's talk as though we were just friends.'

'I've got to go,' said the boy, who had been shifting his weight in the middle of the room.

'I know. Your parents and I did you an injustice. Well, we made a mistake. We misunderstood you. It's not easy for grown-ups to admit to a child that they made a mistake. And it's never easy to forgive –'

He was not laughing. If she had hoped to keep his mirth away by means of sadness and solemnity perhaps she had succeeded. He was looking at the dragon.

'Well,' the hoarse voice proceeded, 'perhaps I can't forgive myself either. Perhaps I can't forgive myself because when a person's done something wrong they need to be punished. Even grown-ups need to be punished, you know, when they do something wrong.'

She went on looking steadily at the blind, if anything, and it was the bristles on her neck and the golden writhing dragon that warned the boy directly that retribution was in the air.

'Grown-ups are punished differently from children. But I don't know that you would understand the grown-up ways of being punished.'

She swung suddenly about and faced him with the red and wrathful face of power upon a cloud.

'But if I were to be punished the way I was when I was a little girl, then you'd understand it, wouldn't you?'

'What,' he asked, 'have you done? I-I-I-I mean what've you done that's wrong?'

She glared at him and chose not to have heard.

'If,' she said, her face changing to deep mournfulness, 'if I were a little girl and had a mother and father to punish me, then I would be able to forgive myself. But I have no father or mother, Simy, darling. None.'

She could not have expected to pluck his heart-strings. And he had no soul to touch. He heard it as a boast, but had no envy in him.

'As you,' she went on, and rose, 'are the injured party, Simy, would you like to feel that you have punished at least one of the culprits?'

She looked so abject, his quarry, it was not yet the moment to strike. And this time there were no followers waiting on the heights of the leather desk or the couch. If old cries of boys lingered on the air, he had no ghostly ear to listen with.

Again pulling upon the cords which were more certainly in her control, she pressed dusk into dark. Carefully she edged round her desk, stepped out of her wedge-heeled mules, tripped to the couch, and let the kimono slip to the parquet. There the dragon lay, coiled upon itself, unrecognisable, a mess of gold in a bog of black.

'And now,' she said, positing her voluminous bum on her solid heels and rummaging under the couch apparently for a box on which was inscribed, in red letters, 'Jeyes Fluid 2 doz'. He went on watching her, waiting for a real laugh to possess him, or an inclination to that other laugh of his, but he felt nothing, not even when she drew out a leather strap from a moraine of glass and china in the Jeyes Fluid box, stood up, and thwacked it across the hide. After that, with care and gentleness, she laid it over the back of the chair which Simon had not taken.

She climbed on to the couch. Her hands reached out and gripped the edge of the precipice, she pressed her face into the leather, and she waited.

His shoes scuffed the kimono.

But there was nothing more here for his senses to learn. His knife stayed where it was. He went away quietly, swiftly. He did not notice until later that he had left something behind.

On the black silk the golden dragon raised its kingly head, and ventured a step.

*

Another week passed before Simon's expulsion from school became known to his family. He set off each morning with Nanny Binny and Josephine, ran ahead, and reappeared beside them on their way home – or if he didn't, "e'll get 'ome on 'is own all right, we'll trot along'. And he did get home all right. At the morning break-times Josephine expected he was risking the koppie again. When one of the boys in Simon's class asked her whether he were ill she thought how he could have missed a whole day's lessons playing up there. Mrs Foster awaited the parents' questioning with her usual resolution, and though she was a little surprised that they were delaying the interview, a week went by before she became suspicious enough to telephone Mrs Leyton.

Since her loss Freda had given up tennis on Wednesday afternoons. She liked to imagine the speculation of the girls.

She feared though that Maisie, the kind soul, probably allowed no gossip about her friend. Maisie was nice. Well Maisie was contented, even happy. But Freda did not envy her. Maisie simply didn't know what she was missing. Her horizons were too narrow. Freda could at least look out of mental windows, see beyond her own fence; could travel in the coaches of books and look out, note that there were spaces; high social mountains; deep poetic chasms. The knowledge oppressed her, but surely it was better to know of them, even though you could never conquer them, than to be, like Maisie, satisfied in the narrow room of matrimony, in a suburban house, in a provincial town. And with Eric as hero! On the very Friday that Mrs Foster made up her mind to speak to her, Maisie did the same, and had been sitting in the blue lounge, where the curtains were half drawn, for two hours, trying to persuade Freda that it was better to get things off one's chest, that she could trust her, and that she was not interfering, only affectionate. But Freda would only sigh and insist that it was impossible to tell some things, even to one's best friend. The sharp Freda was gone, and a new, superior Freda with a quiet voice was in her stead, offering money for the soup kitchen where Maisie did her morning stints.

At four o'clock the telephone rang.

'Be mother,' said Freda, as she went out to the hall, to hear from Mrs Foster's impartial lips the unrepealable sentence that had been carried out on her son.

'But where is he then?'

Mrs Foster could not help her to discover. She telephoned Rayfel's secretary who told her that her husband was in court, but was there any message? Freda returned to Maisie who was quick with sympathy but had no useful suggestion to make except that if he had come home every other day this week he'd be sure to come home today. After all, where else could he go?

Where else was he? Sipping cold tea, Freda wondered if Simon might meet with an accident or develop any ideals.

After a silence which she had been able to alleviate only by an occasional clicking of her tongue, Maisie asked if her Simon had not been 'cleared up' by Dr Weiss.

'Who has been ill for a week,' Maisie told Freda. 'In the General Hospital.'

Maisie never repeated tales of her friends and acquaintances, chiefly because she liked everybody; but after a moment's thought she concluded that there could be no malice in telling poor Freda about poor Dr Weiss's misfortune, of which she had heard from her friend Gertie Hausmann.

'You know,' she admitted, 'I never have understood what is meant by a nervous breakdown.'

'Is that what's happened to Dr Weiss?'

'It seems she was suffering from delusions. Gertie Hausmann says it's a kind of hysteria. She imagined that somebody tried to kill her by setting a poisonous snake on her. I suppose if your profession brings you into contact with mad people all the time anything can happen. Hey?'

'Perhaps,' said Freda eagerly, 'it was true.'

Freda believed in mambas, but not in a civilised context. So she laughed.

And while Maisie felt gratified that she had restored her friend's spirits and helped her to forget for the moment her sorrow and trouble, she also wondered whether she had not after all been guilty of a betrayal, or whether Freda's unhappiness had not begun to warp her. For her part, Freda was irritated by Maisie's earnestness, so the old affection between them, a gate on which they both leant, was temporarily latched with unrespect. She couldn't wait for Maisie to go, and as soon as she had, Freda walked purposefully into the dining room.

'Nanny,' she announced, coming in to where Josephine was turning the handle of the Singer while Nanny guided the sheet which was being sides-to-middled. 'Nanny, I think you ought to know, Josephine stop a minute will you, I think you ought to know that Simon has been expelled from school. Perhaps now you will stop telling me there is nothing wrong with the boy.' She shut her lips but remained standing there. Nanny, grazing her rough hands purposelessly over the sheet which was quite straight and smooth, glared over her spectacles, her nose looking pinched, though this was no sniffing matter. Mrs Leyton glared back at her and longed for reprisals. She had an inspiration, or a temptation, though a dangerous one. Simon with his filthy hands always holding something horrible – frogs, snakes.

'What is more,' she said, against policy, 'it seems quite possible that he has tried to kill somebody.'

She stood for another moment to mark the effect of this wild stab, compressed her lips, went out slowly and drew the door quietly shut behind her.

Nanny continued to stroke the sheet.

'Oh?' she said, looking at the door. 'Well!' And the side of one bony, big-jointed finger rubbed her unavailing lips.

Mrs Leyton felt flushed as she sat on the high chair at her bureau, looked out at the bending branches of the jacaranda, and breathed: but whether with anger or triumph now she could not have said, nor what terrible expectancy was taut in her as the sky, which was the exact colour of her taffeta blouse. Taffeta was a bad choice for a time of emotion; it showed patches of sweat under her arms. She could not remember when last she had sweated.

'Where is he then?' asked Josephine.

'Well, I don't know then, I'm sure, well I never, well I never did,' said Nanny, pleating, folding, pressing the sheet into a neat but complicated, in fact a quite inexplicable shape.

Rayfel Leyton telephoned his wife, and Nanny Binny and Josephine opened the dining room door to listen.

'You must find out,' they heard her. 'Oh he'll be home all right, and I think you should be here when he arrives.'

'Come along now,' said Nanny impatiently, after Mrs Leyton had gone back to her lounge. 'That's it, up we go, come along, there's a good girl, that's the way, yes, come along –'

And 'Well now,' she announced, banging down the linen on a shelf. 'Yes, well,' brushing harshly from the top of this pile and that specks as uncertain as imputations.

Josephine sat on the window sill of the stairs with Alan Jesus, while Nanny bustled and talked about nothing.

Leaving the door of the linen cupboard open – a thing most strange – Nanny marched into her room and came out again wearing her coat and an old beige straw hat pinned on through its petersham ribbon. She bullied her gloves into position as she paused at the top of the stairs.

'You be good now. Frances will get you your tea. 'E can't be far and 'e'll get 'ome on 'is own but if there's something 'e's got to answer for 'e better come right 'ome and face up to it like a man. Yes, yes, there then, you be a good dog then. No you can't come with me this time. If your mother wants to know where I've got to you tell 'er I've 'ad to slip out for a bit and I'll be back just as soon as I can. You'll be all right now? Your bookshelf needs tidying, and' – at the bottom of the stairs Nanny's voice changed to a hoarse whisper – 'there's a bit of that cheesecake you're so fond of in the larder. Blow a kiss, duckie.'

After the bang of the screendoor, the world folded about Josephine. Alan Jesus could only sigh and settle to sleep. Not even a fly teased the edge of the afternoon.

'Simon, where are you?'

The sunlight on the wall was a map of undiscovered depths and distances. She gasped in the air that was crowded with interchanging particles, of which only a few were illumined. She could see where he was. She should have known that he'd been sent away from school. That he didn't tell her only proved that he was not concerned with anything that happened here any more. He was going far, as she had always known he would. But 'Not yet, Simon,' she pleaded, 'not yet.'

*

She had shocked Rayfel with a fiction, yet what Freda needed was a truth, for nothing less it seemed would do: a burnished truth to hold up to their faces in the terrible white silence of avenging innocence. The truth was the one thing that could undo. It was the ultimate weapon. With all kinds of armour, with lock and key, with all wit, didn't everyone try to protect himself from just that? Now she would find the chink. With truth, with proof, judgement must now be given and sentence carried out. By *him*.

It would not be enough, Mrs Leyton felt, merely to send Simon away. It was most important, but not enough. Rayfel was going to have to teach him a lesson. If he was too big for a hiding – and she supposed he was, since he was taller than Rayfel by quite a few inches – he was to be told, it must be driven home to him, that he couldn't get away with it, his selfishness, his lack of consideration, his contempt for anyone else's feelings, his irresponsibility. The truth. She wanted Rayfel's fury to break on Simon, and she wanted to be there when it happened.

Bare stalks, dangling untidily like loose threads, scraped gently at her window. It was an irritating sound, as though someone were trying to attract her attention. In summer it was better when the leaves pressed against the pane – like little hands – and helped to subdue the light.

When he came home he found her standing in the doorway of her dim lounge, her two hands pressing a knob of a handkerchief, so still, it didn't seem that she was bent on

175

making any further accusations. He took out his watch, frowned at it, wound it with absorption as he strode past her with an energy, not urgency, but in deliberate opposition to her mood, and said (locked with the problem of the watch), 'Did you know that the radio wasn't working?'

'Don't tell me he's broken that too.'

'Whoever's broken it, it's not working. It's absolutely essential that I should be able to listen to the news. Will you please see that it is repaired tomorrow?'

She didn't answer. He went to the window and looked out through the gaps of creeper. What was he looking at? Many-towered Camelot?

'Were you waiting for me?' he said.

'I am waiting,' she said, silverly, 'to hear what you are going to do about our son.'

She followed him into the room, sat on the edge of her sofa, her hands still pressed over the handkerchief, and stared, stiff and with jutting chin, out of the window, where, she hardly observed, the taffeta sky was tearing on the jacaranda branches.

For a shield he picked up the evening paper, but only folded it smaller.

'Well,' he said.

'Mrs Foster expelled Simon because he is disobedient, irresponsible, retarded and bloody-minded. A nasty, impossible boy in fact. Look at that horrible thing he did at St James. I know it was him. Who else would have done it?' She hadn't intended to raise her voice. That was clubbing rather than stabbing. She had bungled her ambush. 'I'm sorry.' She dropped her head for only a moment to her fisted hands. 'But I have tried for years and years – I don't say I'm not partly to blame – I've often done the wrong thing, I'm *not* good with children, and I'm not strong enough to cope. I needed some help and I didn't get it. And Nanny has spoilt him and excused him and let him get away with – well – murder!'

'It wasn't help you wanted. You wanted to evade your responsibilities. You wanted to shelve them. Things haven't turned out the way you'd have liked them to and now you're finding scapegoats –'

'He's not only *my* son you know –'

'Well quiet now and listen.'

'He's hardly a child any more. Whatever he's done he's responsible for.'

'Will you be quiet now and listen?'

He took off the new rimless spectacles he had lately assumed, and polished them with the truce flag of his pocket handkerchief.

'It could do me some damage in the election –' He swallowed. Words had seldom failed him, but then he had seldom been afraid. 'Two things,' He cleared his throat, raised his eyebrows and pressed forefinger of right hand to forefinger of left. 'First nobody must know about this.'

'People already know.'

'What people?'

'Mrs Foster.'

'Mrs Foster is a member of the Party. I'll have a chat with her.'

'I shouldn't think that even an Act of Parliament could make Mrs Foster change her mind.'

'She doesn't have to. She simply has to observe a silence as to the reasons for the boy's departure. He's too old to stay on there anyway. But she doesn't have to lie, all she has to say is that he's gone to another school.'

'She might have told her staff.'

'She can impress on her staff the reasons for her own reticence in the matter.'

'Maisie knows. But she would never tell anybody.'

'Who else?'

'That's all I think. Except Nanny.'

'Nanny wouldn't give Simon away in a hundred years.'

'Oh and Josephine.'

'How does she know?'

'I told her – at least she must have heard when I told Nanny.'

'Well if she didn't know before it means that none of the other children at the school could have known. If one knew they'd all have known. She must be told not to repeat it.'

'And what's the other thing then?'

'Oh yes. Simon must be sent away He must go where he can be properly watched over and disciplined –. Where is he?'

'We don't know. He's not back yet anyway.'

'We must find him.'

'How? Go on, how?'

A good point at which to challenge his power.

'Well, I suppose he'll come home eventually. He doesn't know we know, does he? Where has he been every day this last week?'

'Cutting up women and children and putting them in trunks,' said Mrs Leyton, and worn out by the contest, though depending on a lasting victory, she went upstairs to lie down.

Rayfel unfolded the paper. The solution of the Simon problem would require inflexibility, and Rayfel was certain of the rightness of his ends. He must reach Parliament, and stay to serve there, and no impediments would he tolerate, especially when they sprang up in non-political places. He did not doubt himself, his ability to be rigorous when rigour was needed. He settled to the international crisis about which it was expected he would have a good deal to say. It would be Foreign Affairs one day, if it wasn't Justice. Provided that

that delinquent –. No, no. He pursued other notions from the front page round the stout trunks of inner, thickening columns, and at last he had the major dragon cornered, and the lance was in his hand. He delivered thrust after thrust, murmuring: 'Unless the strength of those countries which stand for freedom and justice be opposed unshakeably to the bellicose strength of tyranny *now* and without delay, such a war will be waged upon this earth as the earth in all its history has never known, and if the powers of intolerance, injustice and sadism are the victors of that war, then God help us all, for there is no living man, whatever his political or religious beliefs, who will be safe from destruction.'

The word 'Jew' had sprung at him from several dense patches in the newspaper, but he himself preferred to avoid it. Others besides Jews were oppressed by these madmen in Germany. In any case, he always preferred to be as general as possible. He had a gift for the broad view, and for expressing it. To his cause words recruited words; they came in gangs instead of one by one. He had only to marshal the phrases, throw out an odd weak volunteer, commission a dozen or so sesquipedalian giants and distribute them one to every paragraph, and forward he'd despatch them all to storm the nation's comprehension, assault its ears with such a sound of brass, so many symbols, that it would gasp breathless hurrahs and be content to leave the managing of its multisyllabic problems to them who had the diction for it. Haaaah!

*

As Josephine had made her way down to the kitchen, raised voices had reached her from the lounge. Her father, she gathered, had something to fear from Simon. That Simon should have power even over him came as a surprise to her, but of course she should have visualised the possibility.

179

'Tell me a story, Frances.'

Frances's tales were always of lost children ravaged by wild beasts, stolen by wicked wimmins, eaten by madmen, and skinned and dried by skelms, and so they were this time, until the boiled egg was on the kitchen table (at Josephine's special plea not to have to eat alone in the dining room) and Josephine ate and drank in a warmer and busier place than ever she had before. Alan Jesus lay down in front of the stove. She watched the flickering through the cracks in the iron doors and heard the hurricane rage in it as in deep forests. How terrible it would be to be lost like Hansel and Gretel. But she would be quick and nimble and pitch the old witch head first into the flames before she could cook fat Simon.

*

Not even Nanny Binny herself could have told all the places she explored that afternoon. While it was still light she hunted round the school on her own, climbed all the way to the top of the koppie and came upon a wizened, very old looking African woman suckling a baby. She was not afraid of any encounter.

There were lanes and empty lots she knew of. There was the Zoo, and the Zoo Lake. She walked for miles, in the cold wind, but was used to walking and liked it.

She called on Great-Aunt Jenny and told her that she was just passing, and they hadn't by any chance seen Simon, had they? Great-Aunt Jenny considered. What was today? Friday. No. He hadn't even come on Wednesday, though Josephine had been here. He hadn't come of a Wednesday for ages now. In fact, she had been saying to Freddy only yesterday that they probably wouldn't see Simon again until the spring, and how he would have grown by then. She supposed Nanny just couldn't keep track of him any more. Was there some special reason for her wanting him?

'He hasn't run away, has he?' Uncle Frederick looked up from a task, of oiling a telescope on a tablecloth of pages from old journals, and laughed. 'You haven't lost him?' he asked in a tone of brimming merriment.

Nanny Binny spent the rest of her visit – and she had to sit a while, anxious as she was to get back to their own neighbourhood so as to be sure of intercepting him, for darkness was coming down – reassuring Great-Aunt Jenny that she herself was in no need of reassurance. Yes, she would telephone later, she promised when she could get away at last, to let them know that he was home and all was well.

'If she phones,' said Fred when Jenny returned from the front door, 'get her to put Rayfel on. The news is very serious and I'd like to have his opinion. Not that he's always right, mind you. To tell the truth, if you ask me, Freda and Rayfel are not so badly off with a son like Simon. Just think of the ninny they might have had.'

'Besides,' Great-Aunt Jenny agreed, 'he's not a spoilt namby-pamby like so many other children are nowadays.' Or so she had heard. Jenny herself had not encountered them, nor ever been so unfortunate as actually to know anyone with inexcusable qualities.

An hour later the telephone rang, but it was Lydia complaining that she felt very ill, had they heard the latest about what was happening to the Jews in Germany? At the end of which lament Great-Aunt Jenny was so distressed she went into the kitchen to make strudel, and as a result she did not hear the telephone ring again that evening. And so, as Fred Kronowsky had made it a rule never to answer it, when it rang again it rang in vain.

Wherever Nanny Binny did go that day, there must have been not only disappointment but malice, for by the time she got back to the rise above their own street, her stockings were torn to shreds and tatters, her coat, however industriously she was to ply her needle, would never be the same again, and the bottoms of both her shoes were quite worn through though she'd 'ad them soled-and-'eeled only last month. Six shillings it 'ad corst, and look at them now.

Well things could be 'urt a deal worse than that. Things could be damaged past mending. They 'ad both done wrong, she and 'im. What could they do now but try to make amends? She'd do what good she might, while she 'ad the chance.

The dark – that sudden dark, so different from the twi-lights at Home – was very cold. The wind went right through her coat. She had to take the hat off and clutch it to her chest. Her hands in their thin cloth gloves were the hands of Jack Frost himself. It seemed that there were voices on the wind, distant, wailing, hard to catch. Lost children crying in the dark. She stamped up and down. For herself she was not afraid, though she knew that a white woman alone in the streets in the dark was supposed to be in great danger. If anyone came at her, she'd give them what for.

By and by something did attack her; rose up inside, where all her conflicts had been fought. It was a feeling of home-sickness that had never left her, not in all these years. She could see where the great plain below her ended in a ring of dark mountains against the starlit sky. So many more stars, so much bigger and nearer than she remembered from her youth. The lights of the suburb were really quite a small scattering, like a camp put down for a night. Everyone could easily up and go, and the dust sweep in again over deserted verandas, those rickety wooden sort on the houses of the mining towns where she had lived when she first came out to this country; the veld just out there, starting where the garden ended, two lines of wire and the pumpkin plants straying out underneath. It was under the floorboards, too, under the pavements and the streets. No one had gone very deep in this country. Except to honeycomb the earth with mines. She even remembered when she had first come here to the biggest of all the towns, the wild had started where the Zoo was now, that lake of blackness among the lights.

Perhaps he was already home, she'd missed him, it was too late to find out the truth before they got hold of him. She wondered if she should pray for him. But she had already spent a lot of wind in prayer, and was not sure that she had faith any more. How many prayers were heard? Had He even received all her messages? He certainly hadn't answered – not when she'd been most urgent, anyway. How cold the stars were. You couldn't tell much about Heaven from looking at it from underneath. She would not sing in the street but words ran through her head.

'A man who looks o-on glass,
On it may stay-y his eye,
Or if he plea-eases through it pass
And then the heav'ns espy.'

She stood close to the rock which had been sliced to let the road through, but all the same, after the wind had died down for one peaceful second, it sprang upon her back with claws that went right through the cloth.

'Oof, oof,' she blew, and banged her bony chest.

Someone was coming towards her now. How near or far he was it was hard to tell. A big black brute, probably. (But oh dear, she did hope they'd healed his eyes.) Good gracious, the man was in his shirtsleeves, and on a night like this.

'Nanny?'

'Well there you are at last,' she said. 'And freezing too, I dare say. Whatever 'ave you done with your jacket? And good gracious me, where are your shoes? Well, never mind now, 'urry along. They're all waiting for you. You better tell me what mischief you've been up to. Quick now, and no fibbing. What a fright you've given your poor father and mother. And what's this I 'ear about you being expelled from school?

That Mrs Foster told your mother you'd been expelled from 'er school. And going off like that without a word to anyone. You 'aven't gone and 'ad a fight with some boy, 'ave you? They say you nearly killed someone. They're very very cross with you, and quite right too. You should 'ave told your mother and father, you should. Never mind now. You know it's wrong to 'urt anything or anyone, don't you? And in 'eaven's name where are your shoes and socks? It's a wonder you 'aven't froze to death goodness me. 'Ere now you put this round you and no arguments. Come along now, quick march.'

He made no protest about wearing Nanny's coat hanging from his shoulders like a mantle, and even let her lead him by the hand at her brisk pace.

'Now don't say anything to anyone,' she warned, as they turned in at the gate. 'You can tell me all about it first in the morning.'

The crone led our hero to the kitchen door. Light was pouring through the screen. Yellow Frances was sitting, overflowing the kitchen chair, with her back to the draught and her knees to the stove, waiting up, which was just as well since Nanny had taken no key. Had Frances been told to wait, Nanny wondered, or had she misjudged her. Sometimes one did get a jolt, all one's ideas got shaken up. Frances started as they came in, and began to rise. Nanny signalled silence, and opened the inner door. She managed to smuggle him up the stairs and, rebuking the pipes for their singing, got his bath run, and him into it before going downstairs to tell Mr Leyton of the return of his son.

Mr Leyton stopped snoring in his study armchair, opened his eyes and saw Nanny Binny's wispy, bony, raw head bending over him from the corner of a high square of light.

'Found the scallywag, did you Nanny? Where is he then? All right is he?'

He was weak, he was caught unawares, he was at her mercy, he felt it necessary to seem as Nanny would expect a father should.

''E's all right sir and 'e's in the bath, and if you don't mind me saying so whatever 'as to be said to 'im will keep till morning. 'E's wore out poor child.'

Either Mr Leyton had accomplished more in his weakness than ever he'd thought possible, or else Nanny Binny had a particular and unguessable meaning, but this was the first time she had ever called him 'sir'.

'He needs spanking, Nanny, not cosseting. But if you say so we'll leave it till the morning then.'

He felt relieved – not only because his son was safe.

'Have you told his mother –'

'No, sir, I thought it would be better if you did that. But what I will do if you don't mind is just phone Great-Aunt Jenny and tell 'er 'e's 'ome.'

'Good heavens, what does she know about this?'

'I thought 'e might 'ave gone there as I know 'e's fond of 'is Aunty – 'e 'as gone there sometimes without being made –'

'What did you tell her, Nanny?'

'Only that 'e'd gone out for the afternoon and was bound to be 'ome soon and was just a little late.'

'You're sure that's all you told her? All right, Nanny, we'll say no more tonight. We can all do with some sleep. You don't know what's wrong with the wireless do you by any chance? I couldn't get the news on the air tonight.'

*

Mrs Leyton slept on into the sunny hours next morning.

Nanny Binny was relieved to hear Mr Leyton say that he wouldn't see Simon until lunchtime, as he had to hurry somewhere because of the International Crisis.

By twelve o'clock Simon was in his best grey flannel suit which was very tight on him but was grey flannel and a suit all the same, and his hair was brushed as though for an outing or visitors (for hairbrush and grey flannel placate the vanguards of fury which spring forth with peculiar force if alerted by the appearance of unruliness).

Nanny seated him across from her at the table, and Josephine was allowed to stay, because there were grave moral lessons to be learned this day.

'Now,' said Nanny, 'I'm listening.'

And Simon, who had scented vengeance, told her as best he could. Out of his incoherence her patience and love made sense. He had been expelled for going out of bounds, after he'd already been warned once, and for knocking Mrs Foster down. By accident. He hadn't told because as long as they thought he was at school he could go where he liked and do what he liked. And what was that? Well he went – into the country. And what did he do? Walked. Climbed. Swam. Swam? In this weather? What's wrong with the weather? And last night he'd got a wrong bus, and he'd got lost, that was all. And his jacket and shoes? It had been dark before he'd left and he couldn't find them.

And now, before telling him about facing trial for what you've done, making amends (she was going to set an example), before saying anything about anything, she must hear the worst.

What was this about trying to kill someone?

But Mrs Leyton came in, and Nanny began to bustle about, laying the table. It would keep her busy in here while *she* was at him, and though she knew she must hold her tongue, she still wanted to keep an eye.

Mrs Leyton was wearing a long cream gown and a shawl. She stood in the doorway, one hand to her brow, the other supporting her weight on the doorknob.

'What's the matter with you now?' Nanny wanted to ask her.

'Simon?' she said, without looking up.

'Yes,' said Simon.

His mother did not look at him as she glided to the chair which Nanny had left. Nanny grew brisker yet, and when she had got out the knives and forks she shut the drawer with as rebukingly businesslike, as honest a push as her strong hands could manage, and 'Trong!' said the drawer thus pressed into service.

Mrs Leyton said nothing, but leant elbow on table, chin on wrist, hand, eyelids, feelings all a-droop. She did not even look at him.

In case she were just waiting for him to start, he started.

'You see gosh I-I-I just got lost. Last night. Hey Nanny? I just couldn't get on to the right, the right streets. To get home. Hey Nanny? I-I-I-I got lost, you see.'

Nanny Binny, scorning bells, had to leave the room to fetch the children's lunches. She had a tray loaded in a trice, and Sixpence marshalled. As she led in the stew and dumplings (Simon's recent favourite), Mrs Leyton was saying wearily, '– nothing to be said until your father gets here.'

The smell of the food discovered the shaky excitement in Freda's stomach, and nauseated she rose and went to the window.

But Simon, looking at her apparently indifferent back, raised his voice.

'I lost my things. My shoes and, and, my shoes and, and my socks and. And that thing. My jacket. Because you see I couldn't find them. It was dark. And. I couldn't see in the dark where, where, where they were. You see.'

'Your father,' was the answer, on a sigh, 'will be back any minute, and then you may tell him all about it Simon.'

The way his name was said sounded ominous to Josephine. She knew what a calm could prelude. She felt the tension rising, the hum of mechanical purpose.

Nanny recklessly banged Simon's heaped plate in front of him and shoved and clicked the knives and forks on either side with as sharp, vigorous and impatient a racket as she could, to proclaim that she was not in awe of the woman's quiet hissing, that put-on of long-suffering. She liked people who got on with things, and if something was wrong to deal with it, and if things went against you, stand up and fight!

'Oh,' said Mrs Leyton, putting a hand to her forehead again, and returning to her chair. As she sat, she sighed.

'So you see,' said Simon, with his mouth full and his knife and fork clattering on the plate.

'We are waiting for your father,' she insisted.

'Well anyway I've told you, hey?' The dialogue of metal and china continuing.

Josephine's hands were gripping tightly. She had no appetite. Nanny pushed her plate nearer to her chest once, but did not insist. As an alternative she brought a bowl of green apples from the sideboard. But they too were clenched, their knuckles standing up sharply.

Nothing Simon had done yet had been an enormity. Surely they would not be too severe? Father was a lawyer, and everyone respected him.

Simon's racket went on, but no one said anything. Nanny sniffed, clicked her teeth, and gave sudden little pushes at Simon's plate, though he needed no encouragement, and sometimes jerked it back again, as a rebuke to his greed.

Mrs Leyton's shell-pink fingernail traced the shape of a white lily in the damask. No one would have supposed that she was awaiting a consummation: a small one, but imminent at last.

They heard the front door slam.

Simon went on chewing, grunting a little as he always did when he was enjoying his food.

'Come on, eat up,' said Nanny, brushing invisible crumbs from the cloth.

Josephine held her breath.

'There. Now!' said Mrs Leyton. She sighed again, leant back in her chair and looked expectantly towards the door. Familiar, heavy but faster-than-usual footsteps came up the passage. Josephine felt her face go soft, her stomach tighten. What could they do? What could they do? If only she could see –. What was the worst, the very worst? She saw Simon smile, briefly, broadly, then duck his head and feed it with the last mouthful of dumpling.

The door shook at the near approach. The knob turned, the door was flung open, and Father, still in his hat and coat, cast a wild look about the room, a look that stopped Simon's chewing, a look none of them had ever seen before. He opened his mouth to speak at the moment when his eyes settled upon Josephine and it seemed that it was at her that he proclaimed, with the thunder of a herald, 'War has been declared!'

Nanny Binny and the children sat and looked at him, not at all understanding the literal meaning of the announcement.

But Mrs Leyton, surely to her credit, burst into tears.

*

Nanny Binny sat on Josephine's bed one night before Simon had gone to sleep and instead of reading told them how she had asked for the police to be sent for that day when that boy Willy had been 'taken up', and that whatever he had done, and if he had done what they said it was the worst thing in the world, she was still sorry that she had had any part in it, he was so badly hurt poor man. She would do anything she could for him. Anything, she said again, champing a little like someone tasting something to find out what it was.

'And your father will help me to do the right thing,' she added crossly.

'Oh yes, it will be all right, Nanny, I'm sure it will be all right. You're not to blame,' said Josephine, very firmly, because she had never seen Nanny so distressed before. If it were really that bad for her, of course Father would help her, and no one less than Father could, very likely. No small thing made Nanny's hands shake. It couldn't be regret about Willy only, it must be something newer than that, or something new that had made the regret stronger. Simon, she observed, was looking up at the ceiling and neither met her gaze nor made any comment. His hands were clasped behind his head. People lay like that to think. But his eyes shut suddenly a moment after Josephine had spoken, and a slight parting of his lips and a deepening of breath told the two who were looking at him that he was imperturbably asleep.

Simon was to go to a school far away, and Father and Mother moved more purposefully, spoke in louder clearer voices as though they were not speaking to each other but by telephone to invisible listeners. Nanny Binny was often absent-minded and clicked her tongue and mainly answered 'dear dear, there's a good girl, yes duckie,' no matter what Josephine asked or said. Perhaps it was because of the war.

Now Josephine passed the dining room into which she had seen her father walk (his lips moving). As the door closed she heard him say, 'Well, Nanny, I believe you wanted to see me?'

She went on, up to the nursery. She had come from Simon. She knew where he was, and he was not under the dark pergola. But she had a task.

He had been digging, for no explained reason, a deep narrow hole in the red earth near the tennis court, and at the same time pantingly trying to tell her, without care for chronology or completeness, about the lady doctor who looked like a kangaroo with a moustache, and what he had done, and what he had not. He stopped when his spade struck a stone. He clawed away the dry sand round its edges, lifted it out and staggered with it on to the tennis court, sweat trickling down the brakes of his bare back.

In the hollow where the stone had lain there were white roots and a race of bustling white creatures, questing perhaps for something new to imprison them. Josephine did not consider these things – though she would another time – but observed instead that if you could see right through to somebody's feelings, even somebody you didn't like, then you ought to be able to explain them to other people. You should find the words to tell: words as clear as window-glass, or, better still, windows without glass. As she looked at Simon carrying his purposeless stone, she thought she was ready to try the difficulty herself. She would like to be that kind of interpreter.

So, standing at the nursery table, she carefully removed the jug and opened a new exercise book.

'A Story', she wrote, and underlined it with the aid of a ruler.

A short time ago my brother Hansel took a reptile with him when he went to visit an ugly lady mind-doctor. My brother Hansel is very handsome. He has yellow hair and blue eyes. My Uncle says he is 'the real Aryan type'. I have asked my Uncle how to spell this word, and what it means. Apparently pure-bred Germans are 'real Aryans', and very proud of it. Hansel is not proud. He does not think about his looks at all. Even when he has to brush his hair he does not look in a mirror. He is dirty.

The ugly lady mind-doctor, on the other hand, thinks a lot about her looks. She would like to wash off her ugliness if she could. She looked more at her own face than anyone else ever did, and so she began to think that she was always looking into a mirror when she was facing some other person.

The handsomest face that this poor lady had ever had in front of her own was my brother Hansel's. She felt very proud and glad to have his face, and she stroked it and kissed it. Then she thought, 'The children of a person who is so handsome will be handsome too,' and so she asked him to do what is always done when a baby is wanted.

Hansel thought that her face was very funny, and he laughed at her. But he is not mean, and he did what she wanted.

Very carefully next to the summit of the 'd' she made a star, and at the foot of the page deposited its twin. Down there she wrote in letters half the size of those above, 'It must also be noted that Hansel has said, "It is nice doing it, even with her."'

However, she continued, he did not wish to go on doing this every day for the rest of his life, and so, having given her a fair chance to become pregnant, he stopped going to see her. He had been sent to her in the first place because it was supposed that she could make his mind better. But as it turned out, Hansel had not got the sort of mind that the doctor had learned how to cure in Germany. So when he stopped coming she could not use that excuse to get him back again.

What she did was this. She went to him and said, 'Hansel, I have done wrong. I am an old woman, and you are a very young man, and I should not have asked you to help me make a baby. I must be punished for the wrong I have done. Will you come and see me once more so that I can put everything right in the end?'

Hansel did as she asked, and went once more to see her. She took off all her clothes, lay down on a couch, and asked him to strap her bottom.

Hansel did not wish to and went away.

However, the lizard remained.

As it is known that the lady mind-doctor was frightened of reptiles (and amphibians such as frogs) it is likely that she was very upset when she found the lizard was there instead of Hansel.

I cannot say what became of the lizard. Hansel thinks she must have killed it.

But Josephine was not satisfied that this was the truth. And when she had read again what she had written she knew she had not succeeded in explaining any feelings. She could not have seen the truth herself, she concluded. Or it had not revealed itself to her. Truth would surely always provide the right, the convincing words for its own advancement.

She would wait. When she was sure, she would try again.

*

'If you could just tell me 'ow much it would corst,' Nanny Binny said, with a prim mouth, 'and if I 'ave enough, I will leave the money with you and I want you to see that 'e gets the best man there is since you can't do it yourself. I quite understand that you can't stand up and talk for 'im in the 'Igh Court, but you'll know oo's the best man oo can. And if I 'aven't got enough well I'll leave what I've got and pay the rest later. I'm not stopping working, you know, and I can get a good wage. And more than that I can't do, can I? Whoo!' she said, and she patted her chest, for she was all out of breath; but at once straightened again and was still and respectful but very determined, and only one unreliable lick of hair wilted from under the comb at the back of her head.

'But they can always get legal help free of charge, Nanny. There's really no need for you to worry.' Saying which, Mr Leyton ducked and turned his head as though he were watching a bird out there in the garden.

'Well I can't get it off my mind, and I must do what I can for 'im, and the only thing I can do is pay. The ones oo don't get paid wouldn't try as 'ard as the ones oo do. I'd take it as a very great favour, sir,' and the formality or the urgency was now making her head shake, 'if you'd see 'e gets the best, and if you'd let me know what 'appens. I'll send my address. And if you'd also let me know 'ow Simon comes along. And little Jo of course. All I can say is I did my best –'

'Oh we *know* you did, Nanny. Nobody could have done more. Believe me –'

'But it wasn't enough, and I 'ope 'e now finds a kind strong 'and to rule 'im, and 'e'll turn out a fine man and go far yet. But I've said all I 'ave to say about that, and all that's on my mind now is this business with the boy. Willy, I mean. Now I've got a 'undred pounds. I was saving up for a trip 'ome one of these days, but that will 'ave to wait now, won't it, with the war on. I can be more use to them over 'ere if there are going to be shortages, can't I?'

'Well, Nanny, if you insist, let me arrange the defence and I'll let you know the cost afterwards. How would that be?'

'Yes, well, that will 'ave to do then, thank you, sir. Will it be more than a 'undred pounds do you think, sir? That's all I've got in the 'ole wide world, oh dear,' and because she had to laugh in apology and so let the stiffness go again for a moment, she plucked a little lace handkerchief from her sleeve – it was her best handkerchief and she was wearing her 'Sunday best' – and pushing her forefinger into it she ran it up and down the edge of the table, to treat the inconsiderable dust as it deserved. 'I don't know what made 'im go like that,' she said without meaning to, but quickly stowed the handkerchief away again and lifted her head. 'But I don't believe 'e meant to kill anybody.'

'Well, if he's innocent he'll get off.'

'Oo? Simon?'

'Simon? Simon isn't going on trial.' Was Nanny Binny going senile, he wondered. 'Thank God, he hasn't gone that far. Not yet, anyway.'

'I thought not,' she said. 'I'm glad it was a mistake.'

He looked at her for a second or two, but she was searching his face, and he turned away.

'Well, here's a little present for you, Nanny, and I hope you'll spend it on yourself –' he called heartily into the garden as he took an envelope from a breast pocket and smacked it down on the table. And he strode out, saying, 'I'll see you before I go, of course. If there's anything –'

Nanny Binny rubbed the knuckles of one hand vigorously in the palm of the other, for, one thing seen to, there was much still to be done. It would be a long time yet before she would face an empty future. Oh yes. Yes. While there's life there's 'ope, they say, and that's that.

*

'Nanny, take me with you,' said Josephine.

'I can't do that, duckie.'

'Why not, Nanny? I'll be good and tidy.'

'Well, you see, I'm running off to join the gypsies, and they don't take children. I'll tell you what I'll do. As soon as you're grown up I'll come back and fetch you.'

'And shall we live in a caravan?'

'We shall, and 'ave a 'orse to pull us along.'

Josephine sat beside Nanny Binny on the bed while Nanny took off her comfy shoes and put on her best. She did not believe in this afterlife they were inventing, but words can be tokens.

'There's no discoura-agement
Shall make him once relent
His first avow-wed i-intent –'
Nanny Binny sang in her breathless, soft, croaking voice,
then sprang up, smoothing down her coat, and went to the
dressing table (bare of brush and children and dogs), to
put on her hat. She grimaced as the pin went through, as
though it were truly piercing her head.

'There are the keys, in the drawer, and they've all got a name
tied on. Oh, there, there, Alan Jesus; there, there, poor dog,
you'll remember poor old Nanny won't you then? That's a good
dog. Look at 'im, you could swear 'e knew, couldn't you?'

But Josephine was not there to say. She had gone and
locked herself in the bathroom. And when Nanny's bags
were in the taxi and Nanny herself came up once more and
knocked on the door and called and called, she would not
answer. If I don't say goodbye, she thought, she can't go.

'Goodbye, duckie,' Nanny called. 'I'm blowing you a kiss
through the door.'

Still she did not answer.

Then she heard the taxi engine starting, and she ran
downstairs and out of the front door. She saw the red light
in the back of the taxi go on as it paused in the gateway.
She shouted 'Wait, Nanny, wait!' but the deaf taxi moved
on into the street, and by the time Josephine reached the
gate it was way down at the corner, and though she stood
and waved and called, it turned off into the main road and
was driven out of sight.

She found Nanny's comfy shoes placed neatly side by
side under the bed, each with a small hole in the sole, and
the shape of Nanny's bunions clearly outlined. She opened
the drawer where Nanny had put the keys. There they were,
laid out in a row, all the heads in a straight line, the fintails
on different imaginary lines, like notes of music. And each

had its label strung through its loop. Not one was of name-less possibility.

She took the shoes and placed them upon the cedar-box which held armistice poppies and beads and other things, all lying in there on top of the exercise book with its one story in it. Wouldn't it be nice, she thought, if Nanny could grow up out of her shoes again, like the pelargoniums did from the slips that Nanny planted, or like the thorny Thing did that grows against the kitchen-garden wall?

*

When Simon too was gone, Alan Jesus pined, went off his food. After a few nights sleeping in his usual place on Nanny's bed he moved to Josephine's, with her encourage-ment; for she too felt the absence in the room. Mrs Leyton found him there when she came to shut the windows in the middle of a stormy night when the first rains of summer fell. She was strongly tempted to banish him to the kitchen, and when a simple command and a pointing to the door was ignored by the usually obedient animal, she got so far as to drag him off the bed by the collar and across the floor, his four stiff legs rumpling up the carpet; but finding it difficult to manage the swing-door's stoppage at the same time as the hound-dog's laborious glide, she relented, let go the collar, and Alan Jesus leapt back upon the bed. He lay prone with his back legs folded under him; lowered his head, looked up at her with deep shame, and for apology basted his nose with his tongue.

What an unattractive creature he was, Freda criticised. But sometimes after that when she passed her odd quiet little daughter sitting on the window sill of the stairs with her arm round the undesirable dog, she consoled herself that she had relented to compassion, and so had not been altogether a failure as a mother.

197

After Nanny Binny had run away to join the gypsies, Frances the cook 'saw to' Josephine, who ate alone at the big table in the dining room, except on Sundays and Saturday afternoons. For it was warm enough now for Mrs Leyton to come away from her distractions in the blue lounge and brave again the predictabilities of the Saturday teas. There were some things that it seemed nothing could change. Again Great-Aunt Lydia and Uncle Fred settled down to scones and scorn at the table under the jacaranda, which as yet afforded little shade, but then the sunshine was welcome. And Great-Aunt Jenny who allowed herself neither appetite nor bitterness wore a cardigan over her navy silk and poured (as usual) from the silver pot.

'Ach you should never have let her go, Freda,' said Uncle Fred, starting right in. 'So, she was a bit bossy. She thought she knew best. Nu? Maybe she did. You won't get anyone like her again in a hurry.'

'I can assure you,' sighed his niece, 'I have no wish to find anyone like her.'

'You going to manage the kinderlach all by yourself?' Great-Aunt Lydia's voice scratched suspiciously at the very idea.

'For goodness' sake, there are no children. There's only Josephine now thank God and she's hardly a baby any more.'

Uncle Fred called her bluff. 'What are you talking? That woman did more work around here than you even begin.' Then abandoning emphasis and reaching for his cup he chanted, 'We-ell, good luck to you, that's all I can say-ay.'

But soon Freda was relieved of Lydia.

'She's going in to the hospital, but they won't be able to do much, I'm afraid,' said Jenny.

Fred unfolded a newspaper. He read the front page without comment. There was Europe, and his past.

'How is Simon? Have you heard?' asked Jenny.

'Some school friend wants to take him home for the holidays. To a farm apparently,' Freda answered. 'In Natal.'

Fred was recalled.

'I used to go climbing in Natal once upon a time. Movellous flowers. Bulbs, Iilieees, I'm telling you. In the Drakensberg. I remember once –'

'Don't you want him home?' Jenny asked.

'Not at all. I'm delighted that he should have made a friend and have something to do.'

'Tell me, could she manage him here by herself?' Fred asked his wife humorously, dropping his chin and raising his eyebrows. Then he folded the newspaper a different way.

'Fellow here,' said Uncle Fred, 'reckons, that Africa, is the true cradle of mankind. They've found fossils. On the trail of the Missing Link, hey? Well, well, well. It's probably lying just under our historical veranda at home. Well, well. So Africa is our ancestral home, hey? It turns out it's an old continent for our species after all. The Professor here says it probably had a bottom like the Hottentots. The Missing Link. Did you know, Josephine, that the Hottentots stored food in their buttocks, if you'll excuse me, like camels store water in their humps?'

'Freddy,' Jenny warned.

'Next time you go to Cape Town you must look at them in the museum. They've got them in glass cases. To tell the truth, I don't know whether they're waxworks or real ones preserved. I've been meaning to find out.'

He read again, more about the war, but again brought himself back to where he believed his interest ought to be. Besides, he needed to put up words to shelter him from information. He told the child, 'I saw real live Bushmen once. I wanted to see them when we went up to the Kalahari, but we didn't go far enough. After I shot my hippo near the Limpopo we went on a few hundred miles, but we never found any. The Boers used to shoot them for sport like game once. What you think of that? Hey?'

'Freddy,' his wife signalled again. But there were voices it was seldom necessary to hear. He went on.

'But I saw them at the Empire Exhibition. They had them in big glass cages. Living their usual lives, you know, in a manner of speaking. With their own utensils, and weapons, and everything – only of course they couldn't go hunting down Eloff Street, so I suppose they gave them food. But the landscape, inside the cages, was just like a piece of the Kalahari. If you can imagine a piece of a desert. If it's only a piece, I suppose you could say, it's not a desert. But who's quibbling? As I was telling you, in the time of the old Tyrant, they used to go up to Bechuanaland and hunt Bushmen like animals. Isn't that a shocking thing, hey? The Boers did. "Shoot them down," they said, "they're just vermin." What you think of that, hey? And he's a fine artist, your Bushman. A fine artist. All right, not exactly Rembrandt. But a movellous sense of colour. I've often wondered if they paid those Bushmen for being on show like that. Also like animals, hey? And how the Bushmen felt about it. Men, women and children. But, if you ask me, it's better to put a whole race behind glass than let it become extinct. Hey? But those Bushmen! I'm telling you! Talk about *tough?* There was one old man, ooh, believe me or believe me not, he was over a hundred and twenty years old. That would mean he'd been born, before the eighteen-twenty settlers arrived. Just think of that, hey. And the lives they lead. They drink water would kill any of us. Yes. When it comes to the whole knotty question of survival, when you come to grips with nature, there are tests of a man, of what sort of stuff he's made of, that have nothing to do with how much money he can make, or how many university degrees he can string up.'

His tone was challenging. But he roused no opposition. Lydia's voice was silent.

Yet his heart was not in these back pages of his life; not any more: it was in the front page that he hardly dared return to. It was in Europe. Pigeon heart, it knew its starting place.

And before long he relinquished all claim to Africa. It slipped past him into the future.

One Saturday he did not come to tea. Jenny walked over on her own.

'We have had some terrible news,' she told Freda. Did Freda remember that Jenny had a cousin called Peter who'd run away with a woman whom the family hadn't approved of?

Freda remembered something of the kind. A fortune-teller or something, wasn't she? A crystal-gazer. Oh really? A *circus* performer ? Well, what had happened?

A friend of Peter and the circus performer (who was an old woman now and could not have mounted a horse even in the usual way) had found a letter from Jenny in their apartment and had written to tell her –. They had been living in Strasbourg, did Freda know that? Peter was a schoolteacher.

But what had happened to them?

The Nazis –.

Freda sighed and clicked her tongue. Jenny sobbed. Of course it was worse for Jenny; Jenny had known them personally.

'War – is a dreadful thing,' Freda said, since something had to be said. She too, Jenny might remember, had suffered consequence of war. 'Think of the young. We mustn't cry, Jenny.'

But on the next Saturday Jenny cried again, very quietly and apologetically, with two big wipes of her eyes, and a swift slight blowing of her nose into a lace-edged handkerchief.

It was a surprise to Josephine to hear that Peter and his wife had not died long ago, but all thought of them was stopped by what Uncle Fred (who had come today, despite an attack of rheumatism which he'd never had before) went on to say, rapidly and emphatically, 'And let me tell you, you can doubt me if you like but its perfectly true the Germans –'

He paused, leant forward, hands on knees, eyebrows raised, and finished with a few hushed barks.

'– are, not, human, beings, they, are, beasts.'

He leant back in his chair and nodded.

'Beasts,' he said again, affably, but with a face as serious as Josephine had ever seen.

He waited, looking from one to the other of them. No one could remove her eyes from his.

Again he leant forward, and using the same method of swell and break and scatter, he went on to tell what proved his judgement. The Nazis. The concentration camps. He couldn't hold the knowledge. At last he was whispering, for it foamed, it pussed.

Josephine held her breath, and managed to shut her eyes to everything.

'The child,' Jenny tried.

'She must know. She must know. Everyone must know. You want I should tell you what they do to little Jewish children, hey?' Hoarsely he went on to worse, if there were worse. He had heard, he had heard. He looked furiously about him. Where was denial? Where was a representative? He would have liked to bring his anger and his sorrow home. Great-Uncle Fred.

Freda looked up at the sky through branches, all over which scraps of blue were sticking. She did not sigh. *Germans.* The word conjured up Emma Weiss and reptiles. And inexplicably, a dark, subterranean emotion, a recollection vague and disturbing, as of a promise unfulfilled. So, helped by both revulsion and disappointment she had no difficulty in disliking Germans. But Jews? *Jews.* She shut her eyes. Light and shadow flickered over them. She would get a book about the Germans and the Jews, and find out what she felt about the race to which she unwillingly belonged, in the light of these developments.

Fire. Josephine was afraid that her uncle's words would turn to glass. Hunger, torture, death. She could not put off realisation for ever; it would come suddenly, perhaps in the middle of the night. But not now! She got up and went away, into the spotted, scented shade of the rose-walk, under the airy arches of iron and leaves. The bees buzzed loudly all about, and overhead. Through the loud, loud steady buzz she walked up and down, until the buzz filled her head like a gramophone when the music has stopped, or a radio no longer admitting the voices on the air.

*

Thereafter, Fred Kronowsky, always a thoughtful man, re-tired for the short remainder of his life into his shadowy house, seldom to emerge even to tend the wild hill he had created with love and patience. He was, he discovered, still a European: he had, after all, been landed on an alien shore, far from home, and now home itself was being scuttled and he could never return, and yet the better part of himself was there, the infant Fred was sinking with it, and the old Fred, this remnant, had never been quite a pioneer, never much more than a survivor. Was there, he'd wonder, in idle despondency, regarding his own transparency staked through with guns in the glass doors of the cupboard which preserved his old hunting irons, any place at all for him, with his studious, amateurish, finicky, romantic tastes, his love of nature and books, in a world grown savage. And as for this ideology that could make white gentlemen grow fangs and claws, who could have foreseen that its poison would become so virulent as to threaten the whole earth? Nothing would ever be the same again.

And Mrs Leyton was converted to regret on the issue. For whereas in the days when she had surveyed the future in several possible colours she had been glad that Europe was settling into dust behind her, now that the future was exposed as having no colour or lustre of its own, she felt a pang for parental splendours changed to ugly shapes of death. There had been Beethoven among others. Her mechanical days spun round and round, day-again, day-again, yet surely vibrating with a music that she often found time to be still enough almost to hear.

Another, however, whose place in the scheme was the most obscure, for a while put on deafness and blindness like a shell, and drew into her head all manner of unimportant little curiosities to treasure: grains to irritate the mind and keep it busy and safe. For Josephine too the world would never be the same again. What had hitherto been submerged in depth and darkness, not to be met with unless dug for, was probably after all inhabiting the air.

She was pursued. No matter where she walked, something demanding and dreadful stalked her. Something worse than the old washerwoman had ever been. She dared not pause or it would confront her. When she lay or sat she talked to herself, blazoning the immediate air with the rubric of the words; or sang hymns, letting images of Nanny's Heaven, the hotel-and-country-club grandeur, pass before her mind, a thin flat screen, but a screen. Beyond, just beyond, IT bided in the shadows. If she let that other eye open, which it could upon a breath, she would have to see. She held her breath often, breathed shallowly for most of her waking hours, and was restless in her sleep. She dreamt more than once that she was passing Willy's open door and there was that within which was more terrible than any dragon of jaws and claws and cruellest will, because it was something that did not threaten but suffered: and was more appalling than corpses; black and red, yellow and red – she would not shirk those now; they were done for. And once she dreamt that she was walking on the seashore and IT was about to rise out of the sea and accuse Simon. (But surely he had killed the seal because it was ill, dying like the kitten – so that, even though he were incapable of compassion, it was at least an occasion for mercy which he took as his own opportunity? Hadn't what he had done been right, and merciful, though it had pleased a cruel desire in him?) And then she remembered that Simon had an alibi. 'He's a Jew, a Jew,' she shouted aloud, waking herself, and rising to sit straight up in bed. The room turned and rocked like a roundabout and then stood still. Alan Jesus shot up too with a low growl, a few muffled warnings to whatever it was billowing his jowls but lacking the force to break through. Josephine, fully awake now but remembering what she had shouted, understood perfectly well that *that* was no more a guarantee of innocence than of guilt. It was close then, its breath on her cheek. She leant the side of her face against the cool plaster of the wall. 'No,' she said, the air wheezing in her throat, lids damp with sweat. Alan Jesus slunk up and licked them, and he whined quietly, his little leather nose pushing against her face (his bad-smelling breath replacing for the moment that other), for since he needed reassurance, he gave it.

And through the window in the early morning she saw a world with the bloom of plums upon it, flowers scattered everywhere, a lawn strewn with blue blossoms, powdered with white dew. What kind of heaven was she living in? The amazing routine of the day would begin again: after the rowdy dawn of the birds, a glazed sky, and peace. It would seem a kind of heaven which even losses and absences could not flaw. Yet all the time, in the limitless Unseen, hell was in operation. How can heaven exist if hell does too?

*

When both her hopscotch friends were kept from school by summer colds, rather than wander the playground alone, an open target for the Unthinkable, Josephine stayed in the classroom, against the rules, and read. Hannalore Schultz stood waiting in the hopscotch corner as usual, but Josephine did not like her, and did not want to play with her. The next morning she got her exercise book out of the cedar-box and took it to school, planning to record how Hansel rescued a boy from drowning. This time she wished only to describe what must have been obvious from the end wall of the pool, had she been standing there, looking on calmly. She had no wish to find feelings. She hoped only to ward them off. (And as long as it was Hansel with whom she took the leap, and not the little boy called Simon, there would be no fear to tell of: nothing that could break except bone: nothing that knew its own weakness, or dreaded its own destruction.) But one of her friends was back, and they played hopscotch. Hannalore looked on, expecting nothing. Josephine forgot all about the book for several days.

*

One morning, Miss Pereira fainted.

The children had been tracing the outline of Africa, a colourful Africa with pink-brown mountains resembling stacked shells, and spruce-green valleys, baby-blue lakes and rivers, and yellow deserts; but no names. They themselves had to establish towns and cities with little black dots, and write names all over the tracing paper. But when the transparent sheet was lifted, Josephine found, all you had were dots and names and an outline that you could

206

lay down anywhere, a spectral play-play Africa, all cracked wood on the desk, all navy serge on your lap, while the free, many-coloured, blue-crossed continent was the same as it had always been, cityless, nameless, quite unmarked. She turned to a picture of the globe in the front of the Atlas and admired the shape that Africa had, as right and recognisable and comfortable as a familiar face, and how it was stuck in such a central position. South America was like another, elongated Africa distorted in a side-on mirror, she was thinking, when a noise made her look up, and she saw Miss Pereira lying on the floor.

At once all the children rushed out for help. Although the pretty young lady soon regained consciousness she was carried out on a stretcher by Mrs Foster and a cleaning boy, after Mrs Foster had carefully drawn her skirt down over her knees. Mrs Foster told them to sit quietly until someone came to 'take over'. Their excitement was quenched when Meneer Kruger, frowning and louder-voiced than ever, came in shouting, 'Well, what're you supposed to be doing, hey?'

'Geography,' they chorused.

Meneer Kruger did not care for geography.

'What is your next subject?' he demanded.

'History.'

'What're you doing in History?'

'Draw-ing a laa-ger,' they cried.

'Then take out your History books and get on with the job. Werk! Moenie sit en droom nie. Ons moet ons land opbou.'

The children plied their grease crayons, colouring in their umpteenth drawing of a laager. For they were learning yet again about the Great Trek. They had learned about it every year since their schooling began. It was itself something that had had no beginning, and would never come to an end. Over and over again the children drew pictures of ox-waggons; singly, or in a long straight line going over a pass, through a landscape of aloes and round grass-roofed huts, to drop down beside an orange sun wedged in the hills like a tentacled penny. Or, more often, the waggons were drawn into a circle, and a little square-bearded man in a big cowboy hat pointed a flaming gun between shafts at a leaping stick-figure holding an assegai, while a woman with a bonnet instead of a head stood near him, a draw-string sponge bag dangling from her wrist, a mere onlooker at the game. The significance of this tableau was very ob-scure. They all knew, however, that it was called a laager. It had been faithfully copied, to the point of stylisation, from some preceptive extravaganza which had once, in time im-memorial, been displayed to them.

'You. Brown,' Meneer rapped out. 'What is a laager?'
'It's when the Voortrekkers stopped for a rest.'
'And did what?'
'They put their ox-waggons in a sort of a circle.'
'Why?'
Brown didn't know. A hand shot up.
'Yes, Brittan?'
'So they could shoot between them.'
'At what?'
'The Zulus.'
'Not only the Zulus. Who else?'
A hand.
'Yes? Rousseau?'
'The English.'
'Nee wat. That was the Boer War. Have you learned about the Boer War?'
Silence.
'Rrright. Then I'll tell you about the Boer War.'
It transpired that the Boers had worn khaki so they couldn't be seen, and the English had worn red so the Boers just potted them off like sitting ducks. Despite this, the

English managed to inflict heavy losses, and were particularly cruel to women and children, who, Meneer reported, were put by the English into concentration camps.

'Does anyone know what a concentration camp is?' Meneer enquired.

Josephine was working on her laager with passion. A rosette on the bonnet, bows on the little man's boots. Meneer spoke of barbed wire, hunger, sickness; but eyelashes had to frame the man's eyes as the fiery tentacles did the sun.

Colin Brittan asked, 'Did the King of England know about them?'

'About the concentration camps? Yes, well it was a Queen, not a King. Of course she knew about them. She ordered them.'

Every aloe was a candelabrum, and alight.

Irwin Brown's voice demanded, 'Who won the war?'

'The English won it.'

Out of the south-east a tornado of birds whirled up, a flock of flattening v's.

'Will the English win the war against Germany?' asked Roland Rousseau.

'No they shall not,' the grey oracle ordered. 'Germany will win the war.'

'And then,' Colin Brittan wanted to know, 'will the Germans put the English into concentration camps?'

'Yes. It is only just,' said Meneer.

And an army of stick-figures erupted from the hills, a liquorice lava to flood the earth.

*

'Where is Hannalore?' Josephine asked her confederates that day in the playground, gaspingly, for they had been playing a new kind of hopscotch which Josephine herself had recently invented. Six squares, laid out in a rectangle,

209

had to be stamped upon by each foot and pair of feet, in all possible orders pragmatically worked out by Josephine. Hannalore had quickly grasped the intention of the hoppers, though none of them explained it to her, and had looked on, still with a cold, enlightened eye. Until today.

'Mrs Foster sent for her,' said Isabelle, a very small girl who was the oldest in the school now that Simon had left, and hopped very lightly, raising the least possible dust.

'What for?'

Nobody knew yet. But before the bell sounded again to summon them all back into their classrooms there was a rumour enlarging that Hannalore Schultz had been expelled. She had been seen to collect her books from her desk and could yet be observed waiting at the gate for her stepmother to fetch her in the ugly little battered old car that bore her to school every morning. Waves of observers surged down the sides of the schoolhouse to peer round the corner – the front was out of bounds – where the culprit was indeed sitting on a stone beside the gatepost. Some said she had been up the koppie, but no one had any certain information. Those who called to her were not answered. Some swore she was sitting there blubbing. She did look hunched and woebegone. Nobody felt sorry for her. After all she was such a *drip*, and she looked so silly and so ugly, and she was *German*. But for the first and only time since she had been at Mrs Foster's she was occasioning excitement, enough to upstage the lesser incident of Miss Pereira's fainting fit.

After playtime Miss Pereira was again at her desk. Paul Brittan was the one who hopefully called out, 'Please Miss Pereira, why has Hannalore Schultz been sent home?'

'I don't know, and it is none of your business. Now let's get on shall we?'

Which was unusually sharp for Miss Pereira, but they put it down to her weak condition.

It wasn't until the following day that they knew anything. Isabelle's mother heard it from her niece who was a friend of Miss Pereira's, and Isabelle heard it too since she sat very quietly behind the sofa where all was being unfolded.

'What?' said the hopping girl. 'What did she tell?'

'Miss Pereira,' Isabelle announced for a start, 'is going to be married.'

'Ooooo,' they said. To be a bride in white was the just desert of their princess. 'Who to?'

Isabelle smiled to herself and drew a sun in the sand.

'That's just it,' she said.

'What?' they asked.

'She's going to marry Meneer.'

'Meneer?'

'Meneer *Kruger*?'

Isabelle nodded, still smiling.

'Aaaaah no. She couldn't. You're teasing.'

'They're both going to leave,' Isabelle revealed further. 'And my cousin says that Miss Pereira says that Hannalore has been expelled, because she wrote something and Mrs Foster says it was something terrible dirty. Hannalore left it in the cloakroom and Mrs Foster found it and she says it was pure *filth*. My cousin says that Miss Pereira said that perhaps Hannalore didn't write it, but she says that Mrs Foster says that she knows no one else could have done it, and she's even more angry with Hannalore for telling lies and saying that she didn't write it.'

'But what was it that she wrote?' Janet wanted to know.

'I don't know. And did you know that Hannalore's father has been interred?'

'What does that mean?'

'It means he's been put in prison because he's a German.'

'Where are you going?' Janet asked Josephine.

'It wasn't Hannalore,' said Josephine. 'It was I.'

*

'It was I.'

Mrs Foster looked at the serious face of the child and thought, how ridiculous, such a grown-up sort of tone in such a small skinny little girl. Whatever motive could she have? She looked so different from her brother that Mrs Foster wouldn't be surprised to find that they weren't quite so closely related as everyone was given to understand. The world was a dirty, dishonest place. But perhaps the child was fond of her brother and hoping to use this excuse to be sent after him, wherever he'd gone. Probably a boys' school and she couldn't anyway, silly little thing. But this time she was going to make an example. This time she was not going to have dirt swept under the carpet. For the sake of the school she'd have to keep quiet about things like Anna Pereira and that dreadful man Kruger.

'You mustn't tell lies, my dear.' She felt irritated, but restrained herself from leaning across her desk and pinching the child's thin cheek quite hard.

'I wrote that story. I can tell you the whole thing, if you'll listen.'

'Who told you about it?'

'I wrote it.'

'Who told you about Hannalore?' Mrs Foster persisted. Not that it mattered all that much if it had leaked out. She had intended bringing it up in prayers the next day, without mentioning any actual name, of course. Just by way of a warning. This was where she could wage her war, in the hearts and the heads of the young. Her father had been a colonel.

'Truly I wrote it. I can tell you the story, though I might get some of the words wrong – well, different.'

Three goldfish in a bowl on the desk were kissing.

'So she handed it round for all of you to read, did she? I only hope most of you didn't understand it.'

'I wrote it about my brother. It was a true story.'

'You admire your brother don't you?'

'Yes but –' The muscles in her throat felt taut and sore.

'There's no reason why you shouldn't be fond of him, but he hasn't behaved very admirably you know. I always thought you were a better behaved child. You don't want to follow his example do you? It's a terrible disgrace to be expelled. So much so that your father would be terribly upset and angry if he knew you'd told anybody that Simon had been expelled from this school.'

'I won't tell anybody. The story was about Simon and a lady mind-doctor.'

One of the fish swam into the other two and became a fat scaly serpent.

'Do your father and mother know about Simon and the lady mind-doctor?'

'No. Not what's in the story. But you do believe me, don't you?'

'You don't like being here without Simon. Is that it? You think he's a bit of a hero, don't you? No matter what he's done or what happens to him. If he's pushed out in the cold, that's all right as long as you're with him. Two little orphans in the storm, hey?'

So she did understand.

'Yes,' said Josephine.

The serpent swam round the bowl, shrank, and hid itself in a ruined tower.

'How very unintelligent!' said Mrs Foster.

Josephine looked at the wood-grain of the desk. A shooting fountain, thin and high.

'It was a true story,' she said.

'Do you always tell the truth?'

'No, not always. But Hannalore does,' she said, looking up.

'No little girl always tells the truth. Don't you know that grown-ups can tell when a little girl is fibbing?'

'I did write it,' said Josephine, but no longer expecting to convince Mrs Foster.

Oh the uselessness of truth!

*

By evening she had made up her mind to tell her mother, and if necessary her father. 'After all, what could they do to Simon?' she thought as she came through 'Nanny's room' and along the passage. She couldn't think what, but there was the other difficulty. 'They didn't want anyone to know about Simon going to see Dr Weiss. They'll be furious with me for having written it. At any rate if I tell *them* what the story was about, they'll believe me.'

She would have to dare.

Her father and mother would not allow Mrs Foster to be so cruel to Hannalore once they knew what had happened.

Mr Leyton was about to come into his own. Struggling with a stud, he saw in his mirror that through a top corner pane of his window, in a sky that was most blue and about to be black, one star shone, and was still. Clouds were spreading then. But tomorrow, come else what may, Mr Rayfel Leyton's candidature was to be officially put forward.

And tonight the Leytons were giving a dinner for a pair of ladies who worked for the Party; and a young man named Basil Hirschfield who had edited the political weekly that Rayfel had sometimes written for and who had now joined the army but was still influential; and a revival from the past, no other than Naty Bloch.

He had not been to the house for years, ever since he'd failed some examination. Rayfel had mourned once, in passing, that life had carried them apart. Though not really very far apart. Naty had gone to work in the Public Prosecutor's office, and of course Rayfel had always been delighted to see old Naty, sometimes mentioning to Freda that who did she think he'd happened to encounter, and what a pleasant fellow he was, though limited, and how he was still the same, poor old Naty, not changed at all. But now Naty had changed. He was about to become something important in the Party, though Rayfel hoped he realised he'd never make a Parliamentarian. His reintroduction into their organisation did not disturb Freda, for she never would admit into her universe one whose humour was so coarse, and whose manners were so brash: or anyone at all who was so *fleshy*.

Now, over on her shore, she was dutifully busy with the rouge. She had made no comment when he had told her that Naty was to be entertained. She was, Rayfel found, ever more remote.

In the bathroom he felt his chin which he had scraped over three times with dedication. Would a more public life, he wondered, improve her mournful manner, at least as far as, might one say, a dignified self-containment? That would do very well. And he was sure she would do nothing to humiliate him, since it would harm her too; she must be aware.

Doubt could not linger long with him this evening. He was pleased, and surely his pleasure must brighten her too, linked as they were by matrimony?

'What is it?' Mrs Leyton called in answer to an interrupting knock.

'May I come in, please? I have something I would like to tell you.'

'Well, all right. But I'm in a hurry. There's a dinner.'

Mrs Leyton sat at her dressing table, pinning a sapphire brooch to the shoulder of her blue dress.

'Find me my silver shoes with the peep-toes,' she said. She turned on her stool and leant over to put them on. 'Well, what is it?' She straightened and turned again to screw lids back on to jars, her knees against the curtains that hid the little cupboard, Josephine noticed. One stowed things away in places and left them there, and they fermented danger.

'Mother, I wrote something, and at school they think it was another girl who wrote it, and when I told them the truth they wouldn't believe me.'

'What did you write, dear? Have you had your supper yet? We're having guests tonight and the table will have to be cleared and relaid so you'd better be quick. Unless you have your supper in the kitchen.'

'*I* wrote a story.' The girl's voice rang out. With pride, naturally. The mother quite understood, and answered, 'If you can write good stories, it doesn't matter if someone pretends. You'll be able to write lots more, and she won't. The best way to prove your abilities is to use them.'

'But she has got into *trouble* for it.'

'Ssh! Ssh! Ssh!' said the perfume spray.

'They've expelled her from the school.'

'Nonsense. No one gets expelled from school for writing a story. Though Mrs Foster does seem a little too partial to that rather extreme form of punishment.'

'Well perhaps they *really* expelled her because she's German. Someone told me they'd put her father in gaol because he's German.'

Mrs Leyton rose and went to the full-length mirror in her wardrobe door.

'That,' she said, 'is not something that I would grieve for.'

'Wheeee!' sang a pipe in the wall.

'Is that you?' Freda called. Are you ready?'

The bathroom door opened and he came in, brushing down the fringe of hair about his scalp. It was wet and shone. He was wearing a shirt and trousers, and a towel round his neck. He had no shoes on, so all of his socks showed, smooth and black, except their tops which lurked under the overhang of his trousers. Josephine had never seen him so exposed. His face, though faintly greenish about the chin, glowed.

'I wrote that letter today,' he said, 'by the way.'

'Good. What did you say?'

'I said we were delighted to hear that Simon had behaved himself so well on his last visit that she wished to have him stay with her again. I only hope her son is a good influence on Simon.'

'You didn't say that, did you?'

'No, I'm just saying it to you.'

'Perhaps she'll invite him to spend all his holidays there and we won't see him again until he's left school.'

'Don't be too optimistic. It's out of character. At least,' he said, bending low to peer into the dressing table mirror and further to gloss with his hand and the towel's edge his wreath-shaped tonsure, 'there's one advantage for a politician in having a moronic son. He won't go and join any subversive organisations.'

'Father,' she said.

He sat down, crossed his legs and felt his chin. His toe in its tidy sock knocked against the little doors. The sock had a tiny, neat Nanny Binny darn in it.

'A-ha?' he said, his mouth open to tauten the skin of his jowls.

'I wrote something which Mrs Foster says is dirty, and –'

'*You* did?' He raised his eyebrows, yet the surprise could not have travelled far, for he went on feeling his chin and his hand did not pause. He made no further enquiry, offered no rebuke. But then, whose words should condemn her if not her own?

'Can't you tell us later?' called her mother. Her voice always had a tired sound in it nowadays. She seemed to Josephine to be on the other side of a turbulent river of experience. And unhappy. Josephine would have liked to protect her, but that was impossible.

'I want you to help me,' she said. I want both of you to help me.'

Their eyes assessed her. She was a small person. Usually unobtrusive. What new and threatening development was this?

'Did you say you'd had your supper?' Freda asked.

'No. I'll have it in the kitchen. Can I tell you about the story?'

'Well of course. Tomorrow would be best though. Run along now. Don't keep Frances waiting. She's very busy this evening.'

She took up her silver-edged comb. Father drew back the window curtains. Both of them listened for the shutting of the door.

'Actually it's beyond my comprehension how anyone could wish to invite him twice,' she said, pressing curls to her cheeks.

'Perhaps it's a good sign. Perhaps he's improved.'

'You mean become sensible and reasonable and tidy and considerate –'

'He'll calm down as he gets older. Nature itself is a great tamer.'

'Since when have you had anything to do with Nature? And why don't you say Nature *herself* and have her trussed up in spangles and high-heeled boots?'

'It's probably just that he's chummy with Mrs Whatsername's son, I suppose. They spend the holidays on this farm. Plenty of room on a farm. Boys like to be together.'

He went back into the bathroom, and called, 'Very good for them, farm life. Growing boys. He couldn't do much damage on a farm.'

'Only burn the house down over this hospitable lady's head,' called his wife sweetly. 'Or flood it with bathwater. Or slit the throats of the flocks and herds. And he hasn't got any manners, which is a reflection on us, don't forget – to those who don't know the circumstances.'

'Let's try not to worry unduly.'

'The extent of your ability to ignore what should be faced never ceases to amaze me.' It was out before she'd had time to think. She didn't want to quarrel tonight, but then she didn't want to be compliant either.

'Well for God's sake, what do you want?' He appeared in the doorway. 'Do you want him home here for the holidays? Do you? If you do, go ahead and write to this woman and say you're very sorry you can't let her have him, and haul him back here, and let's see what an uplifting influence he will have on us all. You'll have to look after him on your own, remember. Unless you plan to have a platoon of troops posted here for civil defence. Perhaps you regard Mussolini as small fry compared to your adolescent son?' He disappeared again and the sound of water hitting enamel sounded like tremendous, distant applause.

He stopped it, and called out, 'I wondered whether your enquiries about the family had been fruitful at all. Doesn't one of your tennis friends know her, or know someone who knows her?'

'Oh yes. They're not Durbanites as we thought. The Nathans. But they've divorced and she lives most of the year on this farm they have in Natal. They have a manager on it apparently, but everyone's delighted to know that it's a financial loss. He lives in Johannesburg.'

'Who, the manager?'

'Nathan. I looked him up in the telephone book. He has a big-print entry. Z Nathan and Co, Limited, outsize manufacturers ladies' gowns, coats, suits, lonjereee and perfume.'

'Ho, ho,' he said, coming in, drying an ear. 'Outsize perfume. I like that.'

He went back into his own room.

She waited until he returned in his shoes and then said, leaning towards herself and touching her hair, 'So it's decided is it?' She got up and went to the long mirror. 'We'll sacrifice ourselves to the dear boy's greater benefit – exercise, fresh air, and new opportunities for destruction and slaughter. The darling.'

'Nathan eh?' said her husband, fingering the knot. 'I knew a Nathan at school. What was his name now? Morry Nathan. That was it. Not Z. What name begins with Z? Zachariah. No it couldn't be the same fellow. Actually he wasn't a bad chap. A raging Bolshie. He used to – ho, ho – he used to – it is quite ridiculous really – he used to play revolutionary songs on the mouth organ before and after eating his sandwiches in the playground, as a sort of grace. Nineteen-seventeen it was. He didn't know many of the words but he had us all lined up and humming twice a day. "The people's flag is deepest red, hm, hm, hm, hm, hm, martyr dead." Ho, ho, ho. Splendid. But of course he wouldn't like to be reminded of that now. Not if he's also in the Outsize Trade. "And ere their limbs grew stiff and cold, their heart's blood dyed its every fold." Cut up his red flag by now, probably, and made it into coats for ladies. Cutting his coats according to his ideals. Ho, ho. Outsize Red Coats for Ladies. And the perfume – that's the dye left over – the blood, you see, ho, ho, ho. All the perfumes of Arabia will not sweeten this little coat. Beat your swords into scissors. Ho, ho, ho, ho.'

He had been pacing. Now he stopped, breathless. He turned to the window, rocked and felt his chin.

'I seem to remember,' said Freda, when the last ho had died away, looking at him in the glass, 'that the period of your allegiance to that flag was not limited to the playground singsongs at your school.'

'Hm? What's that?'

His face was serious again. He had moved on.

'I seem to remember,' said his wife, louder but with precisely the same expression as the first time, 'that the period of your allegiance to that flag was not limited to the playground singsongs at your school.'

This was mimicry.

'I don't follow you,' he said.

'Were you, or were you not, a Bolshevist in your own right?'

'Well, all young men –'

'Were you or were you not?'

'I am trying to tell you, if you'll allow me to speak. All young men if they'd had any education and any heart at that time were a shade red. But first of all,' he raised one eyebrow, and crossed his forefingers one over the other, 'let me remind you that times have changed,' he moved one forefinger to a middle finger, 'and secondly.'

'My Lord,' said his wife.

'And secondly,' he said again, taking no notice, but raising his voice to its true courtroom volume, 'as one grows older one has *either* to forget Utopia and attempt what improvements one may, however small, in the status quo, *or* retire completely into cloud cuckoo land, which won't help you or anyone else. Right?'

'I know nothing about it. I take your word for it.'

He rocked again, a little pacified, but feeling somehow cheated of a small victory.

'But I do think the war's terrible,' said Freda, regarding with compassion her own compassionate expression. 'And I think it's a terrible thing that Franco won in Spain.'

Her husband looked down at his chest, brushed it with the side of his small soft white hand, his eyebrows working as though he were raising a dust storm and putting his eyes in danger. 'Yes. Indeed. The triumph of evil. There is no justice on earth. And Fascism is certainly a more hellish doctrine than Marxism. You're not exclusive in your point of view on that issue. Although, of course, I respect the fact that your heart was most particularly engaged in the circumstance of the Spanish scrimmage.' He leant on the window sill, turned his head this way and that, as though looking for weather signs, or to distinguish the constellations. But even the one star had been overwhelmed like all the rest. A still, warm, cloudy night. Nothing was to be read in the sky.

His wife was busy with this and that on the shelves of her wardrobe. She made no answer.

'No, I didn't cling to the dogma for long,' he said, in the right tone for reminiscence. 'That is true enough. In the years of wisdom, which I flatter myself I reached earlier than most, I developed a taste for evolutionary rather than revolutionary means of attaining a socialist order of government. I was, and am, and so far as world politics are concerned will continue to be, a socialist. Unfortunately, as it is ridiculous to attempt to legislate too far ahead of public opinion, in this country I shall have to content myself, for a while at least, with making laws that simply mitigate the worser abuses of our inegalitarian society.'

He turned to see his wife standing like a statue in her long blue dress, with its odd little pleated wings on the shoulders.

'Yes, sir. Thank you, sir,' she said, looking at something above his head. 'A most edifying lecture. It is so nice to be told exactly where you stand. I was most anxious to know.'

'Look here,' he said, raising a forefinger. 'There is no reason to make me the victim of your sarcasm. Admittedly

I haven't thrown my life away in a foreign country fighting for an uncertain cause –'

'So I have noticed,' she sang out, high and clear. Oh, he was so smug, so smug!

He marched off, through the no-man's-land and behind his own lines.

She drew a red shawl from a shelf.

Having rallied, he returned.

'Now listen here,' he said, hands on hip pockets, in the doorway. 'Freda.' It was a trivial, irritating necessity, but for once he had a message to give that must be received.

She turned towards him, but was busy arranging the shawl.

'Just one thing.'

She shook out the fringe impatiently. She knew he was about to sound yet another voice-voluntary.

'Are you listening?'

'M-hm.'

'I am perfectly aware that I have failed to earn your admiration. Perhaps, furthermore, having failed to bare my breast to Fascist bullets I have lost your esteem. But I insist that you be extremely careful of the impression you give the world of our domestic situation.'

'Good Lord,' she thought, 'as if the world cared.' But she said nothing.

'Let me make it quite clear,' he went on, in a voice that could be heard at the back of the hall, 'that I will not have my career jeopardised by you or anyone. I intend to dedicate my abilities to the service of my country. I intend to have a hand in the shaping of its future. And I am not going to have my intention wrecked on a trifle. Is that quite understood? There is nothing to stop you feeling what you like. If you choose to strike up a daily threnody after breakfast, do so by all means, but do it in private. If you've suffered a great loss, if this young man was the subject of your ardour and you refuse to be consoled, that is your business. Just don't make it mine or anyone else's. I do not intend to pour acid into any wounds you might have if I say that I think it strange that your acquaintance with the fellow should have been so short, yet your grief for him should persist so long. But it is an observation I cannot escape.'

He had her attention now. She was looking at him steadily. He went on, he could not stop. It was a geyser of truth, and by sheer force must succeed.

'I'm not as unsympathetic a person as you suppose. But I don't quite see that this is a case for a husband's condolence. And I am certain in my own mind that I have not deserved to be destroyed by you. Don't abuse the power you have – and you do have power in your position as my wife. You have it over me, not in any romantic way, regrettably of course, not in any romantic way, but in a way that matters. I tell you, Freda, I want no moping. No snide remarks. No dispraise however subtle, however ambiguously expressed. People are not altogether fools, I have to suppose, and I am to be in a highly vulnerable position. Highly vulnerable. Naturally, I have my enemies. Nobody can serve a cause without having his enemies. You will not take advantage of that fact. Do I make myself clear?'

She turned again to the full-length mirror and raised her right hand.

'I solemnly swear that neither by word, gesture nor deed –'

She stopped, looked thoughtfully at the neckline of her dress. 'I suppose all the parliamentary wives wear brave fronts most of the time?' she asked, rhetorically.

'Just remember what I've said.'

'What you've *said?* Why, if I forget it, it will surely be recorded in Hansard?'

'That's all right. Say what you like, as long as there's no one else to hear.'

He went back to his room to stow this and that into pockets. That done, he opened the door into the passage.

But she *was* wounded, and must cry out a promise at least of revenge.

'There's something you've forgotten,' she called.

Short acquaintance or not, Benedick *had* fallen in love with her. He had said so in as many words, there could be no doubt of that. She groped for the little doors and shook them, but time had not loosened the lock. Later tonight though, come what may, she'd get the thing. Somewhere there must be a key that fits.

Rayfel banged his door behind him and started down the passage. But as he came alongside her door, he stopped, turned, opened it and said, 'What?'

'Hm?' she said, rising.

'What have I forgotten?'

'Forgotten? Oh yes. You've forgotten – Simon.'

'Simon? I'm sure he'll never cease to be an annoyance but at least for the present he's out of the way. Or is he your secret weapon? Are you perhaps proposing to get him home to stir things up a bit?'

'Get him home?' she said, advancing, passing him, and going on towards the stairs, a Cassandra in that dress. 'No need to do that. Whatever he does and wherever he does it, you'll feel it, you can be sure of that. No matter how stupid he is.'

Reaching the foot of the stairs she turned, and went, feeling a little restored, into the kitchen to remind Frances that the red and green onions must be pierced with toothpicks. There she saw her daughter sitting at one end of the long table, staring at the stove, her plate of cold fish looking inelegant among the Spode dishes of small edible luxuries crowded on beds of shredded lettuce. Was the child, she wondered, lonely?

'*I've* got a good idea,' she said, drawing in her mouth as though on a lump of sugar, and speaking as though Josephine had deflated into a new infancy. 'When you've finished your sup-sups, you hand the plates round, will you dear?'

'All right,' said Josephine.

Freda bent and kissed her quickly on the top of her dark and not at all charming head. Her shawl brushed Josephine's cheek. For a moment perfume overcame fish and oil and parsley, a conquest by another world.

'Who would ever guess,' Mrs Leyton asked herself as she made her way down the passage to the blue lounge full of flowers, 'that I had a touch of sentimentality. Actually, all children are either demanding or pathetic. Destructive horrors, or poor little orphans in the storm.'

'But exactly how,' a young man in army uniform was saying as Josephine crept into the room a little later, 'is it possible to attain a political end if one serves a party that is opposed to that end?'

'But my dear fellow the Party is *not* opposed to that end. Not opposed to it. It is a principle it has not yet embraced,' Mr Leyton explained.

'But they couldn't, could they? I mean if once they adopted it as a principle it would virtually mean the reversal of the major part of their present policy. I mean look at it this way. You're not going to find it exactly easy to maintain your leftist principles within the Party, are you? I mean you surely don't actually expect to?'

'My dear chap!' Mr Leyton pressed his whisky glass down on the mantelshelf between a vase of tulips and the butterfly lady with a careful firmness, turned and rocked forwards and backwards before the empty grate, and said, richly, to the rhythm of his rocking, 'you have my personal assurance that I would not remain in the Party if my principles were thereby to be compromised.'

'But for instance the Trades Unions Act –' the young man specified, indignant, bright and courageous enough, but faltering.

'Politics,' Mr Leyton pointed out, 'is the art of the possible. It would be self-destructive to attempt to legislate too far ahead of public opinion.' And he smiled round at the others, but as if for a camera, and raised and sipped from his glass.

'Oh, I understand that political action is always expedient action. And of course it can be argued that action can sometimes be both expedient and good. Even when it comes to war and killing, I mean, to go to war against Hitler. But I'm also perfectly aware that most politicians hide their motives –'

'Are you accusing me –' Mr Leyton began, his face reddening. This time the glass could have been shattered.

'I'm quite sure,' Mrs Leyton said, rising, tall, and with a kind of weary grace that made her hospitality seem ceremonious, 'that Basil didn't mean to accuse you of anything.' She often despised tact, but she knew that this was not the time to goad. 'Josephine, pass the asparagus.' And she herself carried round the sausages, as though they were an oblation, holding them out with particular reverence to fat Mrs Bath.

'Have you,' asked Mrs Bath, who had heard that Freda Leyton went in for culture, and herself had been a ballet dancer in her youth to the extent of three Eisteddfod awards and one photograph in a Sunday newspaper, 'have you seen the marvellous production of *Cosi Fan Tutte?* Done by the girls of the Catholic Mission School in Roodepoort?'

Mrs Leyton thought of shuddering. Black adolescent girls with their peppercorn hair, in black gym tunics, singing Mozart!

'Do they wear powdered periwigs?' she asked with interest, forgetting to remove the sausages from Mrs Bath's bosom.

'No, no costumes. No thank you, not another just at the moment. But they've got *lovely* voices. So pure. And Miss Peekin lent real eighteenth-century chairs.'

Mrs Leyton moved on to Miss Peekin. Chippendale wobbling on the boards of a church hall in Roodepoort!

'They're doing it once more this Saturday,' said Miss Peekin, piercing a juicy little sausage with a toothpick, and holding it in the air. 'You must go, Mrs Leyton. All in a good cause you know. Comforts for the Troops.'

'Oh yes?' said Freda, moving on to the men and wondering whether Miss Peekin's ornate spectacles were intended to compensate for the drabness of her nature.

'Hello! So you're Josephine are you?'

Turning from Mrs Bath who was imitating laughter in response to something that he had insinuated, Naty Bloch swung his glance vigorously from the asparagus to the face of the child. 'I say, you're not sixteen yet are you?'

'No.'

'Well if you'll let me know when you're sixteen I'll have something to say to you. Hey?'

She did not meet his look.

'Do you know who I am, hey?'

'Yes.'

'Who am I?'

'You are Mr Bloch.'

'Yeah, yeah, that's right, I'm your Uncle Naty. What's the matter, hey? Why do you look so gloomy? You know, the last time I saw you, you sat on my lap without even asking my permission, *and* you did a quick laundering job without being asked or paid.'

Mrs Bath wheezed and shook, but recovered.

'Here,' Mr Bloch went on, tapping his cheek with a ringed middle finger, 'you may give me one kiss just here.'

The skinny, plain, quite swarthy child stared down at the asparagus as though she were looking through them into a deep pool where something swam, hair and shadows helping almost to hide her features. She knew her fate at the hands of this man, it was something she was used to, it would be quickly over, and it would come no matter whether she obeyed or refused. And she could not consider agreement the best way past a trivial demand, since nothing could be depended on to remain insignificant.

'Hey?' he said, cocking his head so that his cheek was a broad target. 'Come on, don't be shy. What about it, hey?'

She breathed in slowly, looked up and said, 'No.'

Before he returned to Mrs Bath with 'I've been turned down, I'm losing my fascination at last', his face became quite flabby for a second, and Josephine turned away. But it was inevitable, and the fingers were in time, seeking their own revenge on the cheek of that arrogant child. Like father like daughter, Naty judged.

'Oh, by the way,' Naty called out, having had satisfaction, 'you asked me to let you know when that murder case came up, you remember, Ray?' Naty always shortened people's names, hoping thus to trick them into believing in his good comradeship. 'Well, it came up today.' Indeed, he had been carrying this news at his side like a lariat all evening. There are never enough bonds to grapple man to man.

'Which one?' Rayfel frowned, pushed a hand into his pocket and clinked.

'Your servant, wasn't it? Murder? Stabbing?' Naty put an ankle on a knee and smoothened his sock, which was grey and white, but quite fine in texture.

'Oh yes. So it's coming up is it?'

'It's come up, old boy. Today.'

'Today? Good Lord. I was going to – Who defended him?'

'Well it was a pro deo of course. A young man called Gish. It was his first criminal trial, I think.'

'Do you hear this, Freda? That boy Willy you remember? The garden boy we used to have? He came up for trial today.'

Everyone was interested. The room, all the apparent world, was quiet. The women enjoyed talking about servants, and everybody took an interest in murder.

'Don't you remember?' Rayfel asked again.

'Oh yes,' said Freda. 'Do take an olive with it, Mrs Bath. Josephine don't stand and stare. If you've been round, put it down.'

'Well the boy insisted on going to one of our colleagues – who shall be nameless – who makes a fortune out of their misfortune without overtaxing himself, I'd conjecture, and then gets a fledgling to lose the case for nothing. What can one do? One's up against ignorance in alliance with obstinacy; a formidable opposition!' said Rayfel, in the tone of one resigned to having his goodwill rejected, clinking energetically and looking at his wife, who had regained the sofa and was looking up at him, possibly with accusation; but there was nothing new in that. 'I couldn't even advise about whom to brief. Though I did intend to discuss the matter, as the boy's employer rather than as a colleague –. How long did you say the sentence was? Seven years? But surely it wasn't impossible to prove self-defence?'

'With one of them a woman? And then the police didn't find a weapon, you see. Neither side could make anything of that, so they both felt well it would be wiser to leave it alone. But ach! on the whole the chap didn't do too badly. I mean put it this way. The wog could have had a better defence, I mean a real brain might have got him off, you know? But the thing is whichever way you look at it he did kill, hey? I mean no one denies that. Ach! I know we feel a bit sorry for these poor kaffirs being practised on like this, but –' He looked round the room for sympathy and spread his hands. 'After all they *do* get a fair trial, hey?'

'And they *do* get a defence,' intoned Mrs Bath.

'Yes, exactly. Hey? And I mean –'

'And I *mean* they're *absolutely* equal before the *law*,' Miss Peekin yelped happily.

'Yes, of course,' others echoed.

For some reason they now all, except young Basil, looked at Mrs Leyton, as though she had expressed, or by her native proclivities inevitably represented, all unfair criticism of the uses of their world. After all culture if taken too seriously was radical all on its own. But though her brooch, somehow an ominous thing, shot barbs of light, she sat immobile in the stalls. She was considering the tulips. They must have been grown in a hot house, or a cold house, or in whatever it was that tulips were grown. She would have one built in the garden. Why had she never thought of it before?

'*And*,' said Naty, 'the judge after all *does* go by the facts. Our bench is unbiased and incorruptible.' He plucked at the cloth over his knees and exercised his legs in turn.

'And it's got some great brains,' Mrs Bath jabbed in, wondering if all present knew that she had a brother-in-law recently elevated.

'But do tell us what exactly happened?' begged Miss Peekin.

'Well,' said Naty. 'You see. You can't say the defendant necessarily struck last, and therefore in defence, simply because he survived and the others didn't.'

They nodded, except Miss Peekin, who with her head inclined towards Mr Leyton was listening to his summary of what was known of the incident itself, while keeping her eyes fixed on Mr Bloch. She would garner every scrap. And Mrs Bath was turning from one to the other. So Naty paused to let the tale be told, and then went on at careful pace.

'Yes. And then, you see, the Crown argued that if he had struck last he must have struck blind, since that would mean his eyes had *already* been damaged.'

Miss Peekin sucked air through her teeth.

'Yes, very logical,' said Mrs Bath, blinking intelligently. *She* was not squeamish. 'I love law,' she explained, 'I wanted to go in for it myself, only I got married instead. Now I satisfy myself with detective stories. Don't you enjoy a detective story, Mrs Leyton? I mean a really *good* one?'

'I'd love to read one where the detective fails to find the culprit,' said Freda, disagreement possibly helping dissociation, which by now she was longing for. Oh, what dreary, stupid, ordinary people! If they did achieve literature, it had to be of this common class. Though she had to admit to herself that after all it seemed this had been quite an important crime, as crimes go, which had happened on her doorstep. She smiled to lessen the bitterness of her offering. 'Another gin?' she asked.

'But tell me,' Naty enquired, 'it was just a sort of coincidence, hey? I mean the police turning up just then? You'd sent for them for something else, isn't that so?'

'Not I, my dear fellow. Good Lord no. I made it *quite* clear to the police that we knew nothing whatever about it. I was away from home and Freda didn't know a thing about it either until it was all over.'

'No, yes, I mean actually it was your housekeeper who phoned for them, wasn't it? There was a statement from her, but she's not available I believe. She wasn't in court and they said something about her being up in Rhodesia.'

'When was the statement taken then?'

'Oh, the police –'

'Did she know when the trial was coming up?'

'What's that? No, I shouldn't think so, why?'

'Let's go and have dinner,' Mrs Leyton proposed. 'Shall we?'

'What school do you go to?' Miss Peekin asked the Leytons' little girl, who was gaping at her father as though she had never seen him before. Could she be a trifle simple?

'Mrs Foster's,' said Josephine, turning quickly towards the irrelevant demand.

'Oh, I know Mrs Foster,' said Miss Peekin as though she knew a private joke about that lady. 'Aren't you a lucky girl?'

Josephine did not need to ponder why Miss Peekin's acquaintance with Mrs Foster should benefit her, for clearly Miss Peekin meant nothing at all by this except a friendly, cheerful noise.

'So you're Joanna are you?' said Mrs Bath, smiling as she went by, and nodding as though knowledge of the child's name established an understanding between them.

And even Mr Hirschfield had his go at a cheek as he passed. From his point of view it was only good manners. But he was not to escape either.

'Come along, come along,' said Mr Leyton heartily, putting an arm round the shoulders of the intrepid Basil, since there were things he, Rayfel, would never choose to forget. 'I know your point of view,' he confided as they made their way down the passage, 'and believe me I sympathise with you. You're a young man, and as they say, if you're not a Communist at twenty, you have no heart, and if you're still a Communist at forty, you have no head.' And he laughed. 'Ho ho,' he said. His mirth was unmitigated, his goodwill boundless.

And the others whose maturing was advanced, or who had even, as in Miss Peekin's case, suffered the solstice, laughed too with easy indulgence.

'I'm thirty-four,' the hothead murmured, but Mr Leyton was shepherding his flock and either he did not hear or remained in any case content with his conclusion of the matter.

The dining room door closed, and Josephine turned towards the stairs.

Josephine did not disturb Nanny Binny's shoes, but raised the lid of her box and pushed one hand down through the narrow opening. It passed over the braille of the sea-egg, and the hesitant beads, and the poppies, and caught the little gold key.

In her mother's room a bedside lamp had been left on. Its light ran down a white satin nightdress laid out on the turned-back sheet, very creamy and immaculate and graceful. Shadows thronged the room but there was enough light for her to see the keyhole. The key turned easily. She lifted out the bundle of clothes which had become oddly stiff, locked the door on the empty cupboard and returned to her own room, leaving the key in the lock.

She pushed the things under her bed, put out the light and lay down. Alan Jesus trod three times round on the eiderdown, settled, sighed and slept.

She had not drawn the blinds across the windows. They were patches of grey, she could not see the sky. It was a muffled night. Cloud pressed against the house. Perhaps there was cloud below her windows too, so that it would seem she was in a high tower, so high that mountain peaks could be looked down upon, protruding here and there through the mist, a palisade to keep giants at bay, or to make escape more difficult. Still she heard the footsteps of the dead, coming up the stairs. They even advanced through Nanny's room to her very door, but she would not again turn to the wall and pull the blankets over her head. They approached no nearer.

She kept looking at the windows, which were all that she could distinguish. They were screens. No shadows moved on them.

Her breath was rapid and shallow. She wanted to keep awake.

Alan Jesus jerked in his sleep, and growled.

She was running after *him* towards the hills, towards a waxen sun, bright orange, which was melting, and darkness was coming down.

She sat up, and felt the enormous stillness of the house, the world. She scooped up the bundle of clothes from under the bed, and with them some scrap of paper, it couldn't matter what. She went through Nanny's room, softly, swiftly, boldly, regardless of who might be waiting there. There was no light on in the passage. The stairs were dimly shown by the grey light of the window. She started down. Alan Jesus came out on to the landing, stood at the top of the stairs and watched her, his ears pricked up. When she was halfway down he followed her, slowly, rather stiffly. Her own breath was noisy, so she stopped breathing until she opened the kitchen door and the silence was over, for here the gusts raged in the forests, the branches crackled.

She left the door open and crossed to where the red light showed round the edges of the iron doors and in circles round the plates at the top. Shadows danced their devil dance on the walls and ceiling, which was washed with a translucent red light.

Alan Jesus sat down in his place.

The rod that Frances used to lift the heavy plates hung on its hook. She fitted the bent end into the slot of the largest lid, lifted it, clanged it down on one side. How hot it was down there, how bright. It was a forest all of fire; the very trees were flames. And there *they* were, in the heart of the furnace, the children. The voices struggled with sibilants, and stuttered with clicking sounds, inarticulate, or foreign; unintelligible, but leaving no doubt as to what they signified. And the heat and noise questioned her directly. She used the rod to poke the bundle of clothes down into the flames. Her head a little to one side, she pushed them through the opening. They subdued the light, the heat and the noise, for a few moments.

There was no need for her to go nearer. What was required of her she could do already, and would, now that she fathomed the necessity. But the voices cried to her again – as though it were her body which was necessary to them! And yet, as she had no words ready to answer their clamour, she bent towards the furnace and pushed in the only possible damper there was to hand, a piece of paper, an envelope she noticed. It lifted and fell in the draught and began to blacken. And although the inflammatory words were not hers, a long arm of fire reached up to her cheek. She gasped for breath, and caught it on a sob, and with it the realisation, long put off, of pain, the word for the whole meaning of the voices. And that should have been enough – had there been gods in this land to be propitiated. But the earth itself, hot and veined with gold, after which men quested with dynamite; the earth itself, without malice and without mercy, brought her down. It rumbled and shook. Alan Jesus started up. The rod fell from her hand on to the dog who darted in front of her as she tried to keep her balance. The earth itself, and understanding, and the dog she loved, all were against her. She fell forward, and grabbed with both hands at the iron stove. Her hair and her long nightclothes were burning as she fell.

And she went on falling into the hollow cave of the world, through the darkness of which she flitted like a bat, close under the roof which was a mass of waving roots fat as fingers and tongues, or so thin and fine they wound up bodies in cocoons of hair. Then she went on down for a very long time, until she lay in the boiling mud at the bottom, which broke in bubbles leaving rings of gold on the surface. Up through a ring the horror was about to rise and she could not escape. It would open its jaws. There it was now, heaving itself out of the mud and mould, muck clinging to its back. Slowly it raised to view a pale and tender underside, gleaming a little with its own fresh secreted slime, and now there opened slowly, not a jawful of terrible teeth, but a wet, bright, swivelling, noticing eye, which proved it was not only living, but also wise.

4
THE KEEP

Mrs Leyton, nerved to the austerity of duty, came downstairs in a new gown of sturdy cotton stuff patterned with a positive trompe l'oeil of twigs and summer leaves, took a trug basket from the cupboard under the stairs, and went out through the kitchen which was full of sizzling, into the still cool day to gather, with her own hands, a posy of wallflowers for her daughter. The shadows of pea-vines fell and fell from her long skirt as she passed, and a row of discarded finches' eggs, the palest of blues, turned to dust under her determined soles. In the trug lay a pair of short-beaked clippers, and with these she assaulted several far-reaching branches of the horrid Unnameable which were growing aslant a clump of golden blooms. And there also, to her surprise and joy, as though it had burgeoned in the warmth of her own determination, was one small, pale, but undeniable tulip. She stood and looked at it. She knelt in the scanty grass and felt it with her fingers, running them up its straight stem and gleaming petals. Soon her conservatory would be built and she would have a satisfaction of tulips. Now with a quick movement she snipped through the stem just above the ground, and laid the lovely colonist on top of the common flowers in her basket, and hurried with little steps right round the house and up to the veranda and through the French windows into her calm blue room, where nothing palpable would ever sizzle, and where the perfect bloom could die a slow elegant death in a coolness which would not be marred even by admiration since only hers would find it. She impaled it on a spike which rose from an oval dish no deeper than a footprint in damp sand. Only the tips of its two wrapping leaves drooped a little: otherwise it remained stoic, northern, aristocratic.

She went up to the Nursery and arranged the wallflowers in a jug.

When the ambulance came, Frances and Sixpence went out to meet it, and got in the stretcher-bearers' way. They were both smiling, and Sixpence said twelve times at least as he followed the retinue upstairs, 'Ow Miss Jossafeen, owwwwa!'

Mr and Mrs Leyton came to the bedside to kiss the small uncovered centre portion of their daughter's bound-up head. The hair that grew in this patch was as soft as lambswool, and curly, and very close to the skin. And it was not black, as the old hair had been, but a dull and dusty beige. It was new hair, and, Freda found, rather nice to feel, to press lightly upon, with the tips of two fingers: but discovery was enough; Freda did not indulge herself with this.

Mr Leyton, finding his daughter still looking as botched as she had in her hospital bed, with only one eye to be seen under an overhang of gauze, unbuttoned his jacket, hooked his thumbs in his waistcoat pocket, and shouted, 'How are you?' as he had on all his visits (after which he had made for the mirror over the washstand and felt his chin). This time he waited for an answer.

And the red mouth – its colour intense under the white and seeming to be smeared beyond the outline of the lip – was speaking.

'What's that?'

'Alan Jesus. Where is he?'

'Oh. Oh I don't know if Sister would allow –. Her dog, Sister. Do you think he should come up here?'

'If it would make her happy. Only we mustn't let him claw at her,' Sister Tonks, brisk and white, permitted.

Sixpence, hovering at the door, went off in a crackle of his own whites to release Alan Jesus from confinement in the pantry.

'Well, I've got to be going,' Mr Leyton shouted. 'I've got to get the train you know. So I'll say goodbye to you my dear. Sister Tonks and your mother will take good care of you, and you mustn't worry about anything.' (Though how worry of any sort came into it, if at all, he could not think.)

He kissed her a second time on the woolly patch, which made the place almost familiar, and went out, frowning at his watch and calling for Sixpence to bring down the bags.

He was leaving that very afternoon for Cape Town. For on a windy day that summer a large number of ladies and gentlemen had driven from their houses to Mrs Foster's Infant and Preparatory School (which had been slightly damaged in an earth tremor but restored by the parents of pupils along more modern lines), and voted for Mr Rayfel Leyton, Attorney-at-Law, to represent them in Parliament. Mr Leyton himself had been there, standing at the gate, to return their smiles and nods. And near him at a table Mrs Bath, and Miss Peekin in white sleeve-protectors, had sat behind piles of paper, some pieces of which, with his picture printed indistinctly on them, had been blown as far as the ridge of the koppie (where they were later turned to ash by trespassers).

After he had gone, Freda stood looking at the swaddled figure.

'Won't you sit down, Mrs Leyton?'

Sister Tonks placed a wicker chair, and she sat obediently.

Alan Jesus came in, choking against Sixpence's restraint. He was prevented from clawing, but with difficulty, and he was slow to subside.

At last Mrs Leyton found herself with the patient in a ready quietness.

'Shall I read to you?' she asked.

'I can smell wallflowers,' said Josephine. It was good enough to disturb the smell of burning flesh and hair which had taken up residence somewhere in a passage or chamber of her head.

'Yes. I picked them this morning. Would you like to look at them?'

'Where are they?'

'On the table.'

The whole body, from the hips to the crown, as though it had no joints, turned, and tilted back. The eye looked out towards the table.

'I can see them.'

'Would you like me to read to you?'

'I had roses in the nursing home.' Red, the colour of cylinders, fire hydrants and unwelcome gifts.

'I sent them.'

And strelitzia had come from Great-Aunt Jenny. They had seemed like tall thin waterbirds, watching her. They might have been birds of prey. And the roses were a dawn, too sweet, threatening. A red sky in the morning.

'What would you like me to read to you?'

'Where is Simon?'

'Back at school by now.'

'Did he come home?'

'No. I think he makes himself useful on this farm. I hope he does. They don't seem to want to be rid of him. They've already written to ask if he can go again.'

Out there, somewhere, Simon was riding a black horse. She could see him, but to see the row of windows she had to turn and tilt her rigid body. She strained, then leant back on the pillows and breathed loudly through her mouth. Here she was, under tented sheets, a positive chrysalis. To await the slow processes of time. She breathed deeply.

Dr Mendelowitz had told Mrs Leyton that the child had some respiratory trouble. He had said that it would clear up, he was certain, or that she would grow out of it, or – at any rate Mrs Leyton wasn't to worry about it.

*

In fact Freda found herself still less troubled than ever she had been, especially as Sister Tonks turned out unexceptionable, a presence formal enough to be impersonal, but light enough to be unimpressive. Flimsy and stiff in fact, as her veil had promised. And thanks to her arrangement of her patient's day, the mother was permitted only one hour in the mornings and two in the afternoons at the bedside.

'I think you'd enjoy *Henry Esmond,*' she offered.

The mower stuttered its sentences below. Banality, Mrs Leyton supposed, would always be at it, just outside the door.

'I'd prefer draughts or snakes and ladders,' Josephine said, as much at a loss as to how to cross these small Karoos as her mother was.

So they played draughts or snakes and ladders, each for the other's entertainment. Mrs Leyton was better at draughts, but Josephine encountered more drama in the other, chancier game. Josephine had some difficulty gripping the shaker. All her movements were slow. Mrs Leyton found it hard to concentrate on the game. She was able to feel no joy as her white bone button (the coloured counters had all found unknown graves) soared up a ladder, nor the least distress when it landed in the serpent-jaws; nor was she able to feel envy when the black button flew along the firmament, while her white moved on the recurring summons of a dot, from room to room along the second storey.

As long as they remained within the frame. (But the board itself was coming apart at the centrefold, and would soon have to be patched together.)

Josephine shook, and the die shot up and was lost somewhere in the bed, on the floor, under the table, no one could discover where, not even the reliable Tonks.

'I lost control,' Josephine said.

'I wondered how it happened,' said Mrs Leyton.

'It was an accident.'

'Your father wanted me to ask you, actually,' Freda substituted. 'What were you doing there at *all*, I mean. And how did you manage –'

'There was the tremor.'

'But –'

'And it was your fault, Alan Jesus, you dreadful beast, wasn't it? Yes, be ashamed, so you should!'

'Don't let it lick your hand.'

'He doesn't mind how horrid it looks.'

'Yes,' Mrs Leyton sighed. 'But on the whole you know you have been terribly, terribly lucky.'

'Yes, here I am, alive, aren't I, Alan Jesus?'

'Do you know that really is the stupidest name for a dog I've ever heard. Quite ridiculous. I've always thought so, I must admit.'

Freda was always glad to see teacups arrive, after what arduous ascent by Frances, or swift transportation by the electric Tonks.

Every evening at six o'clock the good Sister went downstairs for the news on the radio, so she might follow the progress of the war. And as the curtains were zipping across the windows all over the house under Sixpence's despatch, Josephine also heard the voice coming up through the floorboards. Freda did not go down to listen. Of course she wanted the Germans to get what was coming to them, but the war itself seemed nothing but an endless, unnecessary transaction; an exchange of bones.

*

After a while, as Josephine seemed less helpless, and her repertoire of occupations surely enlarged (though the skin was still rather nasty really, for the poor child; forbidding to look at too – maroon, rucked, even in places quilted) Freda's hours at the bedside became fewer and shorter. She went back to reading and listening to music in her lounge, where a poetic but featureless spirit was her adoring familiar. And sometimes, especially at six o'clock, she strolled down to that part of the garden where nothing decisive had ever been done before, where there had only been weeds and bonfires, but where now the conservatory was going up.

One day, as she was returning (the last pane of glass was in place, and soon the plants would be growing), she passed under the jacaranda tree, and remembered how, that day when *he* had called, Fred had taken a photograph.

(Oh, who could have unlocked her secret doors with a golden key and stolen the evidence of love away?)

She would ask Jenny for it. She would say – that she wanted every picture she could have of Josephine before the accident, for whatever soothing things the doctors said, she knew the child's face would never be the same again.

*

Josephine did not ask for a looking glass. Her fingers shunned her cheeks. But she did sometimes search the faces of others to see how her own must appear.

In Great-Aunt Jenny's when she came to tea one Saturday, she saw distress.

Fred did not come, nor Lydia who was very ill. But Jenny brought the chocolate, to represent her it would seem, for she couldn't have imagined it was indispensable to Josephine.

'How is she?' Josephine asked, unwrapping one of the delegates out of pity for the Great-Aunt she had never liked.

'She's having a bad time poor Lydia I'm afraid,' said Jenny, rearranging the cups on the Nursery table. 'A bad time.'

But Josephine had to be spared the misfortunes of others, so she quickly went on, 'Oh Freda dear, it's a funny thing but you remember you telephoned me about that photograph Freddy took on the lawn one day? Well do you know we just can't lay our hands on it? Of course it must be somewhere, we could never have lost it. It's bound to turn up, and as soon as it does I'll bring it along to you.'

And since she was always glad for other people to have and do what they wanted, she told Freda that if she would like to be off to Cape Town, Josephine was more than welcome to come to her house, and have Freda's old room in the tower.

But Freda said she would wait, at least until Josephine was up and about. And there was the conservatory.

*

When it was finished, lined with shelves, and stocked, Freda walked up and down inside it. The tulips flowered, waxen and cool in the safe, green light.

*

One morning, while Tonks was 'taking an off', Josephine woke to see the door opening slowly. A voice called 'Cooee, can I come in?'

And round the door came a hat, and below it grew a face. 'Nanny!'

Alan Jesus, for some moments rigid and snuffling, leapt from the foot of the bed and bolted to the door. He whimpered and leapt and licked the face. Nanny. Just the same as ever, in her best black hat.

She had brought a deep bag of fruit and a new set of snakes and ladders because she'd thought the old one must be almost worn out. She kissed Josephine on the lips and both cheeks as though there were nothing particular about them. Lovely brisk kisses as always, and the most wonderful, the dearest smell of her, of skin and soap, of clean newly pressed cotton. It sent the smell of burning up into the attics of memory for ever. And these were the first kisses on the new skin. Now it was familiar with the best that the old skin had known. It couldn't be too bad, the new skin; Nanny didn't seem to mind it.

But soon Nanny Binny was furious because there were crumbs in the bed and the reading-light was too dim and Josephine's hair hadn't been washed for months.

'It hasn't been there very long Nanny.'

'Well and how old does something 'ave to be before it's safe in a tub?'

She took Josephine off to the bathroom, sat her on a table at the basin, and scrubbed her head with her lovely hard fingers.

'– Oh help us to see

'Tis on-ly the splen-dour of light hideth thee!'

'There now. The bandage is wet at the back and I better not try changing it, but that bit of damp will soon dry in this 'eat.'

Then she remade the bed, and changed the bulb in the lamp. Then they played snakes and ladders with the new set, a stiff board and all the colours to choose from. And Josephine loved it.

Frances brought up the supper tray and Nanny Binny said it was disgusting that a young girl should be fed like that. 'And the pudding will be cold before she's finished 'er stew.'

Frances explained about her feet and how they were taxed by the stairs. Especially in the heat. And how she had too much to do, even the polishing now.

'Things must be ordered different,' said Nanny Binny to Josephine. 'I'm going to 'ave a word or two with your mother.'

'What's the trouble, Nanny,' said Mrs Leyton, coming in, floating muslin.

Frances creaked off.

'Look what the child is given to eat. A dog would turn up 'is nose at it. And I may as well tell you Mrs Leyton that I've washed the child's 'air. She's been neglected, she 'as, and if no one else will say so, I will. Everyone's always been too busy to worry about the children in this 'ouse, that's the trouble. And poor little Simon being sent off like that when 'e 'adn't done any 'arm to anyone as it turned out. It wasn't Simon as needed 'is 'ead seen to, if you ask me.'

Nanny Binny's hands were trembling.

'Nobody was asking you, Nanny. And I don't want a lecture from you thank you. If you think Josephine's not getting the right food I'll speak to Frances. I'll tell her to give her whatever you order. But it seems to me that she's not doing very badly if one considers that there's a war on. And if her hair hasn't been washed there must be a good reason for it. She has a trained nurse to look after her.'

And Mrs Leyton went out and pulled the door shut after her before Nanny Binny could reply.

'Will you come back and stay with me, Nanny?'

'She won't 'ave me so it's no use asking,' said Nanny Binny, still furious. But she kissed Josephine again and said, 'I'm looking after two nice little babies. In Salisbury. The family's on their way to Port Elizabeth now. We're going to spend a holiday with Grandfather. We'll be passing through on our way back again. And I'll never forget you – or poor little Simon.'

She straightened the sheet again, her hands scraping over the smoothness.

'Whoo! Isn't it hot? Think of those poor polar bears in the Zoo! There. That's better. Now what happened to you? Were you trying to burn something?'

'Yes.'

But Nanny Binny did not ask what or why. Children had no motives. They came by natural force to whatever harm there was to come to, unless prevented.

'Fancy the kitchen door not being locked! I knew as soon as I was gone nothing would be taken care of properly. You need fresh air and exercise now, that's what you need. And proper nourishing food. They do such wonderful things the doctors do nowadays. They'll get you right in the end. Oo's this nurse they've got you, and why doesn't she see to your food? Well, I'll 'ave a talk to Frances, but she's the one oo should see to things. Your mother, I mean. Well now. I shouldn't say that, should I? They're your father and mother and you're to show them proper respect, d'you 'ear?'

'Yes, Nanny,' said Josephine meekly. But she did not respect her father any more.

And what's become of your brother?'

'I think he's happy Nanny. He spends his holidays on a farm.'

'I wonder what 'e's up to then? No good I shouldn't wonder. Well they can't just push 'im away. They'll 'ear from 'im. Oh they'll 'ear from 'im all right. Poor Simon. I don't know what went wrong with 'im, I really don't. It was that Willy, poor boy. I do 'ope 'e won't be blinded. What a 'orrid business that was. 'Orrid.'

Her fingers combed up her back hair and pushed it under her hat.

'I wrote to your father about Willy. I wondered whatever 'appened to 'im. Of course your father's a very busy man. I don't expect 'e found the time to answer.'

'He went to gaol for seven years Nanny.'

'Oo? Willy? Well I never. That's a very long time with 'is eyes so bad. 'Ave you ever 'eard the like? Well I never did. Fancy that now. Couldn't they get 'im off? 'E must 'ave done something to be sent off like that for seven years.'

Her hands were trembling again, and even her head shook so that the back hair came out again.

'Father let you down. I'm sorry Nanny.'

'I always thought 'e was such a clever man your father. And always sticking up for the underdog, making speeches and all. Well never you mind then. I'm sure 'e must be very busy. 'E must 'ave 'is 'ands full as they say. Don't you worry about anything now. Don't let anything upset you. You just get well and strong again. Well now. Fancy that. Well I never did.'

*

Summer came to an end, and so did the regency of Sister Tonks, who moved on to Great-Aunt Lydia at the Kronowsky house. Lydia had been unhappy in the hospital, Great-Aunt Jenny explained, and as they could do no more for her there than a good nurse could do at home, Jenny had had her brought to her large old house and carried up to the room with the best view, the high and final corner which Josephine might have had: the tower room – to Freda's unspoken, irrational chagrin.

Every afternoon Josephine, still wearing that one cunning bandage which would seem to rule out all but a little vision, sat at the window and watched, with her hooded eye, clouds and birds and the changing colours of the hills; blue, mauve, and amethyst, and black. On some days they were glacial, hard and sheer; on others they were mounds, confections. One of them sometimes held a silver stud, which dazzled her; a window reflecting the sun perhaps, returning her hopes, mocking her speculation.

At night she lay quietly in the great shrill silence, looking out at the cricket-stars, no cough or stir or cast of light coming from the next room. Only at a late hour she'd hear the footsteps coming up the stairs. She breathed evenly. Here she was, with the dead. But of course it wasn't the old washerwoman she heard but only her mother going to her bedroom.

One Wednesday morning Josephine woke up to find that the disc of the garden and its glass cover of sky had been tipped, and white flakes were floating everywhere. This alone would have made it an unusual day, for no event could be rarer than snow which she had never seen. But furthermore this was to be the day on which she could put on daytime clothes and walk about. Her shoes felt tight. The floor seemed far off.

She took her hairbrush to the window, and as she stood there brushing the thick boy's length of tangles, the snow fell more swiftly, became so fine it might have been sleet only, and it seemed to her she was standing on a platform that was rising as the flakes sped downward. She felt the hair with her hand, traced the parting with a forefinger, but she knew the time had come to look at the fact of her own face. Very well then. She would go to the biggest, clearest mirror in the house. The one in her father's room.

She wanted not to be disturbed while she met her new reflection, so she made her way very quietly along the passage and carefully shut the door behind her. She crossed the room and in the silence of the snow (which fell in the mirror too, so white, so swift), she stood close to the glass and looked at all that the one bandage did not conceal. What she saw was worse than what she'd already learned of her hands and arms and chest. It was as though another, redder face had been pressed to her own and had left part of itself stuck there for ever. Her mouth looked stretched and pierced and torn as though by a cluster of large thorns. She stared as long and hard and steadfastly as any prince new-risen from a frog. And so closely that she did not see the reflection of her mother who had come into her bathroom on slippered feet and now caught sight of Josephine, and what she was at. Vaguely Freda thought that some word, gesture, action would be becoming to her now; that surely it was a moment for sympathy. But what could be said or done that would neither confirm nor rebuke self-pity? To do the first would be unwise, and the second harsh. So she went away, back into her bedroom, put on her shoes and went down to the lounge. ('Ditto, ditto,' her heels salvoed along the passages, on the landings, going down every morning, and up again each night.)

This time, as she reached the hall, the doorbell rang.

The Kronowskys, both of them, came in with snow on their shoulders, carrying tins and newspapers and stuffed birds or something under domes, and looking solemn. Jenny had been weeping.

'We thought we'd come ourselves to congratulate you on Rayfel's speech. And to tell you the news. We didn't think the telephone would be right,' Jenny said, quietly but earnestly.

'Tell me what news?'

'Your Aunt Lydia. She passed away at seven o'clock this morning.'

'Jenny had been up all night with her. She wouldn't have Sister near her,' Fred elaborated. He had been tempted out by the importance of what there was to be announced and commented upon. And also by the snow which he accepted as a personal gift.

Freda led the way up. Josephine met them at the top of the stairs.

'Well! What a lovely surprise.' Jenny's voice brightened. 'We've brought something nice for tea since we knew we wouldn't be expected. Well, what do you think of the snow?'

Uncle Fred, who had glared at Josephine and grunted when he had first looked up and seen her, now very gently laid down on the Nursery table a plate with a glass dome, and beside it Jenny placed another and lifted the covers. Not birds but cakes, a chocolate cake and a yeast cake. And in the tins were meringues, and ginger-snaps filled with whipped cream. And in a jar there were pickled cucumbers. Imperishables!

'There. A little celebration feast. For your recovery and your father's success. But what do you think of this weather? Isn't it beautiful, the snow? I'd almost forgotten how beautiful it was.'

'There should be troikas,' said Josephine.

'And that's a fact!' Uncle Fred agreed. 'The tyres wouldn't grip. We nearly had a nasty skid.' He held both arms of a chair as he lowered himself into it. 'Nu, that was a fine speech your husband made, Freda. A fine speech. We brought our copy of the journal for you to keep. I'm not saying I agree with everything he said, but did he say it! Oyoyoyoy, he's got a fine turn of phrase, Rayfel. I'm telling you.'

With her one eye Josephine read her father's speech. The words were like boulders falling down a mountain on a silent screen. But the reporter who had been there to hear them seemed delighted. 'A new star has risen,' he pointed out.

'Lovely,' said Great-Aunt Jenny of the speech or the snow. But her cameo went up and down.

Uncle Fred grunted.

'Well, I baked as usual yesterday, although –'

'No need, no need,' said Uncle Fred, frowning, irritable. This time it was he who was on guard.

'Well, Josephine will enjoy it, won't you dear. You must eat well and build up your strength. Nanny Binny popped in the other day to see us. I didn't take her up to Lydia though –'

'What are you going on about?' Fred interrupted again.

Josephine saw how it was.

'Oh I know that Great-Aunt Lydia died this morning. I heard what you said.'

'She was *old* and she was *ill* and it's *a mercy*,' Fred intoned. Death above all mustn't be made too much of to the child, not now: she had bought her exemption, it seemed to him.

'It must have been just before seven,' Jenny said, and started to nod, with the look she put on for reminiscence. 'At daybreak. I was in my big chair and I think I must have dozed off. But I heard her calling quite loudly – and you know she'd hardly had the strength to whisper an hour or two before. Dr Mendelowitz had been in during the evening and told us what we might expect. So it wasn't a surprise when it came of course. But I was telling you. "Look! –" she was calling out, and craning forward like this, "look, they've set fire to the village. They're here." Something like that. Well, she was looking at the window. I'd drawn the blind down but it doesn't cover the edges where the coloured glass is, you remember dear. And there was this most peculiar moving light shining through. To me it looked as though water were pouring down the other side, but it was red you see, so she must have thought it was flame flickering. And when I let it up I couldn't believe it. "It's snowing, Lydia," I told her. "Oh yes, then they're coming," she said, or something like that, I can't remember exactly. But then, do you remember what I told you she said next Freddy? Her last words. Do you remember Fred?'

'I remember what you told me.'

'Go on Freddy, tell Freda.'

For Jenny would not seem to be inventing.

Fred leant forward.

' "Vu bist du given di gantze tzait?" Where have you been all this time? What you think of that, hey? A Jewish girl!'

'That's right. That's exactly what she said.'

'But who did she mean?' Freda asked, shrugging, not seeing any point at all in the story of Lydia's death, any more than in her life.

'Do you know, I believe she meant the Cossacks.'

'The Cossacks? Why Cossacks for goodness' sake? Was she in love with a Cossack?'

'It's only conjecture,' said Fred, 'but it seems to me yes, very possibly she was once in love with a Cossack.'

'And we'd always been under the impression that they were the terror of her life ever since she'd been – attacked, you know? If you see what I mean. Or at least we *thought* she'd been attacked. You follow?'

'Well, well,' said Freda. 'What a wonderful way to go. *Did* she go then? After that announcement?'

'Yes. I went to the bed to put the pillows up behind her so that she could see better without craning her neck, and I saw that her head had just fallen back. I called in Sister Tonks, and she felt the pulse and everything and said well we'd been expecting it. So there we are. Poor Lydia!'

'She had a bad time,' said Fred, and he sighed. It was an afternoon of sighs.

Josephine went to the window and watched the snow. How quickly Simon would have spoilt it.

'Legs a bit shaky dear?' Jenny called.

Josephine turned.

'A little,' she said.

'Can you see with that thing right down over your eye?'

'Yes, thank you. I'm glad she was happy when she was dying.'

When the white horseman seized her.

'Shall I be mother, Freda dear? The funeral will be to-morrow dear. Do you think you could manage it? I'm sure Sister Tonks would come and sit with Josephine.'

'She'll be all right by herself.'

'There's the sugar. So you will come?'

'I think they've forgotten the cake forks. I'll ring.'

'Oh, by the way Freda, you asked me for that photograph. You remember I said that I couldn't find it but that it was bound to turn up?'

'Yes?'

'Well it did. Fred had put it away in a special box for the ones that have a fault in them but are not so spoilt as to be thrown out altogether. One likes to keep them even if they are bad pictures because so many of the snaps are unique – if you see what I mean? A group of friends – pass the sugar to Uncle Fred too, please Josephine dear – who're unlikely to be all together again. It's a way of keeping alive – which cake Freddy? – old memories.'

'Yes? Well?' Freda drove, pressing both toes into the carpet.

'Well Fred thought he remembered putting it in there because something was wrong but it wasn't too bad and –. What will you have, Josephine? Some of Frances's nice bread and butter? To start?'

'Well, and have you got it?'

'Yes. We did find it. Freddy had tried printing it twice, but it's the negative that's got the mistake in it.'

'Not a *mistake*!. An unforeseeable, interference, by the light,' Fred corrected her, and sipped his tea loudly.

'You can recognise some of the group. But I'm afraid Josephine is not clear at all. Ah Frances, cake forks please. Cake forks. No, I'm afraid they're not here.'

'Oh dear. What a pity. Still, I'd love to have a look at it, actually, if you have got it.'

'Oh you've come out beautifully, so I brought it for you to see. I'll show you after tea. It's in my handbag.'

'Josephine can pass it. I'd like to have a look.'

'There's no hurry. We'll get the tea things cleared away first. A meringue dear? And what about you Freddy? And Josephine? Ready for another cup?'

'Pass me Jenny's bag, Josephine. Now may I look for it, or have you got secret love-letters or bombs or something in here that no one must see?'

'Oh if you can find it in there please do. I only brought the one print. They were both exactly the same. I don't know if you remember Freda but that nice young man was here that day. I know his death was a blow to you –'

Freda's hand found the smooth rectangle of the print. Josephine put down her cup and went again to the window. She did hope that the time would come when she would have a use, when what she was capable of would be needed. Or was she really to be filed away among the Dead? In a special box for the damaged but recognisable?

'Come and look, Josephine. Mother's found it,' Jenny called.

Josephine looked with one eye at the picture of a past summer that was shaking slightly in her mother's hand.

A fine pencil of sunlight had drawn a cancelling device on the surface of the scene. It was ruled direct through all the fine leaves and twigs and tangled branches, down to the bench, where lay the goggles, things one had supposed quite superfluous. But one of its lenses shot the beam diagonally upwards to the opposite corner of the picture. On its course it crossed the left eye of Josephine much as her bandage did now. With strange relief she saw that the white line made her sufficiently unrecognisable to be struck from this particular record. She was not yet held ready for the files. Merciful light.

And the same ray of it passed across the centre of Benedick Colley's face, who, standing beside Josephine, and being taller, was caught by the rising line. Mrs Leyton stared in disbelief. How could fate be so cruel?

Part of Jenny's face too was scored out.

But Lydia, who was sitting, was plain to see, the light behaving most decorously on the buckle of her hat. A clear and sufficient memento.

And Freda's face too was perfectly distinct.

'You can keep that one Freda dear. We have the other for our collection,' said Jenny.

But was there anything worth Freda's keeping?

*

Freda, still protected, but threatened by realities on all sides, felt compelled to admit Josephine into her lounge sometimes in her quiet hours. It was no great intrusion. The child sat so quietly on the leather pouffe, her bandaged head bent, she could have been made of stone.

But then Josephine (let in at last to this sanctum where she found nothing after all but stuffiness and time) had no choice but patience. And it was Freda who came to wonder, in the spring, whether there might not yet be opportunities.

And then one afternoon, while Josephine was upstairs sleeping, Simon came back.

She was dreaming that she was safely back in the landscape of life. Flat lands of golden grass, orange rocks here and there, avoidable, and mauve mountains, cleft by a narrow valley. She was walking towards the mountains. The going was hard. No cool white clouds known also by the name of Tonks, which could scatter rains to bring up flowers, passed over the clear sky.

A sky too clear. She had never known daylight so hot. There was no mud, but when she'd come through the grass she was on sand as dry as a desert. And the sun came down in front of the mountains and stood on its edge, a ciliated gong the size of the desert itself. It was, however, very thin, and through it she could see something advancing, a man on horseback, and when he emerged through the yellow heat she saw that it was him at last. He was all the colour of winter grass, except for his hair which was made of the same substance as the fallen sun. And he was carrying the knife. Had she forgotten the knife, when she had thought that she had done all that was necessary to protect his innocence?

'Simon.'

She was flat on her back looking up at him.

His bulk was between her and the sunlight that came in through the open window.

He was dressed in crumpled shirt and trousers, the colour of dust. His face was a dull dark gold, and his hair brighter than ever, so bright that its edges were quite indistinguishable from the sun behind him, and the rest that peculiar black that lies at the heart of light.

'You, you, you, you were making a noise,' he said, and his voice was Simon's voice but sounding over a new depth, with vibrations, as though his throat were hard and deep, a grotto, a ravine, and all of bone.

'Was I?' she said, staring at him, accustoming herself to the changed appearance of reality.

'They, they told me you'd had a bit of an accident. Hey? Did you? You do look funny.'

'Yes, I do. Are you going to stay?'

'Well no, you see. She brought me. Rhona. That's Benny's mother, you see. And they'll fetch me again in a few days. On the way home.'

'Home?'

He turned and took a step to the window. The room was become as tiny as a cell.

'Yeah. Home to the farm. When, when, when they've bought the horse. They're going to buy a horse. For me.'

'But why –'

'Benny said he would you see. He said if I joined something that he belongs to he'd give me a horse of my own.'

Did this Benny, she wondered, whom she had clear knowledge of as weak, spectacled, pale and talkative, want Simon beside him wherever he proceeded? Or what other reasons could he have?

'Join what?'

'I d'know. He says they want a-a-a-a revolution. I d'know.'

It did not seem impossible, since Simon had become so very big, so very tall, that the tops of mountains, or even stars, need not be beyond his reach.

'Simon.'

'Yeah?'

'Where is the knife?'

'What knife?'

'From Willy's room.'

'Why?'

'Throw it away where no one will ever find it.'

'Naaa. Why?'

'Willy's in gaol for murder, and if they find that you've got the knife –'

'Alpheus is drunk,' Simon remembered. 'I saw them. They're playing a gramophone. She'll be bloody angry if she finds out, hey?'

'Doesn't Mother know you're here?'

'Where is she?'

'In the lounge or the –'

'Is, is she shut up still? Because of the man who died in St James? That time. Hey? Was it the one with the fat face and the black spot?' He gargled a syllable or two of his old false laugh. 'I'll, I'll, I'll ask her if it was the one with the fat face and, and, and, and the black spot.'

But a stronger desire had to be answered first.

'Hey! I'm going to have a taste. The stuff they make. You coming with?'

It was not because he felt the lack of what she could supply that he was willing to grant her oldest wish, but because he did not care. And as she had broken through the barriers, even of skin, and gone through stinging air and hot earth, to confirm that Being With was not effected by touching, or made easier by being near, 'No,' she said.

*

When the sun was going down and the whole garden was burnished, Freda was tempted out of her lounge at last and set off to look at her tulips. An old dissatisfaction moved her. She was being too much detained between her daughter's dull spirit and the vacant view from all the windows. There was still something she had to achieve.

Now the garden seemed to be giving rather than receiving light. As though they were expelling what had long been stored in them, a hidden truth, flowers glowed, clumps of foliage, grass, a red patch of earth where someone had dug an unnecessary hole, and even stones which showed unexpected colours. It was a dramatic, almost a lurid light. The rhythm of her steps started words in her memory, or her hope: 'O I'd rather have –'

What would she rather have? She strove to recall the preference of someone else or discover her own. What was it? It seemed very familiar, and even more her own than many other poems had become. What could the alternatives have been?

But now her uncertainty was claimed by a rival throb, an alien rhythm, which was quickening in a covert beyond the visible garden, near the kitchen perhaps; and was one thing to be avoided.

So it was as much to escape an ambush as because she was eager for new paths that she went towards the tennis court, rather than across the lawn and down the rose-walk, and holding up the front of her long gown she crossed the sandy waste and came to the neglected pergola where untrained creepers hung like jungle plants and formed a kind of cave at one end, its entrance almost overgrown. She went past it into the orchard, aware of an excitement in the branches overhead, but not noticing how her skirt was trailing real twigs and leaves, or that a web was caught in her hair, or that a narrow black snake had come out of the potent compost of flowers and leaves and mud and was following her through the orchard, where there was a smell of rotting peaches; and there were so many weeds, yellow and red; and blackjacks. How wild it all seemed. She hardly recognised this as her own garden. And now the throb had declared itself as music: singing, and jangling instruments. However was it made?

She stood before the door of the inevitable conservatory, and listened. One high-pitched, keen, female voice strove to be heard above an opposing strength of drilled and united voices, deep, of a submerged fraternity. But it wasn't a sound she cared for, and she had already lingered too long on the threshold. For shelter and protection, and being resigned, she finally opened the door and went in. She breathed the smells of wet earth and pollen, and started towards the tulips, but remembered that the door must not be left open. She shut it, turned again, and the snake bit into her ankle.

She screamed, because of the horror of the thing flowing away under a low shelf, and because of the pain which was intense, and because she had probably been poisoned. And yet disbelief superseded terror. She could not be going to die. Not she, Freda Levin. Why she hadn't even, she had not begun to. Someone must come and help her. Josephine – it would take her hours to grope her way down here, if she heard at all. But the servants, where were they? The garden boy? Anybody!

She gripped the edges of seed boxes, her fingers sinking into soil, to hold herself up, since that thing must still be in here, on the concrete under the shelves; but whatever had always allowed her to be upright was being slowly withdrawn, and she was brought to her knees.

She wailed, 'Who's there? Can you hear me?'

The music was still struggling on.

But at last her voice, her ringing voice, did penetrate the glass, and was heard by the conspirators in the kitchen garden.

Simon, who had just had his first taste of Alpheus's brew, ran down beside the wall, brushing through thorny branches, and when he came to the glasshouse he stopped, surprised at its being there, and seeing himself, sectioned by struts which held panes of green glass.

The voice was coming from inside it, so he did not look for a door but seized a stone and used it to knock out a pane, and another and another until he could look in, and there he saw his mother, kneeling on the floor and screaming.

'A snake,' she called, not knowing who this was who was breaking the glass, but that here was help at last.

Simon took out his knife.

'Where?' he said, and put his strength to the wooden struts.

Finding himself barred he suggested, 'Get up and run.'

'It bit me,' was all she could articulate, before breath became impossible and froth spilled from her lips instead of words. Why didn't that giant of a man, with all those black faces gathering behind him, break in and save her? Tears were squeezed out and ran down her cheeks.

He saw them; and he saw the snake, pouring upwards from one shelf to another, the sort of snake it was. He knew there were remedies to attempt, like cutting into the wound. But he put away his knife. He stopped trying to break the resisting wood. He just stood and looked. This would be the first time he'd ever watched a person dying.

She lay on her side on the floor. Her mouth stretched open (for even the most abstemious must take in air). But Simon, even now, though he could see her eloquence, was still not informed. Her eyes, he observed, were bulging, and the muscles of her neck. She jerked. One arm reached up, its hand snatching. If this were evidence of something else that was happening, it did not explain.

'Ow!' Sixpence commented, and clicked his tongue – a sound which would do either for contempt or sympathy: for although he stood on a stone and craned, he could not see past big Mosser Simon whether it were wickedness or tragedy which they had been summoned to attend.

Frances was patient but unsteady on her feet, and frequently lifted her apron to wipe the sweat from her face.

Simon waited until there was nothing more to watch. Then he did fetch her out, and carried her up the rose-walk, looking closely at her face, until Frances, weeping drunkenly, took off her dishonoured apron and hung it over her mistress's head, because she looked so strained and bloated, and had turned such an undignified colour.

The snake went back through the orchard to its hole. The sun found the tulips, and they opened wide and hungry as tropical flowers, and their purple stamens and crinkled pistils stuck out naked, obvious, had there been anyone to see. But by the time the sun went down, they were all dead.

No one looked out of the windows of neighbouring houses to discover what the screaming had been about. Perhaps no scream could penetrate the walls of such houses, built as they were to withstand assaults, even by time, hail, pests, earth tremors or the black menace.

Josephine at her open window had heard, but was still making her way down the stone steps as the counter-marchers came out on to the big lawn and through the shade of the jacaranda.

After Simon had gone with his escort and his horse, and Mr Leyton returned to the business of government, the house in the valley was shut up and a watchman set at the gates. Passers-by, and women with babies on their backs who sat on the kerb and looked up at walls, could see the hills reflected in the windows, but no face. Frances, Sixpence and Alpheus packed their cardboard suitcases, rolled up their blankets, drew lots for the gramophone, and walked away.

Josephine (with Alan Jesus) was carried off to the Kronowsky house of relics. She did not, however, sleep in the tower, but chose instead a small white room looking on to the koppie. To which Uncle Fred added no more. But sometimes he went and stood among the cacti and the aloes and looked about him frowningly, as though he were nervous of what might come up through this unpredictable soil.

When she wasn't reading or writing, or studying Uncle Fred's theories on history and botany and zoology and anthropology (until proper arrangements could be made for the poor child with her face), Josephine could look through the albums at leisure, but found that she preferred the window, from where she could see not only that representative piece of the continent, but other, distant parts as well. She did not choose where to look. But she drew no blinds. Once she saw right into the huts on the Karoo. There was yellow newspaper, and the kind of transparent paper that Frances used to wrap food in, stuffed between the tin walls and the tin roof. And she felt the cold that crept along the ground where the children slept, pressing against one another. Africa. It too would be a tale, for her to tell to a child, perhaps.

And though the picture was too big for her to see much of it yet, perhaps in time it could be constructed, deserts from a square of red earth, plains from a clump of uncut grass, even cliffs of granite from a garden stone: a country added to the little space, the few and partial ranges, the sand and water, the plants and beasts she knew already: a wide world extending before Simon, who was out in it, free in it, and oh, as dangerous in it as fang and horn and flame.

She saw him, once, riding down a green valley, beside a river, through long grass. Small wild pink lilies were crushed under his horse's hooves. The horse's mane was blowing the same way as the grass. Over the nek towards which he rode was a waterfall, whose sound was composed of drums and shouting voices. She let him ride out of sight, but before she looked away he had reached the nek, and his horse was stepping high, legs on legs, through the bands of reflecting heat stretched between the mountains. He seemed a skeleton rider on a skeleton horse. Or were they the legs of many horses? An army of skeletons, shouting and drumming? Uncle Fred, with a bush hat and a telescope, waved to her from under an acacia tree. Whatever had *he* been looking at? In which direction? Ahead was only that unused wilderness, the miniature of Africa, which was now, from his present standpoint, a barrier to any forward view.

For some undiscoverable reason – unless it were the Kronowsky custom of sequestering the chattels of the dead – the pouffe was brought from the other house and put in the room with Josephine.

Although Freda was spoken of, usually in the present tense, her death was never mentioned. Nor any other death; not even the most remote in space or time. For the old people reached an agreement that the child must be sheltered from any reminder of death.

As though dying would never happen again.

As though Africa were indeed a heaven such as the one Nanny Binny thought highly of; or mortality nothing but a fable, once told by the spirit to the bone.

www.ingramcontent.com/pod-product-compliance
Lightning Source LLC
Chambersburg PA
CBHW050237110726
47898CB00007B/2182